Building a House in Thailand

Building a House in Thailand

A Novel

by

Ken Klein

Three Pagoda Press

Distributed by:
White Lotus Co., Ltd.
G.P.O. Box 1141
Bangkok 10501
Thailand

Telephone: 6638-239883 and 6638-239884
Fax: 6638-239885
E-mail: ande@loxinfo.co.th
Website: http://thailine.com/lotus

Printed in Thailand

ISBN 10:974 480 1077
ISBN 13:978 974 480 107 4

Dedicated to:

Mother and father, aunts Rose and Madeline,
this is for you; and, for my Thai family,
in appreciation of their grace and dignity.

In *Loving Memory of:*

Bruce Colman, Jane Davis and Jan Bauer:
We will meet again.

This is a memoir of a fiction writer. Fact and fiction flow together. Memory is merely a perceived notion of an event. And therefore, all characters and events are fictional.

Leaving Chicken - Watching Fish - Killing Will

The greens are brilliant. There have to be a billion shades that swash through a spectrum from golden and shimmering, to flat and dull. The rainy season created a milk-green marshy bog that slid from creamy white-green to ink-dark forest. As I strolled down a forgotten country lane, my eyes danced from shimmering rice paddies to pale washed-out green eucalyptus leaves; so much frivolous lushness, I thought. That, and what a Neanderthal pin-head Jefferson Davis Lee turned out to be.

Can you imagine this?

Right in the middle of what could be a nasty divorce, he's two hours away from a reasonable offer from her lawyer, and he's leaving his hometown in South Carolina and getting on a plane for Thailand. He's married for thirty years to his high school sweetheart, and he has a couple of grown kids and a small fortune to lose in terms of financial assets if the divorce turns sour.

He might just as well be telling her, excuse me, but before we make this multi-million dollar agreement final, I need to get laid by my Thai girlfriend. I humbly apologize, but I can't wait another two hours. I have a flight booked, and she's waiting for me at the airport.

I know that's not what he said. But he might just as well. For sure, that was what his wife heard. It was my assumption too. What he actually said was that his friend Will was dying and he wanted to see him before he passed on.

I had told him that Will would surely hang on for another day while he caught the next flight out. I had told him that it was more important that he finished up that divorce before it got really ugly. He had an opportunity to get it over with, and should avail himself of the chance. What a pin-head.

In spite of my well intentioned advice, Jefferson Davis Lee got on that plane, and he didn't have a girl waiting for him at the airport.

* * *

It is a rare village in Thailand that has one. Amongst the millions of cards that get shuffled everyday, one undoubtedly will pop from the deck and fall into an irretrievable spot; an unmatched sock in the laundry bag of life. A three of diamonds or four of clubs that has been lodged too long next to a joker and gets caught in a cosmic swirl, and then is whisked about the planet until it alights in a small village in Central Thailand where it finds peace in a slow paced existence that hasn't changed in centuries, and certainly hasn't seen the likes of him.

As a three of diamonds, he is barely noticeable in the deck, but as a white face in a sea of brown, he is quite the card. Thai villages revolve around generations of family, descended and unmoved from their ancestral abodes. One day fades into the next, as surely as generations pass along. On a local level, one insignificant card becomes more than noticeable, a Martian walking in the midday sun awed by the varied shades of green that surround him.

Thai people don't walk unless they have to, and the sight of a white guy strolling down a back road in a small village is something that does not come along every day. They see me and smile, wave and wonder why anyone would be crazy enough to be walking in the noon heat.

Thai people are engaging, magnetically friendly, and as I proceed along my journey, they laugh and call out to me.

"*Pie nai?*" - Where are you going?

"*Ork gumlung gai,*" I call back. They are very happy that I can speak at least some of their language, as it has virtually no function in the outside world other than neighboring Laos which taps into their TV stations.

"*Ork*" is to leave. "*Gumlung*" indicates present tense. "*Ork gumlung*" would mean to be in the process of leaving. In my world of limited language abilities, "*Gai*" is chicken, and here's where the fine points take over. For me, to "*ork gumlung gai*" would translate as "leaving chicken". There is a barely detectable change in tone, a rising inflection that turns "*gai*" into "*gaii*" an entirely different word. What that word means, I have no idea. However, as I stroll down the road and shout to people that I am "leaving chicken" they understand, having easily interpreted the meaning as "exercising."

I would later learn that "*gaii*" is another way to say "*dtua*" which means body. That has become my method for learning Thai, an amusing process of butchery, curiosity and correction.

As I stroll along, "leaving chicken," passing school children and shopkeepers, people are left smiling and laughing in my wake. Lightness flows through my body, and the heft of my legs disappears as motion becomes effortless. My mind darts from thoughts of greenery and chickens, and plods heavily onward, mildly distressed envisioning a friend, Will, lying wasted from cancer.

When I think back, he never was quite well. I can hear his easy laugh roll into a hacking cough.

Will is a philosopher with the here and now being of primary focus. Too cowboy Texan to have gone hippie during the sixties, the philosophy took hold later in life after a military career carried him to the Philippines and on to Thailand. Older now, he has the awareness to embrace a simple mantra from many years ago – if it feels good, do it.

Booze feels good. Cigarettes feel good. The round rump of his thirty year old deep-honey brown Phillipino wife is delightful. Eating is OK. "Leaving chicken" is a burden that quickly leaves him breathless, but a slow paced meander along the beach in the early dusk is lovely, and so, he lives near the shore in Pattaya indulging a life in which excess is success.

Will spends his days tinkering with his computer, producing volumes of downloaded music and photos which he pieces together into homemade movies. He took a turn at writing, with an odd predilection for setting the world straight as to religion. There were unique twists, but the general idea was that there are five billion of us, and if you think that you are worth a rat's hair more than anyone else, if there even is a god, you are sadly mistaken. It was certainly not a new concept.

The writings seemed more of a purge to me, a way for him to unburden himself from a religious past that haunted and disturbed. He was brought into a world where he would now be considered a sinner, and felt a need to set the record straight. Thailand is a world of orange-robed monks and gaudily ornate temples. Buddhism is imbued into the relaxed nature of the people. Sins are an assumption, accepted with a shrug, not hellfire and eternal damnation.

What did set Will apart was a fantastic curiosity as to what might happen next. Is there an after life? And if so, what odd form might our existence take. Thailand is beset by ghosts and few people have not experienced an encounter, but do we all become ghosts? Are there alternatives? Do we have choices? Do we go to the movies and watch a video of our life, seeing ourselves from the outside, complete with remote control, fast forward and replay?

Will told me that even though that might sound like fun, there would probably be surprises. The action parts, our fondest memories, may play out more clumsily than we envision. We might find that the periods of sleep, especially as a baby, unaware of bills, obligations and expectations, are incredibly peaceful to watch and experience again. But that was just one of a myriad of afterlife possibilities.

Do we slip into other worlds of existence similar to an adventure novel or video game? He had a hundred amusing possibilities that he liked to expand and expound upon. Will concluded that the most likely after death occurrence was far beyond our wildest imagination.

We must still deal with the "here and now," he would remind. And that was always set-up by the "before."

* * *

Two years before - I received a call one day about noon. It was Will calling from Pattaya. He met a fellow southerner on the bus. Nice guy, but completely lost. He needs help. I had books to deliver to Pattaya. I told him I will be there tomorrow. That was when I would first meet Jefferson Davis Lee.

The here - Two hours from Bangkok, Pattaya is a beach resort of mammoth proportions; Las Vegas by the sea, an abundance of guesthouses, luxury hotels, multi-national cuisine and bars. Anybody's guess, but mine is that there are more than 10,000 bars where alcohol is not the only intoxicant.

Will had offered Jeff a prescription. "Three girls a day, whether you are in the mood or not." I asked to speak with Jeff.

I told him not to feel compelled to follow that advice. I told him to do what felt right for him, and maybe therein was the core of his problem. Too many possibilities, too many things that seemed right, but ran head on into behavior that he had been taught was irrefutably wrong. Carolina was half a world away, and three months buried in his past. It seemed a distant lifetime ago.

Pattaya was shining bright as a day on the beach in front of him, smiling wide and welcoming through an ocean of bargirls. An embarrassment of choice as lovely ladies, laughing and joyful, beautiful and beguiling, engaging and entertaining, competed for his attention. Dancing dark eyes flashed a radiant, believable flirtatious presence and availability, pleading for his companionship. And he acquiesced.

* * *

The movie Big Fish begins with a song that my grandfather wrote about seventy years ago. When you think about it, not too much beyond a few classics has survived for that long in the field of pop music. The name of the song is "Dinah" and it states that "there is nobody fine-ah, in the state of Carolina..." and on and on.

My grandfather died fifty years ago when I was four years old. His music, however remotely, lives on in this delightful movie about a man who tells fantastic stories of his life using an almost believable hyperbole. I went to the film with Jeff.

Jefferson Davis Lee the Fourth is a pillar of the small South Carolina town where he and his ancestors were born. A direct descendent of Harry Lighthorse Lee, great nephew of Robert E. Lee, he received an extra dose of respect, a hero of the south by breeding alone, and he carried that dignity in his demeanor.

Jeff built a small chain of restaurants. He was a solid businessman, a regular churchgoer, a father of two and devoted husband. His wife was a perfect southern belle, a lovely debutante, sweet as mint, fresh as the aroma of spring and nearly as untouchable.

They were an enviable couple until the bedroom door closed. Touching and intimacy was suddenly distasteful, sex transpired fully clothed and with time concerns.

"You're a good man," his wife would tell him. "Do what you want, but get it over with as fast as possible." The act was a near sterile incision, an emotional and physical deflation, less intimate than a warm handshake and as infrequent as a harvest moon.

An unseen chill ran through the center of Jeff's life, and he drowned himself in work. In the quiet of late evenings, he read. Though active in the Southern Baptist Church that cocooned the community, his interest turned to a fascination with the Far East and Buddhist philosophy. At age 50, Jeff's eldest son took the reigns of business and set him free to embark on a mid-life pilgrimage, a poetic stroll of dreams to fantastic locations, even the names intricately spiced and totally enthralling; Bombay India, Kathmandu Nepal, Bangkok Thailand and Tokyo Japan.

"He says he's a Buddhist," Will had warned me before I met Jeff.

"A practicing Buddhist?" I queried.

"I didn't ask," Will had replied, and then paused. "I was afraid that he might tell me." Jefferson Davis Lee is a good talker.

Seratonin is a chemical that is released into the brain by the act of touching, a natural intoxicant that simply makes you feel good. When Will brought Jeff to his favorite bar, his aptly named friend Joy was all over the Southern hero. She was laughing and hugging, swirling across his lap, her brief tank top leaving her arms and midriff exposed, available for touch; the first few steps in the journey to the promised land.

Jeff's interior dam broke wide, and several decades of serotonin coursed like a mountain stream. He could not remember being this happy in his entire life. She called him "handsome man" - "the good man, good heart." She said that she "loved him too much" in choppy English and pressed her cheek against his. Bliss cascaded through his cells. Joy was perky, lovely and affectionate, and the twenty dollars for the night was shuffled to the side, a minor detail.

The twilight hours with Joy produced fun, romance, giggling and much needed intimacy; more than he had received in thirty years of marriage. This is what he confided to me at lunch the next day. That, and every detail of his night, reliving the fascination, the experience, and I let him go on. The conversation shifted to his wife and home in South Carolina, his community and church. His smile, as wide as a fresh-baked loaf of cornbread, broke down. The indiscreet pleasures that a few moments before had felt so natural, were suddenly troubling in the backdrop of the rest of his life.

He had done nothing wrong. Right? Joy had a wonderful time. He was in a previously unimaginable semblance of heaven. When she had left in the morning, parting like lovers on a honeymoon, they had made arrangements to meet for dinner. They had the perfect date, and she was his girlfriend. He had no idea that sin could feel so normal.

I could see his eyes drift back through narrow recesses, slipping away to South Carolina, a now uncomfortable distant world. What was common in Pattaya, was unconscionable in Carolina. His mind raced through a vocabulary list of sins; adultery, consorting with a prostitute, improper tasting of body parts.

He remembered back to Jimmy Swaggert, the televangelist, and his tearful confession after being caught with a young prostitute in a motel. Disdain. Disgust. It was sordid, and yet, his time with Joy seemed pure. The twenty dollars was not payment for sex, but a token of his affections, help with the rent, cab fare.

"If my friends in church could see me," he confided, "if they could see me with an Asian woman, a prostitute." He put his head in his powerful hands and sobbed. An east meets west collision of worlds tear rolled down his cheek as realities swirled and ran uneasily together. No comfortable rationalization could reconcile the clash of physical love and family. One was loose and laughing, the other tight and restrictive. I had no doubts as to which felt more right as he sat across from me choking for air, tears now in full stream.

He went again with Joy that night, another girl the next day, and then Joy again the following night. After three decades in a physical vacuum, Jefferson Davis Lee was alive and out there. He told me that back home they would pity him, call him a fallen soul. People would pray for forgiveness of his weakness and the perversions to which he had succumbed. But it just felt too good, too comfortable and happiness won out.

Big Fish was a movie about a man who told stories. When I spoke to Jeff in the United States, several months later, he mentioned having finished reading my book. He told me that I was a storyteller. I had never thought of myself that way before, but I realized the truth of it, and now look at life from that perspective.

There is a story that resonates through my family history. My grandfather wrote a song called "Dinah." It was a big hit in its day. His friend Harry Akst borrowed the song to use in the Cotton Club Review. My grandfather had a trunk full of songs. When Harry Akst borrowed it, it wasn't a big hit, just another unpublished song. Harry Akst put his name on the song, as if he had written it.

After it became a big hit, Harry Akst made a lot of money from it. More than likely my grandmother bemoaned the loss of money they could have made. I can imagine that she used that to berate my grandfather. He wrote a great song, and surely received more grief than joy for his effort. Toward the end of his life, he spent time in a state run mental institution. I don't know what happened to Harry Akst.

My grandfather wrote many songs. He played drums with the big bands, and wrote a song called "It isn't Fair." It was a hit twice. When it was re-made in 1950, it sold a million copies, but "Dinah" was the big fish that got away.

When I saw my grandfather's song listed in the credits, an emotional twitter sparked deep inside; a moment of holding hands with a grandfather I never knew. It was as if this song emanated from an ancestral homeland more imaginary than real, a forgotten past, a changing scenario of people and places. For a brief instant, the sensation of words and music stood my hair on end.

Jefferson Davis Lee and I went our separate ways and parted in Pattaya. I met up with Jeff a year later. He was traveling through Northern Thailand. He was courting conversation with other travelers and Thais alike, his genteel good manners winning the day and his smile contagious.

And two years later, as I walked about the enchanting myriad of greens, my mind wandered to the inevitable future when Jefferson Davis Lee was going to return, and we would visit Will and sit by the side of our now semi-lucid friend. The cancer that undoubtedly had started in his lungs had metastasized and was busily ravishing his body. It had spread to his pancreas, liver, and he suspected was working its way into his brain, creating a fuzziness of vision and thought that combined with pain killers to distort his realization of time and place.

I told Jeff in a brief phone call that I had not seen Will since the diagnosis, but that I spoke with his neighbor, Shark Fin Sammy, and he said it was awful. Will was wasting slowly. Though perfectly lucid some days, he even had the energy to have dinner out one night, on most days he floundered in bed. Just awful Shark Fin told me.

I reminded Jeff of my opinion of his own actions. That he was most likely mentally ill for not postponing the flight for a day to finalize his divorce, and maybe even a couple of days so he could get some serious psychological help. I told him that Will would forgive him a few days.

He said no, he was coming, and he would meet me in Pattaya, and we would go to see Will together.

As I wandered past the Buddhist Temple that perches on a lone hill overlooking my small village, the loveliness of yellow-green fields of rice held my vision, but Will captured my thoughts. What should I say to a friend who undoubtedly knew that his days were a short calendar sheet in number?

I could imagine Will lying there, aged and worn far beyond his fifty-six years. Jeff is tall, a six foot two straw of a man, and I am short, more mutt-like. I could imagine Will's eyes lighting up as we walk through the door.

"Guess what. This is what happens when you die. You enter into the world of a Mutt and Jeff cartoon," I thought of telling an old friend with a great sense of humor, a wonderful ice-breaker for an uncomfortable moment and a buddy who loved to laugh.

I dismissed the thought as a disrespectful ponderance on an afternoon walk, a wrong and callous thing to think or even consider saying in a somber moment. Shark Fin Sammy had called last night and told me that the wasting was a horrible thing to see.

When we entered, it was just as I had pictured. Will's torso lay in the center of the bed, his arms and legs reduced to frail appendages that looked like they belonged to a hundred year old man. Oxygen tubes were fed through his nostrils. His wife flitted nervously around the room, uneasy, as though she must do something, but having no idea what that something might be. I had the feeling that she had been in that state for several days.

And yet, when we approached his bed, there was more than a spark of recognition in his eyes. He tried to talk, but his voice hung dry and lacked volume. He flapped an arm for us to sit on the bed. A smile leaked from his mouth. Then, logic and reason slipped away from my ability to tactfully process thought and deed.

Maybe it wasn't a proper thing to say. Who knows? But the concept had already been formulated, the words repeatedly rehearsed like a dumb joke or a bad song lyric that echoes and won't fade away no matter how hard you try to drive it from your head.

And yes, as we sat on the edge of his bed, I said it. "Welcome to the after life," I informed him with the joyous inflection of a tour guide. "You have just entered the world of a Mutt and Jeff cartoon. If you will all look to your left..."

Well, the first thing that I noticed was that Jeff's jaw dropped in total shock. I thought he was going to wind up and sock me, but there was an immediate positive reaction from Will. It registered like a lighthouse through the fog. Will liked it and broke into a wide grin taking respite from the world of the slowly dying. He was now alive again, and joking with friends. That was what had been missing the last few weeks. Moments of normalcy, times when life was worth living, when you could look straight ahead without the reminder of the axe that way too obviously hung over his head. Will was back.

Shark Fin Sammy started a chuckle, and I couldn't help but smile. For Jeff, after a long plane ride with his own demons heavily draping about, and the shock of seeing his once normal-sized friend now reduced, he too needed a release. An unwanted laugh started to leak out of him like steam from a radiator, and as he was making an effort to suppress it, his shoulders bounced up and down as Will's smile grew wider and tears of joy began to fill his eyes.

Laughter is contagious, and this was beginning to be a good one. Shark Fin Sammy is a big guy, and he can really howl. I can let go a good one too, especially filled with pride as it was my joke that was wiping out the room. Jefferson Davis Lee could barely keep his breath, like a train puttering into the station his laughs came in choking staccato bursts that could have been mistaken as cries. The stress of a crumbling life in Carolina gushed out in odd noises that sounded so funny that we were all starting to lose it.

Will's smile had grown seemingly wider than his face, and the tears were overflowing the banks and cutting a path down his cheek. He was clearly getting a kick out of this and contributed weak laughter to the raucous procession. It rumbled into a faint mixture of cough/laugh and then maybe gasp/laugh. None of us could easily stop, and Will was now, for the first time in a long time, one of us.

Though maybe it was more gasp than laugh. It was a flickering moment. It is difficult to recount the millisecond when it turned, though I think we would all be haunted by the feeling that it took us too long to react.

Gasp sure. Turn up the oxygen. Call an ambulance. Do something. Do what?

Jefferson Davis Lee called me an idiot, and said it was my fault. He would later call from America and apologize. Shark Fin Sammy said

Will had been suffering for a long time, and if he had to go, having a good kick ass laugh with a couple of buddies wasn't too bad a way to pass on, though he added that he would rather be hit by a bus or something like that. Yeah, a bus would be better.

1

Cocks don't only crow at mornings first light. They call out whenever in the mood to let the world know they are alive, light or dark.

An eerie howl knifes through the night. The neighborhood dogs go crazy. I had not yet turned-in, nor had my wife. I had heard ghost stories from the village, but this noise alarmed no one.

An hour later, unable to sleep while the others had fallen off, there were three distinct knocks in succession against the tin gate that encloses the compound. I am staying at the house of my wife's father, a large teak home built on stilts at the entrance of the compound, nearest the river. There are three other homes bunched in the small complex.

The knocks are unmistakable. The dogs go wild again, barking and growling. Nobody else seems to hear. I consider waking my wife, but there is no further noise. The wails of the dogs stop in unison, suddenly, as if on cue. I wonder what the hell I am doing here.

We have just moved our few possessions to this small agrarian village in Central Thailand. Tomorrow, I will pack a carry-on sized suitcase, and find my way to the nearby small city, where I can stay in a hotel while being near enough to oversee the construction of my home.

Father's 100 year old teak house has no western toilet. I don't like to intrude on the space of others, though they don't mind. Sharing with family is normal. My wife sleeps peacefully while I lie awake and wonder about the direction we have chosen. I want to be back in Bangkok. I am glad to be out of Bangkok; contradictions envelope my world. I hope I remember to ask my wife about the rapping in the night.

I never do ask. I sit around the house during the day writing, reading and watching. It is my job to detach and observe. I am hoping to continue to learn and assimilate. It is not that I have rejected my culture. Thailand feels more comfortable for me in a way that transcends words and logic. It always has since the first time I set foot here as a young backpacker on a round the world journey in 1974.

For my wife, family is everything, and that is why we are building a home in her village.

I do love the greens, so many different shades that ease into hues of yellow. Towering coconut palms bend gracefully. The setting is superbly peaceful. I drift easily atop a smooth 100cc Honda that barely qualifies as a motorcycle. I have no interest in speed.

Pre-historic looking oxen graze casually, moving with resolved deliberation as if they were part of the landscape. Everything moves slowly. The confounding concepts of time and purpose are off the local maps. The sun weighs heavy, pounding through the afternoon. The hot air pressing against my face is an experience of being inside an oven stuck on bake.

There are no English language newspapers nearby. If there is up to the minute news, it is visible to someone else. Bulletins won't reach me quickly. They will not likely affect me, no matter how big the story.

The corn is ready to be picked, and my family and neighbors are decked out in straw hats. Their faces are covered with cloth, wrapped tight leaving only dark eyes exposed. They wear long baggy pants and long sleeve shirts to keep the sun off their skin. I bring a bottle of Orange Fanta soda and a bucket of ice. A bag of small tangerines for 50 cents a kilo is a treat, and they smile. The snack cost $1.25, the equivalent of half one person's wage for a day.

There is a Thai way of thought that does not run parallel to the workings of our Western mind. The differences begin with language. English and Thai do not always translate directly.

After dating in Bangkok for a couple of months, I asked my wife-to-be if she could cook. No, she told me. The first time we were together in the village, I found out that she was an excellent cook. Why did you tell me you couldn't cook? I asked. Because I didn't have time, she answered.

These types of miscommunication are common. My Thai has improved through the years. She has learned a respectable amount of English. We could have a similar conversation today. Meaningless misunderstandings over words put things in perspective. Intent is the only important element. We shrug.

In Thai language they "open" and "close" not only a book or a window, but the light and television. I taught my wife that in English language we "turn on" and "turn off" the television and the light. We walked around the room for five minutes "turning off" and "turning on" various appliances. She liked the game, and it served as a valuable memory aid. When we left to go out for dinner that evening she told me to "turn off" the television. When we exited the room, she told me to "turn off" the door.

Auntie watches the little ones while the family is at work on the farm. She is sixty years old, frail but steady. She is the one who is there for the children, as she was for their mothers; an ever present security blanket of lanky arms that represent home. She wears an old shirt and a traditional sari-type skirt. She sleeps in a small, rickety structure of weathered boards unevenly nailed together. Her appearance has a forever dusty quality. Her eyes are soft and weary.

I think every family in the village has an auntie who performs these functions. Ours is a bit different. She speaks in a barely audible hoarse, but magnified garble through a small electro-larynx on the exterior of her throat. The obvious first thought is cancer. This is incorrect.

My family likes to plant things, most often food. They have a five rai parcel where they planted eucalyptus trees. They are making a lovely garden on my property now. Chili peppers grow behind my house, near the banana trees. We can purchase ten-foot high palm trees for $5 from a local tree farm. – Ah, but I get ahead of myself here, but then, maybe sequence isn't so important.

The Thai genetic makeup is different. They work hard, they are thin and fit. Children like to rub my stomach. It is a novelty for them. A prominent nose and white skin are points of interest. Anxiety and neurosis are rare. Along with my Grandfather who wrote Dinah, I share a familial thread of instability. It entangles each member of my immediate family. A spider navigates his web by knowing which strand is the sticky one. We have no such facility. My cousins have it worse.

I once heard it said that when you come to the realization that everyone is crazy, then the mystery is solved and life stands explained. My craziness is not manifest in a way in which it interferes with others. After that, not too many people really care what you do with your life. I think that there is no sane path to follow, and so, I do what I want. I learned this from my best friend. At an early age, he went outside the bounds of what was considered normal behavior. He was Bruce, and never tried to be who other people thought he should be.

Bruce and Willie

Bruce could return to the old neighborhood, Rockaway Beach, and go to the Amusement Park. He could stroll out near the old wooden rollercoaster where the speakers were blaring and, as the only white kid in the area, dance to the Motown music with all the cool black guys showing off their moves on Saturday Night. He was that good.

We both started out in Rockaway Beach, before the neighborhood transitioned. As babies, our mothers walked us in strollers along the boardwalk. There was a connection formed in those early days that went beyond time and place. We were best friends – even if at points in our lives we hung around with other best friends, or didn't see each other for a long time, there was no breaking that bond.

There was something else in the 1951 air in New York. It was a life infusing buzz in the person of Willie Mays. We were only a year old at the time when Willie was tearing up the minor leagues. The Giants were floundering at the start of the season, which was beginning to look increasingly like the last thirteen seasons [they hadn't won a pennant since 1937] – when the manager made the call to the farm team in Minneapolis to bring Willie up to the big leagues.

When it came to baseball, Willie had all the skills and more. There was a visceral energy, an excitement that came with him. You could never be sure what he might accomplish next or how, but if the play could be made, and some that couldn't, Willie would find a way. You might say Bruce and I were raised in this era of Mays magic. It was compounded by a feeling that anything was possible as technology was blooming all around us.

Willie could do it. Scientists could do it. We could do it too. Only, like I said, we were not even toddlers yet, and maybe, the fact that we were infants at the moment of his entering the major leagues, maybe we were more sensitive to the vibrations that were rocking the city.

Willie went on to inspire the Giants to a remarkable come from behind season. We may have been newly arrived in the world, but I think we knew. I don't recall becoming a Willie Mays fan. I just always was. Throughout my boyhood, my first phone call every morning was to Bruce. My first question every day was, "How did Willie do last night?"

My parents moved out of Rockaway Beach, and a year later, Bruce's family followed not far behind. That was the beginning of a decade long exodus which changed the Rockaway neighborhood demographic to black. I went back in the daytime on rare occasions, but Bruce, he could go at night alone, and he could dance.

I have class pictures dating back to kindergarten. Bruce always managed to have an 'oh yeahhhh' expression on his face, which was usually propped on an arm bent at the elbow, leaning on a desk while all the others stood tall.

If I stood out in any of the photos, it was because I usually forgot to put on a tie that day for the photo shoot. Once they caught me with my finger in my ear. Maybe I was slightly noteworthy, but Bruce always looked like a wise-guy character straight from The Little Rascals.

In fifth grade, Mr. Andretti's class, that's where things really started to happen. You might say in our ten year old pre-pubescent state we reached a simple philosophical plateau that I am not sure I ever surpassed; everything was hysterically funny.

Words or jokes could be useful, but we didn't need stimulation to recognize the ridiculous and sublime. Looking at Bruce was about all it took for me. Of course, there were triggers. The National Anthem, which began the weekly assembly hall, was the height of scintillation. It was the funniest song ever written, and the dramatic rising and falling nature of the musical score added to the absurdity. The fact that someone had written the song in a serious vein, and that it was not something to be laughed at, made it even funnier. It was not our fault that they chose to open the assembly with a group rendition.

Bruce would sing along with an exaggerated patriotic fervor, and I'll be damned if Mr. Andretti didn't have us by the back of the neck and in the Principal's office before the rockets red glare ever shone through the night, and it was a good thing because singing the high notes would have probably killed us both.

Bruce would start out with a rousing "Ho-Jose can you see," and that was usually it. If Mr. Andretti didn't get to us quickly, though usually he did, we would be doubled over in laughter rolling on the gymnasium floor, gasping for breath, while our classmates were proudly hailing the dawns early light. This went beyond fun. It hurt like hell to laugh that hard. We would be in tears, gripping our stomachs; it was painful. We weren't trying to act-up or cause trouble. They were provoking us by using that song week after week to begin the assembly.

Mr. Andretti was a good guy, and we liked him, but you could see that it really pissed him off. It was the late 1950s. We had won the war. Maybe he had participated. There were still duck and cover drills where we would file into the hall and keep away from the windows in case the Russians bombed us. It was a serious time, though Bruce and I never got that. We lived in a nice suburban neighborhood filled with kids. The war was ancient history.

It amused Bruce that he would see me get a powerful swat in the back of the head, and then know he was next. He would scrunch up his neck. The funny thing was that we both had the feeling that Mr Andretti secretly liked us, that we were his favorites, even though we disrupted his classroom on a daily basis, and he had us write out the words to the Star Spangled Banner after school hundreds of times.

Well, think about it. "O'er the ramparts we watched," – Where is that coming from? I'm over 50 years old, and I have never watched o'er ramparts. It might have been a good choice for a national anthem in the 1800s, but for the 1950s or today, they should be able to do better. I still find it kind of funny, and I bet Bruce would too, if he were still alive.

2

I send this story along to Bruce's mother. She tells me to write more about Bruce. I promise her that I will, but warn that we were mischievous children. I can see her smile even though there is a phone line and uncountable miles between us. She called us angels, but she delighted in our devils.

Many years had passed where I hadn't contacted her. I knew that she enjoyed seeing me, but she would cry afterwards. A mother is not meant to outlive her children. It is a hurt that cuts too deep and heals too slowly.

Bruce's mother is in a nursing home now. Her grandchildren visit, and she forgets that they were there. She tells me that the name of the teacher was Mr. Kaufman, not Andretti. I tell her she is correct. I tell her it is a story, fiction, though for this tale, the only thing that I changed was the name of the teacher. Otherwise, it is true to my memory.

The lines between fiction and memoir are blurry. Old paned glass settles and refracts. Memory dances then hazes over, the original moment impossible to revisit.

Fiction can be subtly revealing.

* * *

In 1951, people were talking about Faulkner, hydrogen bombs, summer camps for the kids and Willie Mays. Bruce and I were babies at the time, but we grew up with those sounds.

Willie made plays that nobody else could; one hand grabs, amazing throws and his speed and daring running the bases drove the opposing players to error and distraction. Willie played the game with so much enthusiasm, that his Manager, Leo Durocher, called it "a contagious happiness."

These are the things that make the molecules swirl and get people worked up. This is the potion that put frenzy in the air that Bruce and I breathed. I don't remember a time in my life when I didn't love

Willie Mays. He hasn't played ball in over thirty years, and I still love Willie Mays.

It was in Brooklyn, in the bottom of the ninth with two on, when Bobby Morgan drilled a ball into left center. It would have hit the wall about belt high, but Willie managed to get there. He dove. Stretched fully extended, Willie grabbed the ball in the fingertips of his glove. He landed hard. His right elbow jammed into his stomach and knocked him out cold. Durocher ran out of the dugout and rolled the unconscious Mays onto his back. He still had the ball.

When you grow up with an idol like that, it does something for you. And yet, at age thirty, Bruce would take his life. He would be the first of three close friends to do so. The most recent was Jane.

Sail Away

There are not many pleasures in life as fine as relaxing into the world of a good book. Though I have brought one along, it rests untouched. A consuming read would be a distraction from the ultimate of luxuries; a Thai foot massage. I soon surrender, allowing myself to sink into the plush, velvet atmosphere.

It begins with a basin of warm perfumed water, a finger-sized scrub brush, and a smiling masseuse who cleans my feet. My master of reflexology is in her late 20s, stockier than the typical Thai and from a farming family in the poor Issan region of Thailand. After exchanging pleasantries, I close my eyes and open my sails.

Beginning with my right leg, a mixture of oil, cream and a warming tiger balm is smoothed in sweeping strokes from my knee down and around my calf, descending to my ankle. Soon, her slow steady strokes extend to my feet as the heat of the balm begins to take hold. After five minutes, my entire leg slides into a state approaching Nirvanic repose. A towel is used to create a womb-like seal as my foot is bundled and left to silent relaxation. Then, work begins in earnest on my other leg beginning with the application of the warm, creamy mixture.

"*Nok*?" Heavy, she asks my preference.

"*Tumadah*." Normal, I reply.

Just right. She kneads never too strong, applying acupressure to my spots. Rubbing, then releasing in easy flowing strokes, waves lightly lapping, barely perceptible, gentle but firm, a light breeze catches my sail and whisks me further from the shore, transcending time and place, oddly, disconnectedly, returning me to a phone conversation several months in my past.

"Sarah, how are you?"

"Do you really want to know or is that just like a greeting?"

"Just a greeting," I tell her. Surely, she must know that. I cringe with the realization of where we are going, and feel sorry that I chose the wrong moment to call. We've had this conversation before.

Her life is empty; a vacant vessel only capable of holding angst. There are financial concerns and emotional pain which leads to drugs in an attempt to subdue sensation and bring sleep; an escape into a less troubled world of subconscious. She is lonely and wants the pain to stop. Twice in the last six months, probably twenty times in the last thirty years, she has tried to kill herself.

Classic depression. We discuss the solution, but she knows the answers. A career in brain research, a lifetime of therapy, but somehow, without intent, she has tossed the problem to me. She knows it is the function of the brain to try and solve problems, and yet, she rejects all my positive suggestions, or at least has in the past. And so, my brain sets course on the solution to a present moment dilemma. How do I comfortably end this uneasy conversation? How do I get off the phone?

What is she really after? Am I to drop everything and say – Don't worry. Don't do anything rash. I will pay all your bills. We can play scrabble until midnight. I am yearning to join your despair.

"What is it you want?" I ask hoping she will provide the answer to her problems.

"I want the pain to stop. I want to sleep."

"Sleep well," I tell her.

She will later feel badly about the conversation. She will realize that it only serves to drive people away. She is nothing if not smart.

Using a dowel, my masseuse presses on the tops of my toes, and then slowly eases off. She has an innate sense of the appropriate amount of pressure to apply, inducing a smidgen of pain, and then lightly backing down. Her hands, oiled and warm with balm, slide easily up and down my foot. The aches from miles of walking, endless exploration of Bangkok streets are receding to an electric tingle.

In the past, I have emerged from a foot massage with renewed vigor, a bounce in my step, but now, a thick mist has formed; an opium-like, dreamy aura has washed-over my senses. I am falling beneath heavy eyelids. I need sleep. I don't have the necessary minimal use of facilities to face the outside world. I don't want the massage to end.

My left foot is finished. She cocoons it in a towel, and returns to my right foot. I consider asking for an extension, a two hour massage. Yes, that would be wonderful. I inhale deep as the shoreline disappears from view. I am floating.

Sure, the problem was tossed out to me months ago, but it has not disappeared, just remained dormant; lurking in the recesses of my cranial web. The traditional answers to depression have never yielded sustainable results for Sarah. Do something with your time, your life. Help others. Be constructive. Do anything but wallow. Treat yourself, have fun. If you can't get a life, at least - get a foot massage!

The calculations streak like lightning bolts, each one a direct hit. It is not only do-able, but easily. Sell her condo in Philadelphia. Invest in bonds and add to her state sponsored income. She could rent a decent apartment in Bangkok, and, after expenses, there would be more than plenty left over for massage. Not just one a day but a bevy, a veritable beehive of pampering. Thai massage, oil massage, face massage – at $5 per hour and less the possibilities are limitless. She can indulge herself eight hours a day if she wants, search out the best masseuses in town.

A foot massage does not end at the knee. Distributing her weight evenly, my masseuse leans forward placing both hands on my leg and walks her way upward toward my pelvis. She stops, concentrating her full weight on my femoral vein, cutting off the circulation. She holds this position for a long minute, and then releases. The warm blood, let loose, flows rapidly through my leg. After repeating the process on my other leg, she moves to my side and begins work on my shoulder and arm. I consider switching to an oil massage when the hour is done as my masseuse moves along with seemingly little effort.

It is noon, and I am most certainly her first customer of the day. The shop is empty, but for me. My masseuse will receive half of the $5 hourly fee, and I will give her a $2 tip as well. She will be thrilled. If there is a second customer today, or another hour from me, it will equal what her father makes in a back crunching week of rice farming. She has a good job, and the rare time I open my eyes, her entire face lights with joy.

Open my eyes – why? Her rhythmic movements provide the undulating motion to simulate soft waves. Flowing breezes whisk me to other levels, not conscious, not subconscious, not quite sleep or dream, an easy place of imagination, beyond hurt, wafting in the arms of Morpheus, languidly drifting inside my head.

* * *

The most popular name for private boats is Obsession. Not far behind is Escape. And yet, for most it remains a weekend passion, an indulgent fragment, but not a lifestyle. The unrealized dreams of man slide through my thoughts as warm hands gently exorcise the stress accumulated in my calf.

For most, those names are a written representation of an unreachable dream. The visions fade and trickle through fingers like coins on a beach, disappearing back into the sands, never to be found again. The few who realize the dream become like a lone apparition met at a foggy crossroad at midnight, leaving you to wonder if they ever really existed. You vaguely recall a face, a flurry of words, but only in a misty sense as if encountered in a different dimension, and all that you are left with is a story that begins with the phrase: I once met a guy.

I once met a guy who was a successful lawyer in Holland. One day, he sold everything and moved to Thailand. Working alone, by hand, he built a boat. I met him off the coast of a small island in the Gulf of Siam. He lives on the boat, fishes for food and wanders uncharted islands. He knew nothing of politics, or current events, nor had cares about governments or taxes. We had a drink and traded stories until dusk turned to dark. In the morning, he was gone.

He is one of a handful. They are not trail blazers, and do not expect others to follow. They are disconnected wanderers, totally devoted to their unique, inimitable road. They are consumed with their path, unconcerned with what others might think or do. They appear to us in stories, almost mythological in stature, fleeting in nature.

And I wonder if that too could be an answer for Sarah. Not a life at sea or a round the world journey, but an existence consumed in massage. If things had been different, the stories might have gone like this:

I once met a woman who knew every masseuse in Bangkok. She indulges herself, all day, every day in massage. She says the continual touch on her body frees her mind to venture to amazing places. When I met her, she was having both a foot massage, and a face massage, at the same time. She laughed and called it a "massage- a-trois." I later heard that she used to live in Philadelphia, and was once irreconcilably depressed.

But this odd solution won't work. It emanates from me, not her. Our lives, outlook and approach are not the same. Passions don't change planes in Tokyo and transfer on arrival in Philadelphia. It is my dream, and I have a seemingly limitless cascade of them, for better or worse, realistic or not, they are mine to pursue.

My masseuse seats me on a footstool and trumpets a scale up and down my spine. She slaps and pats my back over and again, finally coming to rest on my shoulders. She smiles wide and beautifully and gives me a little hug. It is over, and I feel revived, excited to re-enter the world, curious as to where my now youthful feet will take me.

In loving memory of Jane Davis – sleep well

3

I write this essay about Jane, and make a weak attempt at selling it to a massage magazine. They reply that they are too busy to consider even looking at the piece. A second magazine does not return a reply. I send it along to Jane's cousin. She returns a mournful appreciation. We all miss the happy, silly, smart Jane, but the sad aspect of her persona was becoming the increasingly largest portion. We exchange the 'I hope she is somewhere peaceful now' sentiments. There isn't anything more you can say. Life goes on for the rest of us.

My wife accompanied me to visit Jane in Philadelphia. She could not understand her wanting to kill herself. She had food. She had a nice apartment. My wife has always had a close-knit family, and a small circle of devoted friends. I am not sure that she can fully comprehend the chasm of loneliness and despair, especially when someone apparently has so much.

My wife is the oldest of four sisters. If they need anything accomplished off the family homestead, she is the one. Unlike father and mother, she can read and write. She knows how to talk with government officials if there is business to be transacted, such as getting a deed for land, or securing a mandatory ID card. Auntie doesn't have an ID card, but she rarely leaves the family compound. Auntie sits home watchfully as my four-year old nephews invent games from string and sticks as they dawdle through endless summer days before school begins next year.

My wife watched after her three younger sisters from the time she was a toddler. When she was 13, she left home to work as a housekeeper for a Chinese family in Bangkok, and was later brought into the family business as a saleslady, selling eyeglass frames. When the family closed the business, she was left without education and decent work. She found a job in a bank making coffee, cleaning up and assisting the manager.

We met through an introduction. An American friend had dated her cousin. He told me she came from a wonderful family. After a formal courtship, two months of chaperoned dates, we moved-in together. Eventually, I paid her salary, which allowed her to quit work and continue to send money home to the family. Two years later, I was fortunate enough to obtain a tourist visa for her to enter America.

When we arrived in Central Pennsylvania my cousin telephoned. He asked excitedly if I had taken my wife to the mall. He wanted to know if she went crazy. If she had never left the village, never lived in Bangkok, this might have been true. The local mall in State College is old and tired. In Bangkok, we lived near The Emporium which is home to Versace, Gucci and hundreds of fashionable stores. There are six sparkling floors, if you include the plush state of the art movie theatres upstairs. It dazzles.

We went to the movies in State College. We sat in a small cramped theatre, which had once been a large movie house, but now contained five screens. The seats were small and uncomfortable. You could hear the music from the movie in the next cinema. My wife had heard that America was a leader in technology. She was puzzled. I think one of the most difficult things for Americans to understand is that while we have been standing still, the world has been catching up and exceeding, and that extends to what we refer to as the third world.

In Bangkok, the hospitals are world class and nicer than any I have seen in America. People come from all over the world to use these facilities. The food throughout Thailand is fresh and excellent. You can indulge in a terrific $3 buffet lunch in a fancy hotel while a piano player glides through show tunes on a baby grand. Luxury is affordable.

There are digital clocks connected to the stoplights at intersections, and they count down the seconds, so that you know how long you have to cross the street. Sometimes, they connect them backwards, and they count upwards. Yes, it is Thailand. Internet Cafes are everywhere. Mercedes Benz and BMW's crowd the streets. On occasion, you can see an elephant walking in the road with a reflector attached to his tail.

My wife is thirty-five and has been to America three times. What impressed her the most was that there were sixty and seventy year old people working in supermarkets. Her twenty-nine year old sister is too old to get a factory job.

I think America is no longer fun for my wife. The food is not good. There is no Thai television. There are no Thai people to talk with. And yet, she is happy. That is her disposition. She walks around the house singing. It cheers me.

Having ventured to America gives her prestige in the village. Ever since she began learning a few words of English, she has delighted in growing her vocabulary. On the farm, she is an encyclopedia of worldliness, in an airport, she would be lost.

4

We arrived in the village on the evening of January 19th 2005. Somchai, a motorcycle taxi driver from Bangkok, transported us in his pick-up truck. The village is thirty-five kilometers past Tak. He complained mildly about the extra distance, begging a tip. My wife loaded his truck with three ten-kilo sacks of rice to deliver to youngest sister in Bangkok.

For Thai people, for my family, rice is life. They have two fields of rice located outside the village, about ten minutes away by motorcycle. They eat rice daily. It is not a satisfying meal without rice. When they call on the phone, they greet each other with, "Did you eat rice yet?"

Somchai grouses as the fee negotiation proceeds with steady calm. We are paying $100 for the five hour drive. After gas, it is a good days pay. It is 3 p.m., and he will drive back to Bangkok. He puts his arm around my shoulder. He rubs my belly, and tells me that I should buy him beer when I next come to Bangkok.

I borrow my nephew's bicycle and ride to the small makeshift spirit house for the locals in the woods. There is a large Buddhist Wat a few doors down from the house, but other than New Year or special holidays, the family goes to the shrine in the woods. That is the magical place.

When we returned safely from our journey to America, this is where we went with family and neighbors to give thanks. They lit candles. There is an altar with hundreds of old toy soldiers and horses lined up neatly. The paint is chipped on most of them. They look kind of cool, in an eerie way. The elders chanted. Then, we went back to the house where a pig was slaughtered, and the neighbors gathered for a welcome home party.

Father is one of eleven children. Most of the neighbors are family. I'm not sure who is who. He has a younger sister the same age as my wife. There are about 600 homes in the village. I estimate that twenty percent of the village is family or extended family. My wife agrees with this figure. If I estimated ten percent or thirty percent, she would agree with that too. Accuracy is not as important to her as being agreeable. This keeps life free of petty controversy while creating factual confusion.

The builder chose January 22nd as the auspicious day to begin construction. My wife assured me he is *Mor Dtoo*, a clairvoyant. When I think back to the builder, I can picture a distant, knowing look in his eye.

I have confidence in my builder. After having viewed several homes with several builders, we assessed that his were the nicest. One, he built for another American who was not present during the process. One was built for a Thai policeman. It was open and spacious downstairs. The parquet floors were lovely. Upstairs there were three bedrooms and a half-size Buddha room. We told him to build that house on our land. That was it. He had built it once; the second time should be easier.

When I return from the shrine, there are trays of food ceremoniously displayed on the benches on the outside porch of Father's home. There are hammered silver-colored bowls. One large bowl is filled with un-husked rice. A smaller bowl of rice sits atop. Another tray holds candles, a natural gum and leaves. Alongside sits a plate with bananas and incense. My wife tells me that the Monks are coming to bless the land before we build our house.

At 5 o'clock, they spread mats along the floor of Father's home awaiting the monk's arrival. At 5:30, the neighbor shows up and informs us that the monks are not coming to Father's house, but have been waiting for us at the land. I am heartened that communication problems in Thailand are not mine alone. We load into a pick-up and proceed to the land.

The parcel that we have purchased is more than two football fields long and thin. It is directly across the street from the elementary school. We have chosen to build in the back of the land, giving the front half to two of the sisters. As the oldest of four sisters, it would be improper for my wife to build in the front. This custom works well for me.

Though it is not yet January 22nd, work has begun. Five cement poles have been set to carry electric from the road to the house. Township water has been brought to the back of the property. There are stakes in the ground and wooden boards roughly framing out where the house will be positioned. There are two holes dug inside the framework.

The sun rests large and orange directly behind the monks. My inseparable nephews throw rocks at a piece of scrap rubber. Auntie is the only family member not present. She remains at home to watch over the compound.

The food and a bottle of whiskey are set upon a small platform where the monks sit. There are two older monks in saffron robes and three younger monks in lighter, brighter orange robes. They are given several bottles of orange soda as well. There is a large bowl of water and a smaller one next to it. The eldest monk melts candle wax into the water. He whispers a prayer, and blows gently on the large bowl of water, then the smaller one. He repeats this ritual for the next thirty minutes.

The sun falls low in the sky behind him. Now yellow-orange, it peaks out from a smattering of scattered clouds. Rays shoot in all directions. I remember as a young child seeing this depicted in religious paintings. When I first saw it in nature, I thought it was god. As the chanting continues, the sun turns to brilliant orange and slips toward the horizon.

Second sister is sent back to the house to get more candles. Shortly after she returns, Father is sent home to get a small branch with leaves. Our land is 1 kilometer from the family homestead. I can't help but notice how the lack of planning created the need for the second trip. This is my Western, businessman nature kicking in. You don't waste time or effort. I am the only one here who would think this way. My logic would be near inexplicable to them. They have time. When father returns, it is well into dusk and turning dark.

My family had been preparing for the ceremony all day. They made small boxes from banana leaves, and filled them with a mixture of chili peppers and rice. Tiny poles made from toothpicks with folded newspaper flags adorn the boat boxes.

Candles and incense are placed in the boxes and positioned at each corner of the house. We light the candles. The monks split into two groups, chant over the candles, and then use the branch and leaves to splash now holy water in all directions. They laugh and joke with each other while they do this.

They return to the platform, and a string is run from the house frame to the monks. It is thread through their fingers like a string of beads, and each holds a piece. Candles light the dark. They began to chant in Pali, the language of the monks.

It is a beautiful Gregorian sounding chant, and I feel warmly special to be on my newly purchased land, sitting in the dark candlelit scene. I imagine that this same ceremony has been performed through the centuries.

My mobile phone rings. It is my mother from America, half a world away. Six months prior, my eighty-five year old parents had come to visit the village and meet my new family. My mother can picture the land as I describe the scene. I hold the phone near the monks so that she can listen to the melodious chant.

The Man Wearing Lime Green Pants

My builder is not unique in being *Mor Dtoo*, clairvoyant. Thai people are naturally gifted with a strong sixth sense. There are card readers, palm readers, face readers, aura readers, future seers, luck changers, mysterious ladies with black magic, ghost keepers and Monks with power. I am sure this is just scratching the surface. Sorting superstition from sensory perception is an unending fascination for me.

Once, I was sitting on the beach, when a man with lime green pants wandered past, near the waters edge. I was parallel to the water's edge. He was approaching from my rear and would not have been able to see me. After passing, and walking ten yards down the beach, he stopped. He put out his hands with palms facing down toward the sand, as though he were feeling for something. He slowly circled looking about, and then spotted me lounging in my chair. The transcendental little man with the lime green pants broke into a wide and joyous grin, "Lucky! Lucky!!" he exclaimed.

I have always been blessed with good fortune. When I asked my companion what precisely was going on, she explained that he is *Mor Dtoo*. *Mor* means doctor, and *dtoo* is to see. And, only in Thailand would they bestow the title of Doctor on a clairvoyant or Doctor of Seeing, as he might be called.

Thailand is an ancient culture. Fortune tellers are treated with respect, and visited regularly. The man with the lime green pants was not looking for business, just acknowledging my presence. He was happy to see me.

My wife went to a reader and was told that she should not play the lottery. I thought the odds were well in favor of the psychic on that one. However, these are Thai people, and part of what makes them unique is a mildly contradictory nature. Though gentle, they can be combustible. There is more than a spark of defiance and rebellion. In my experience, telling a Thai person not to do something can be the equivalent of daring a teenager to do it. My wife usually indulges in one lottery ticket, but with this ominous forecast, the time seemed right for her to buy two tickets. The fortune teller was correct. Both tickets were losers.

Third sister went to a medium near the village. It was a lady who becomes possessed during a reading. A spirit speaks through her, with the voice of a child. She was told that she would meet a *farang,* a foreigner, but he would be a jerk. There would come along a second *farang,* and he would be a good match. Third sister went to a different fortune teller two months later who told her the exact same thing without a tip off or prompting from her. So far, the first half is correct.

Youngest sister went with a friend to a *Mor dtoo* in Bangkok. The clairvoyant said that her friend, who was sitting next to her, had stolen her money. The friend confessed on the spot.

My wife and I were standing along the highway waiting for the local bus that runs from the Dam at Sam Ngao to Tak. A man from the next village approached her. He knew the family. He saw me. He told her that her luck was down, and that she should come to see him. He would take care of it. I couldn't help but think that he saw a *farang* and wanted a piece of the spoils.

The next day, my wife did indeed visit his house. He and his wife put on special robes; there was smoke and incantations. Two hours of hocus-pocus ensued. He charged her $5 for the elaborate service. A typical reading might be fifty cents, but not last that long. When my wife told me the price, I winced and rolled my eyes, feeling she was taken.

She told me he is poor, and has a "not nice" house. She told me that if I had been there and seen how he lives, I would have felt sorry and been generous too. I knew she was right. It was a good deed. My good fortune is to have a thoughtful wife.

Bruce 2

As boys, we learned to leave our hats on loose so they would fly off when we sped around the ball field, just like Willie Mays. It was as if Willie was so fast that his cap couldn't keep up with him. Bruce learned to copy his pigeon-toed trot onto the field, and I learned it from him.

There were a ton of us 1950 babies, and by 1959, the schoolyard was a full and happening place. Pick-up games were a constant, and Bruce was always selected as a captain to choose up the sides. My physique would later fill out, but back then, I was scrawny. More a mid-range or lower-end pick as the teams were drawn up. Except when Bruce was there, he chose me first. It felt good. At age nine, he knew that. For him, making his best friend feel good was more important than winning.

Later that year, in fifth grade, Bruce would quit Little League. He became the only kid in the neighborhood who was not on a team. There was talk of him not liking to get up on Saturday morning for the early game. There was talk that he was annoyed with a couple of the parents serving as managers who took the game too seriously.

One time, Mike Hoyt struck out for the final out in the game. His dad was the manager, and took Mike's bat and smashed it to splinters against the metal backstop. He could have been smashing someone's head. To witness someone as big as Mike's dad with a bat in his hand smashing stuff, well, it wasn't our game anymore.

The week before, Mike Hoyt's dad got in a fist fight with one of the other managers. The other fathers had to break it up. We were just kids who wanted to play ball for the fun of it. We didn't know that one asshole could ruin the fun for everyone. When Bruce found out, he quit.

Bruce didn't have a need to talk about it. He quit, and he was right. It wasn't as much fun as it should have been. I quit three months later. Before that, I didn't know you could quit organized stuff like that. Once I found out, I quit the Cub Scouts too.

5

There have been too many places in my life for me to locate or easily relate them in conjunction with dates and times. I don't remember precisely where I was when Kennedy was shot in 1963, but I can place a few events in the landscape of time.

In 1961, I was behind the back seat of my parent's station wagon, lying down pretending to be asleep when the news came over the radio that Willie Mays had hit his third homerun of the game and would get a chance at four. I lay there hoping. When the news came that he hit his fourth home run, I could barely choke back my tearful cheers.

I was in Afghanistan in 1974 when Nixon resigned. That is the only way I can trace back to what year I circled the globe for the first time. I had just arrived in Kabul. It had been dirty and rough travel via local livestock-laden buses crossing from Kandehar. I had heard that there was a restaurant where you could get a good, American-style cheeseburger and French Fries for twenty-five cents. This was exciting. I also heard that Nixon resigned.

I observe politics in the same manner in which others follow sports. I am amazed at how much importance people place on it, and how little they can do about it. One friend in New Jersey tells me that he did not think he could hate a politician more than he hated Nixon, but now his anger and distrust of George W. Bush far exceeds those levels. He is nostalgic for when he used to hate Nixon. He wants me to be sure to register and vote from overseas.

I tell him there is an old story about an interview that Jack Paar had with a little old lady from Maine. When asked whom she would vote for, she replied, "I never vote. It only encourages them."

The real reason I don't vote is not as funny as the Jack Paar story, so I don't tell him. The first election in which I was eligible to vote was in 1972. It was circumstance that kept me from the ballot box.

I Never Vote. It Only Encourages Them
Nixon vs. McGovern 1972

My nights were a psychotic rage of tears and tumult that culminated in passionate release. There was lust and rapture delightfully packaged in olive skin tones and complemented by big, rich-brown save the children eyes that could slide from fathomless need to devilish seduction. After the feverish peak, came a spectacular dreamy state of drift, a detached, near nirvanic lack of desire.

I wasn't a non-voter then. I was a recent college graduate unable to suffer the confinements of a sensible job. My choice to abstain in my first opportunity to vote could be partly attributed to an attractive, but troubled girlfriend. Life existed in drama and emotion, a rollercoaster rising higher and falling steeper than a twenty-two year old youth is equipped to handle, and far more exciting than McGovern vs. Nixon.

* * *

I remember Richard Nixon dying on the television. He lost to John Kennedy and said that the media was not going to have him to kick around anymore. I was 12 years old. I thought his career in politics was over. I took him at his word. I was surprised when he returned in 1968 and won the Presidency. It was a more innocent time in life. I didn't know you could do that; lose, quit, and then come back.

John F. Kennedy died for real. But he didn't die either. There was more news/talk than ever before. There would be endless debate about his assassination. To this day, politicians strive to emulate him. You could make an argument that he is more alive in death.

The war did not loom heavily in front of me. I had only one friend who went to Vietnam, and I think he enlisted in the Navy because it was safer than being around his step-mother. Nobody from our upper-middle class suburb was inducted into the military.

One friend put on a dress for his appointment with the draft board, another went into blood pressure training, smoking cigarettes and staying up all night before his physical to elevate the levels. He went on to Medical School. It was not people from our social class who were getting drafted. It was the poor.

The choice could not have been plainer. McGovern was not Richard Nixon, and that was enough. McGovern was anti-war. Everyone I knew was anti-war. Tricky Dick was not only paranoid, but flat out evil.

New York City and liberal Ivy League universities are less a representation of main stream Americana than French Fries. Polling my friends, I believed it was McGovern who was going to win in a landslide. However, if he needed my vote to carry him past this supposed silent majority, a few imagined hold-outs to reason somewhere in Wyoming or Utah, then, OK, I would lend my support on Election Day. It was the least I could do for someone who was working to save my butt from getting shot to hell in Vietnam.

I was young and un-informed, which leads me to an important question all the more valid today. Who exactly is informed, and are they properly informed? I did not attend the anti-war rallies of the day. I was too independent minded to partake in a mass anything. I would have made a lousy soldier, and I trusted the Military Establishment to recognize that fact. I like to ask questions. Taking orders is not my nature. I don't care for giving them either. Killing strangers is a violation of my temperament.

I remember seeing a hippy van with a hulking, bearded, obviously pot smoking, smiling fellow at the wheel. On the back, a bumper sticker read: **"My Vote Cancels Out Your Vote."** There had to be more to it than that simple fact of math.

It was during the last couple of weeks, before the '72 election, that I learned the truth, though at first difficult to believe. It was Nixon who was going to win in a landslide. It was projected that McGovern might not carry one state.

I was staying at a friend's house in the Long Island town where I grew up. My parents had purchased a hideaway farm in New Jersey and, for tax purposes, had made it our permanent address. On an earlier visit, I filled out voter registration forms. I had been suitably indoctrinated into the concept that voting was a privilege. However, on Election Day, there were two larger issues.

First, I was in New York and the price of gas was high. It would have cost me $10 to drive to Western New Jersey, cast my vote and drive back. McGovern was a certain loser. My vote would not have brought him a state. It would not have delivered him a county, or even our small township.

Second, emotions were peaking with my girlfriend. We had a nightly routine of her crying, my feeling terrible and guilty, but not wanting to commit. I wanted to travel. A suburban life of normalcy was not the hand I wanted to play – a world was trumpeting in front of me.

My mother had taught me that I could be anything I wanted. Her thoughts likely went to Doctor, Lawyer, Businessman – mine to Wandering Minstrel. When I mentioned this to her later in life, her reply was an expression of surprise, "I said that?"

Having a girlfriend was an anchor that dragged in direct contrast to my need for motion. There were tantrums and breakdowns, which I met with confused, stunned silence. I learned that slipping deep inside brought peace. Outside, there were psychosis and neurosis far beyond my capacity to understand. There was a hurricane of fear, issues of protection, disappointment and abandonment swirling about. I was under the youthful illusion that love was supposed to be a good thing. It was present, but not working for either one of us. The rains came in cascades, and the sun cooked a pot that would bubble and boil passion into a steamy, sweaty release.

Was I going to leave this melodrama for even one night to vote for some loser, mosquito-bitten liberal from frozen Minnesota? My vote would not change his life, or mine, in any measurable way. But really, it all came down to the ten bucks. I didn't talk about it much. I didn't proclaim myself a non-voter due to high moral principles. Voting would have been a waste of money, and I needed the ten dollars more than I needed to issue an inaudible call from the woods: "Don't Kill Vietnamese, Don't Kill Me."

6

Tak is the small city in Central Thailand that is nearest our village. There are several places to stay, including a luxury first class hotel near the River Ping. I have stayed there before, but for a longer residence, I choose a less-expensive small resort with beautiful gardens.

I will check-in and check-out on a regular basis. Around the corner from my resort is an excellent, outdoor, noodle soup restaurant. A bowl of soup costs twenty-five cents. There is a Buddhist Temple nearby, where for $2.50 an hour, they give therapeutic massage.

My wife tells me that I must come to our land on January 22nd. The builder will be holding a ceremony before beginning construction. When I arrive, I am surprised to find that there are many holes already dug. Twenty workers are busily pounding with picks.

The workers are both male and female, and their bodies are covered entirely. A cloth is worn across their faces so that they don't inhale the dirt and dust. They all look at me. They are curious. We exchange pleasantries. They are surprised that I can speak Thai. Most of the workers are older, but there is one young girl dressed in blue jeans and wearing a baseball cap. I can't see much of her, but she attracts my attention. She smiles wide when I walk near. I cannot see her face, but her eyes shine and narrow, as they might if she were smiling.

The builder arrives on time. He has many silver dishes filled with candles, flowers and accessories. He asks for my necklace. Several Buddha amulets and one King Rama V are worn under my shirt daily. They were gifts for good deeds, given to protect me. The builder takes my wife's necklace of amulets too. He hangs them both on a nail attached to a long board. He puts the board in one of the holes and raises it 15' into the air. The workers pour cement to affix it in place. The necklaces must remain there overnight. There will be a guard at night watching over everything.

The builder lights candles as the family sits on mats in front of him. Once more, Auntie has remained behind. The builder chants. The Thai word for builder [or any professional such as a carpenter, electrician or plumber] is *Chang*. If you make an imperceptible, to my ear, change of the tone, *Chang* is also the word for elephant. I am sure there are many times that I must have asked my wife if the elephant was finished working in the bathroom.

When the builder has finished chanting, he hands my wife and me a plate full of rose petals. My family hands us a dish full of coins. There are sixteen large hand dug holes inside the boundary of what will be the house. We are told to sprinkle the rose petals and coins, a few in each hole. There are more blessings, and cement is poured into each of the holes. The foundation of my house is embedded with coins and rose petals.

As I am leaving, I walk past the young girl. I catch her eye, and she smiles. I wonder if she is thinking that the only way that she could afford a house such as she will be building, would be if she too could find a foreign husband. This is probably not a unique thought for young Thai ladies. Foreigners represent money. We are a house. We are a car. This makes us fascinating.

I return to Tak. There is an internet shop near my resort. Children noisily play games, screaming along with each kill. I sit and write emails. When I tell my ex-wife, in an email, of the lovely traditions associated with building the house, she writes back that it is similar to American Indian ceremonies. This does not surprise. I have been to dress-up Cowboy and Indian parties in Bangkok where it would be difficult to separate-out a Thai person from an actual American Indian. I believe it was Thai people who walked across the Bering Strait to Alaska and filtered down through the Americas. I have a friend who is an Otavalan Indian from Ecuador. When he came to visit me in Thailand, everyone thought he was Thai.

In lighter moments, I think the Thai people may be the lost tribe of the Jews, gone wild. They love chicken soup and *shtick*, but they are not as neurotic as my ancestors.

One day a week, I check the construction. A friend had advised me to go every day and watch, so that in the future, I will know where they screwed-up, and be able to rectify the mistake. One day a week is enough for me. Two days a week, I walk to the local Buddhist temple for a massage. The temple houses a radio station, a small factory for making clothing and a primary school. My masseuse likes that I can speak Thai. She wants to learn English. There is an American song on the radio. She asks me the meaning of the word "funky."

Often, I can talk in circles and arrive at the meaning from the back side, but I am not sure I can explain "funky" in English language. I want to tell her it is like cool, but that does not translate either. I don't know any Thai words for hip, jive or cool. I nod my head, wrinkle my nose and snap my fingers – "funky" – but I don't think I've done it justice. She nods as if she understands. I think she is being polite.

My builder says, "Yesterday…" in English before reverting to future tense in Thai. "Yesterday, I will come to pick you up." I have no idea when he is coming. We like each other, though communication is difficult. I can converse fluidly with most Thai people. Some, I cannot understand anything they say. The builder is near totally incomprehensible to me. "OK," I tell him and smile. When he comes tomorrow, or at three o'clock today, if I am not there, he will wait. It will not trouble him.

I asked a German friend who was building a house in Bangkok, how it was going. "Going," he responded in a thick German accent. "What is going? Nothing is going." He explained that one day all the workers walked out – that was it.

Another friend, who had just completed his house, had a problem with a flickering light and was told that it was a ghost. The electrician said there was nothing that he could do.

My time in Tak can be lonely. It is an opportunity for reflection. It is a chance to write. As we enter hot season, my room becomes an escape from the heat. My walks become shorter as humidity drives the mind set to groggy and dripping sweat bleeds salt into my eyes. Even sitting in the shade, beads of perspiration will materialize on my arms. I can sit and watch them form in seconds. Air-con is the only relief. I nap often, sleeping fitfully, sometimes unable to distinguish my dreams from reality. One particular wry smile rings through my memory clear as day.

It was at an outdoor restaurant in Bangkok. The waitress took a cigarette lighter, and on her hands and knees, went under the table to light the anti-mosquito coil. Thai people have trouble with the sp sound. They drag it out and alter it. Spoon, becomes Sssa poon. I pay no attention to the waitress under the table, until I get a nose full of the smoke from the coil. Her head is between my knees when I tell her, *Mais chorb*, don't like – I hesitate. What is the word for smoke? I fake it – *mais chorbp sssa-moke,* I attempt to say the English word with a Thai sound to it. She looks up in shock, and then rises from under the table with a major league smile. Someone at the table helps me with my error. *Samoke* means blowjob. They tell me there is a blow job bar around the corner from the restaurant.

I go out for walks in Tak. I retreat to my room and watch the only English language station available, Fox. *Fock New* the Thai's call it. I have my laptop and write stories. In the quiet normalcy of Tak, my imagination craves excitement, and my daylight hours take hold of my collar and sweep me toward creating Bangkok based stories about friends who frequent bars.

The Staggering Reality of Red Fred
A Mystery of Sorts

This is a mystery where there is no deceased and no body count; however, there is a profound passing on. Youth, innocence, love; the things that fade slowly as people age and weariness overcomes hope. They usually pass away gradually, the causes vague and tangled in threads of disappointment. Where does hope go? Maybe that is the real mystery. Pay attention to the clues, and tell me what you think, because I don't know, and I'm telling you that right up front.

Here are the cast of players in our strange cross-cultural story:

Ning; our heroine, our devil, I'll let you decide. When we meet her she is attractive, smart, twenty-five years old and working in the infamous red light district of Bangkok, *Patpong*. Sometimes it seems as if half of Bangkok is an evening entertainment complex, but *Patpong*, that's the one on all the tourist maps.

Ning works as a hostess, which means that she doesn't have to take off her clothing and dance on the go-go stage. Sometimes, she is the greeter or roper, as they say, working outside the bar as the lure; classy, nicely attired, a seeming taste of what you might find if you came into the bar for a drink. She takes your hand and leads you in. Only a fool or a dead man would not be tempted to follow, as she allows you to feel that you will be with her, but after you are seated, she quickly finds her way back outside the bar to snare another passerby.

So, what I want you to see right off, is that, though this is only a minor ruse, a simple deception; conning the weak minded foreigner is part of the job and Thais don't think too much about it being wrong or right. The customers don't think about it too long either. This is not an industry that follows any particular dictate of moral standards. The gents accept a moment of disappointment, and then concentrate on the bouncing ladies up on the stage. For the girls, bait and switch, or any ruse, becomes an accepted part of life.

Ning can sit with a customer and hustle a drink, if she wants, and can go with him for the night, if so inclined, but mostly they are just stupid guys here to bang a Thai girl or two during their two week vacation and then go home, possibly to their wives. Ning's command of English and outright hot appearance makes her most valuable in front of the bar, and that's pretty much where she stays.

Fred; Or Red Fred, as his friends called him, though the days of nicknames are rapidly falling away, more often now, to a small flinch, it is Mr. Frederick. The boyhood Deadhead days that slipped into his late twenties have faded from a tie-dyed past to an established jacket and tie corporate future. His shock of long, flowing red hair is cropped presentably neat every other week by an accomplished stylist. It is unsettling, in a lost youth sort of way, but mostly boring. The Grateful Dead died with Garcia and by thirty, the word "security" had crept into his mindset.

That was what came to be missing for Jennifer, his long time partner and Deadhead companion who bailed and left him for a square accountant. Red Fred was stunned by her departure from his life. It was sudden and not lacking irony. After she left, he fell in line with a more conservative, corporate-type of existence. It was the only choice that made sense. The heads who switched to Fish, the guys who were still doing the same gig past forty, looked pretty sorry. It was a change they could have made together, but Jennifer was gone. The wound went deep; the pain never knew where to go for healing.

Fred found a 'real job' and worked his way up. He worked hard, but never relinquished the idea of dropping out again. When we meet him, he is still bummed by having lost Jennifer, and that was two full years ago. He thought they were forever, and the disappointment, like a stubborn morning fog, is not easily melting away. That's one of the problems for a youthful guy who is smart and decent with a strong sense of self confidence. They have trouble believing that their lady could possibly prefer someone else.

Fred thought he knew the scene in Bangkok, at least how it played out in words on the page. He had read up and been versed in all aspects of the game, but there is nothing that can adequately prepare you for being one of the players. Even the girls get too involved. They fall in love too, which makes things more confusing. The game is real, off the playing field, beyond any set of rules of proper conduct, fast-paced, and the stakes are the essence of your life; how you spend your time, your emotions and money.

Red Fred was invited to Siam by Party Paul, an old friend who was experienced and knew the players. And with Fred's best interest at heart, Paul decided to bring a girl to the airport, a welcome to Bangkok first night gift. But, if this mystery is to have a Lucifer, a fuse to set the explosion in motion, then it just as well might be Party Paul, because without him, none of this goes down.

Party Paul Kingsley and Red Fred were long time friends. Party Paul had made a few bucks selling "stuff" at the dead shows, but he had gone straight now too. He was working as a chef, saving money for his own restaurant, like everyone told him to open, but he never seemed to get much stashed. The amount of money needed was a vast and distant vision. His small nest-egg never grew because blowing it on a good time always made more momentary sense. The restaurant may never be. How many good times are there in this lifetime? Why waste even one for a few bucks in the bank? Party Paul had a strong feeling that his future was happening now.

Paul had been to Bangkok several times on vacation, a stationary Dead Show, an entire city where the party never stopped. He knew how to have a good time, without hurting or getting hurt, and his current good time was one of the wildest, craziest, downright funniest girls in any Patpong bar. She was a lively, sexy dancer who had enough energy for three girls, and while the other girls were shuffling through their shift onstage, Pen had a firecracker up her butt and was dancing as well as playfully harassing the customers and other girls. Paul watched and laughed as Pen was the main attraction, center stage in the three ring circus of a bar.

Paul was on a high because Pen was coming with him to meet Fred and the midnight flight from America. That meant two things: He was going to be able to show off "his" really hot looking Thai girl to his friend Fred in his first moments in Bangkok, and he would have the chance to spend the night with Pen.

Pen was spectacular, but Paul was certainly not the first guy to notice that fact. The testimony was that she had a cell phone that went off seemingly every time the second hand crossed twelve, and sometimes she would have to disappear pronto. Now, you can believe the lines about her girlfriend having to go to the hospital, or her brother coming in on the three a.m. bus, but it is kind of like religion. You better be imbued with an abundance of faith, and Paul only held a thimble full, and that was on good nights. This girl had customers.

He knew her game well enough and accepted. When you have a chance to spend time with a dazzling entertainment package like Pen, you have to accept certain things; otherwise it can make you crazy. The choice was this. He could enjoy whatever time she would give him, know it will cost, spend his time hoping the phone doesn't go off, and he could not get upset when it inevitably does. Or, he could forget about her and never see her again unless she haunts an early morning dream. The first option was more fun.

"Here's the deal," he told her. "I'll pay your bar fine, and the bar fine for one of your friends, and we all go meet Fred at the airport, but you have to spend the whole night with me. You have to turn off your phone. No flaking off at two a.m. and I'll double your nightly fee." Pen agreed. The trip to the airport added excitement to the evening for her. And then, afterwards, there'll be food, a lot of drinking, maybe a late night disco; Party Paul was always down for a good time.

But which friend should they invite along? Paul said that Ning would be perfect for Fred. Her English was good, and she would be the girl that Fred would choose if he were here. And OK, Ning doesn't "go" too often with customers, but Fred was young, tall, thin and handsome, and he would be just the kind of guy that Ning would like. He was a nice guy; it was his first time, and he didn't know the scene, which is of great value to a clever bargirl.

Fred wasn't typical. Ning wasn't typical. If they were both not typical in a manner that fit well, they would be a great couple. But Ning refused to go. She wasn't the type to go with a customer whom she never met before. And all the talk about the perfect this or that was fine, but she wasn't buying into it. She would allow only this; bring him to the bar, and she'll think about it.

Now, when you look back at this story, this is one of the things that you wonder about. But getting into the head of a nighttime worker from *Patpong* is not an easy chore. They do everything they can so that you won't judge them on the fact that they work in a bar, and it is amazingly easy to forget. The girls quickly present who they are, in part; poor girls, from small villages, trying to earn money to send to mama and papa. And that part tugs on your heart strings. They are joyful and making the best of it, and you easily come to respect that. The other part is a charming night hostess, all the more alluring because the class and elegance is natural, and the combination of dutiful daughter and entertaining hostess can be fatal.

Bargirls; I invite them in as a chorus line of sorts, not any specific one, but I bring them in to our mystery as a group figure. They are a teaching/learning experience for other bargirls. Normally, an oppressed majority, women are responsible to bring up the children and help support their mother and father. So, there is a lot of responsibility thrust their way.

They go to work, and like to talk. If the normal nightly fee is about $50, and one of the girls comes home with $75, then they all want to know what she did, or more often than not, what fairytale story she got the customer to fall for. Hospitals and sick mothers were always good. But, as the customers became known, hooked you might say, there is room for curving pathways which lead to the opening of wallets. And there is always a room full of coaches to guide you - bargirls.

So - that about gives you the cast of characters, except maybe one, me, a shadow watching from the sidelines. I am the antidote for the Thai ladies, as I have been around long enough to know what they are probably filling each other's heads with. It is not that I am up on the latest scam, just that I am aware that tom-foolery exists on a constant basis. It is part of the job, part of the fantasy they are selling. I make no judgment.

So, this is how our mystery plays out.

Ning is not going to the airport, and Red Fred's fate is hanging on who is available. But OK. This is *Patpong*, and it is still a matter of good and better. Party Paul chooses on looks and gets a young, thin lady who, later on, nobody would remember her name because after the first night, the story is all Ning.

The second night Red Fred would go to the bar with Party Paul and meet Ning, and then, every night for the rest of his vacation, he would pay her bar fine and take her out. It was love or some reasonable facsimile from then on. And this continued for three years. They would spend every second together during his one week vacation from work, three times a year.

Ning was quick witted, clever and had her own convoluted brand of logic. She was a five-foot-two bundle of fun. There was Ning humor, Ning style, Ning this and that, which was always geared toward whatever she might want at the moment. A puppet master contortionist, twisting a willing Fred, Ning held all the strings.

Fred was pretty damned charmed by the whole exotic nature of everything. He had a Thai girlfriend, he was learning to speak Thai language, he loved to eat Thai food, and you might say, he was in love with a whole culture, an entire country and Ning was the harpoon stuck in his heart that kept him connected. He would spend his three vacation weeks in Thailand, but not with Paul or me, or any other friends who might be there. Fred was lost in Ning Ning land. And it was OK with all of us because he was happy.

Here's what we did know. Fred was in love, though none of us had the maturity to define the term. Definitions ranged from enamored to pussy whipped. He could tell you a half hour story about Ning buying a bowl of noodle soup on the street. Though a rather ordinary occurrence, it was enough to charm the daylights out of him. He was always smiling whenever we saw him, which wasn't that often. Like I said, he was either with Ning, or back home working overtime to save the money to go and see Ning.

There was an occasional fight, but it seemed to be one of those elements that added spice, a chili pepper tossed into the already hot mix. But the fights were about real issues for Ning, and gradually she won each one and would go on to the next issue, and here they are, in as close as I can get to any semblance of order:

1. If you pay my salary, then I don't have to work at the bar. $250 per month, though the bar only paid her $150.

2. I'm bored. If you pay for me to go to school, then I can learn English and get a good job. An additional $250 per month, though the lessons only cost $125.

3. Money. How about an extra $100? A gold necklace would be nice?

4. Momma knows I have a rich boyfriend and now she wants me to help her out too. $150

5. More money. [It is easier for me to bother you about money, than for you to resist – if you resist the fantasy turns ugly – you ruin everything.]

6. I want to live in America with you. [Are you sure you don't have a girlfriend back home who is getting some of your money?]

7. I want to get married. [I want all of your money.]

Well, I think you get the picture from my angle, but I am not sure what the view looks like for you. Ning had told Fred that she previously worked in a gold shop, and that was why her English was so good. I had told Fred, if a bargirl's English is good, that they had probably been working in the bar for a long time. Poor girls from farming families learn English from customers, and the ones who speak well had more than likely lived with a foreigner. Like I said, you believe what you want. Fred did.

Ning working in a gold shop was easy to swallow and legitimized the whole affair back home. If you lop off the few months that she was a roper in the bar, then she had a pretty legit career, but not enough so as to be able to pass her off at the Embassy. He would need a fianc e visa to get her into America. And that takes a commitment. And just as a point, I live here, and the few times that I have been in a gold shop it was not an oasis of English language. It was Thai people, speaking Thai language.

Her English was already pretty good, so I doubt the few months time frame that she offered about working in the bar. I got the rest of the story in pieces. For a while, Ning pushed hard for the marriage option, but then she seemed to almost lose interest, not willing to go to the embassy on her own and file the papers in his absence. I started to hear stories about her name not being her real name, though she never legally changed it.

Nobody cared much when things were going well, it didn't cause commotion, but that was about to change. A September trip planned well in advance was the time, and Bangkok was once more the place, except this time, there was a glitch. During his one week visit, Ning had to return home for family business, and Fred was not invited.

It was a pot coming to boil. Fred had been at this with her for three years and, for whatever reason, was not ready to pull the marriage trigger. He didn't believe her line about going home. Actually, he thought she was just kidding around, and when he got there, she would spend every minute with him, as usual. That didn't happen. He had consulted me beforehand. I told him there were two possibilities. She was pissed off and trying to teach him a lesson, which was not likely. Or, she had another guy, which seemed likely, though extremely difficult for Red Fred to believe. Youth holds onto ideals, and Red was young in the ways of Bangkok bargirls. Besides, they were in love, right? She wouldn't do that.

The first couple of days were OK, but then she really did have to go home. And here is how things played out. Red Fred gave her $200 for the trip, which is actually only a $3 bus fare and $5 worth of obligatory food treats for the family. Even though Ning was no longer working the bar, his first night alone, without Ning, Fred went there anyway. Where else could he go? He didn't know anyone else in Bangkok.

He caught her. Sure enough, there she was, sitting with a young Englishman. She said it was someone that she knew from a long time ago, [could this have been a man she had lived with] an old customer who came back to town. She didn't cancel her date with him. Ning and Fred talked outside for twenty minutes, and she apologized with profusion. Red Fred went home with only a hollow feeling to accompany his profound sadness. Ning stayed with the Englishman. I am quite sure she never returned the two hundred dollars that he gave her to visit the family. There is a Thai proverb that says: What the elephant eats, he does not give back.

Fred was left angry and resentful, and this is not a good thing to be left with when you are in your thirties and have your life tied up in a Thai bargirl. Party Paul had been kicked around, and so had I, but you have to work through these things. We had all explained to Fred about bargirls selling a fantasy, but he never quite grasped their ability to make it seem so damn real. It was real.

Here are the questions that make this all a mystery to me: Why would Ning blow Fred off on his one week vacation? Was he just a customer? If so, he had to be a good customer, paying her $500 a month and bonuses for a no-show job. Was the other guy sending her monthly money too, and she got caught in a time vise? She wouldn't be the first bargirl to pull this trick. It is easy and quite profitable. Were there others? And if so; how many others were there? That first night that she didn't meet him at the airport - Was that all part of the game? She is a good girl, and doesn't do that sort of thing – Was that part of the ruse? Could she have been that clever and calculating right from the start?

For me, there are no good answers that she can give to those questions. Obviously, blowing off the other customer wasn't worth it to her, she's not stupid. But you have to wonder. Was there ever any sincerity at all? Was there ever a genuine desire to pursue the marriage option for reasons beyond finance? But for me, the mystery goes one step deeper. Why does life not get sweeter as we learn and progress? Have we all had a Jennifer or Ning to crush our youthful hopes? Why does life so often sour for most of us, and is that the real challenge? What do you do to keep your life fresh and vibrant? We all want our lives to be special.

Hope is what keeps us going. And is that what life is all about, getting a job, progressing up the ladder, occupying your mind with that brutal task so that you don't have to wonder, you don't have to deal with the simplest of questions – Where does hope go? Being in

Bangkok made Red Fred, Party Paul and I feel alive, but why, if you open your eyes, does life so often suck?

After returning home, depressed and discouraged, Red Fred sent an email to Party Paul asking a rhetorical question. "Do I have the word 'sucker' tattooed on my forehead and only women can see it?"

"No," Paul returned an answer. "I think everyone can see it."

Well, like I said in the beginning, you tell me what you think, because I don't really know – and here's why. It seems to be the way with mysteries that they have an unexpected twist to the end, an unrevealed fact that changes the vantage point. And so, though all the other facts are true, I present this one nearly lost piece of information along with one last character; a vixen who passes through the life of Red Fred and Ning with the speed of a shooting star, and the effect of gasoline thrown on an already overheated relationship.

Shana Day was a soft breeze who blew into the desert of Central Pennsylvania from the Caribbean Sea. Tall and lithe, she was the spicy salsa amongst the white bread conservative world around her. You might say she didn't groove to the same funereal march as the other women who worked in the company, and who cloaked their femininity in business attire. There always seemed to be a touch of lemon or lime in her wardrobe to match her youthful vivacity. The company had brought her in for a week, to work on layout designs for an advertising campaign, and she and Fred were spontaneously combustible. She had a boyfriend, he had a girlfriend; it was only a week.

It was more than once that Ning telephonically intruded on Red Fred in his sleep from half a world away. The time difference is twelve hours, making noon in Thailand, midnight in America. For Red Fred, it was a playful interruption of slumber. A phone call from another world; his lover calling in the night because she missed him; it was an endearing surprise, irregular, infrequent, but the type of intrusion that warms your heart. Ning missed him and needed to hear his voice at that moment, and he was pleased to oblige.

Visas for young, single Thai ladies are near impossible. When a customer leaves Bangkok for home, it could well be to a wife or girlfriend. Just as the girls are practiced in deception, so are many of the customers, though sometimes it boggles the mind as to why. The girls would go with them anyway. It is their job.

But when a guy talks about marriage, well, a girl has every right to know as much as she can about what is on the other side of the impenetrable door that her man passes through after his eight day vacation in Thailand. They tend to envision the loose moral structure of Bangkok, and easy availability of lovely ladies as existing in the Western World too. They just don't know.

A home phone number is a big prize. If there were a wife, she would not tolerate middle of the night calls, and it also serves as a fishing rod. The week that Red Fred spent at Shana Day's hotel, there was no answer when his phone rang in the middle of the night, though he did answer at work the next day. Ning tried every night, her anger rising.

So, just maybe, she didn't really care that Red Fred found her out when she blew him off that day in September and went to the most likely place that she could have been found. Maybe she was really pissed, and her temper got the better of her reason until she saw how hurt Red Fred looked when he came in the door and found her with her other date. Maybe, as fate tends to be quirky, especially in a place like Bangkok, an international city with so much to add to the mix; her other customer called her the same week that she had been unable to find Red Fred at home, the same week that she knew he was staying with someone else. All that good for the goose and gander stuff may have been playing on her mind. So, she blew him off.

And maybe, the old couple sitting over there, together on the park bench, they too went through rough times, and then patched things up. Sort of. They bicker over the tiniest of things, insignificant timelines and old wounds that have scarred over long ago. They bicker over their own version of Shana Day, who in the entire scheme of things meant nothing more than a momentary satisfaction of a biological urge, but created a lasting hurt to hold on to and make life suck just a little more than need be.

And so, the answer to the mystery of what screwed up the relationship might simply be that of life. It is human nature to screw up, and it happens to us all, and, on some level, we know that it will again. And that's where hope goes. Age replaces it with calm resignation. Youth keeps on hoping.

Party Paul, Red Fred and I never discuss Ning. It is difficult to imagine what their relationship has morphed into as two years have past since the painful incident in the bar. Surely, it must cost. Surely, there is hurt and emotion still being swirled through a tie-dyed mix of fun and wild Bangkok nights. Fred, like a fighter answering the bell for the next round, still goes back to it every chance he gets, and this is his punch drunk, staggering reality.

Entrepreneur's Quiz

Take a moment and consider this question. The answer is on the following page.

An attractive young bargirl had been collecting customers for three years. She had marriage proposals, but turned them down because work was more lucrative than nuptials.

Sue Lyn had five different boyfriends; two from England, one each from Sweden, Germany and Venezuela. They all sent monthly money ranging from 20,000 to 50,000 baht, so that she would no longer have to work in a bar. The largest amount came from the Swede. The Venezuelan was the easiest customer, because he rarely came to visit. He had initially contributed a lovely apartment, but came for only one week a year. When none of her boyfriends were in town, Sue Lyn went back to work at the bar, where she mined for new monthly customers and picked up nightly fees.

Here is the breakdown:

Sweden	–	50,000
England	–	40,000
England #2	–	30,000
Venezuela	–	35,000
Germany	–	20,000
Total	=	175,000 baht or $4,375 a month

And there were times when boyfriends would volunteer, or could be coerced, to send a little extra. Plus, she made money when they were out of town which was 80% of the year. Best guess is that Sue Lyn was reeling in near $70,000 a year. A tax free fortune in a land of fifty cent lunches and $2 taxi rides.

It was December when she received a troublesome surprise. All five of her boyfriends were coming to visit in the same week. Both of the

Englishmen stay in the same hotel. Only the Venezuelan is aware of her apartment.

Take a minute and consider the options. If you were Sue Lyn, what would you do? Her solution is on the next page.

Sue Lyn's Answer

The answer was simple. First, she turned off her phone and abandoned Bangkok for the seclusion of her mother's house in the countryside of Khon Kaen. Nobody would be able to find her, and there would be no unfortunate mishaps. She waited forty eight hours, enough time for the guys to be suitably worried before having a friend show-up at their hotel.

"There was an accident. Sue Lyn was on her way to see ***you*** when the car went off the road." Her friend did not know the name of the hospital. No, she would be in the hospital for at least a month. No, she had no phone. But she had been so looking forward to your visit. In addition to her monthly money, there will be doctor bills that need to be paid.

For the month of December Sue Lyn cleared over 400,000 baht or $10,000 – and didn't have to do a days work.

Well? How did you do?

As far as I can see, the only better answer might have been that she was driving and responsible for the damage to the car. She thought of that too. When I flashed my eyebrows, smiled and asked her why she didn't employ this technique, she gave me a stern look. "I'm not like that," she told me.

7

I bring a bag of oranges for the workers at my construction site. The men ask for whiskey. It is impolite to give a direct 'no', and so I tell them, when the house is finished, we will have a party. Postponement is a proper way to rebuff. There is a sign posted that says: "No Whiskey." Booze and beer seem to be the only things that they think about, which leaves no wonder as to why the foreigner frequented bars of Bangkok are well-populated by young ladies in their 20s with a child or two and no husband.

There are timbers everywhere. They are used as supports and to build scaffolding. I look for the young girl with the baseball cap. She is waiting for me to find her. When I finally locate her; a smile lights-up her eyes.

Work is being done by hand that I think could be more efficiently accomplished by machine. Labor is cheap; $2.50 per day. Renting large machines is expensive. I am wrong. What would be foolish in the West is cost efficient here.

I spend the night in the village, but it is too hot to sleep well. The shower is a large plastic garbage pail of cool water and a scoop. It is refreshing, but not long after, I am hot again. I am concerned that my laptop will melt.

In the early morning, shortly after the sun's first light, at 6 a.m., the Wat broadcasts old style Thai music from its PA system. It has an air of summer camp; rise and shine – the dress for the day is shorts and shorts.

I think about Party Paul. I was responsible for bringing him to Bangkok the first time. We went out to bars together. It was fun. At the conclusion of his first trip, when he left to go back to America, he said to me, "Hey man, keep the party going. I'll be back," as if Bangkok was an extension of his fraternity days, and if everybody falls asleep, the party is over.

After a few trips, Party Paul settled in with one lady. She was robust, had a broad smile and a great, hoarse throaty laugh. She was a terrific dancer. It was fun to watch her. She was quick-witted and a frolicking monkey parade of laughs. When Party Paul was visiting Bangkok, she lived with him. When he left, she moved back in with her Thai boyfriend. I think Paul knew, but didn't care.

When I was first dating my wife, we went out to hear Thai music. Party Paul came with his girlfriend. One of the bargirls, and her Thai husband, came with us too. She was angry at her husband. Party Paul's girlfriend had a fork stuck up her ass and did little more than grimace and snarl all night. She would not get up and dance.

It became a defining moment for Paul when a group of eight girls came in who work in the bar where we hang out. They had paid their own bar fines, and bought themselves out for the night. They came to let loose and go wild, and in minutes, they were waving their arms over their heads, singing and dancing.

Being with them would have been more fun than being at our table. My wife is quiet in public, but it seemed that both the other ladies were dealing with a butt load of cutlery, and ours was a dour table. Party Paul wanted to be at the bargirl table, and in the future, he would. He came to Bangkok to have a good time, not hassles.

Thai bargirls are unique. They defy Western definition. They are affectionate, engaging, and a downright comic hit parade. They laugh a lot, and giggle like school girls, but have the alluring, enticing eyes of a sexy woman. Put it all together, and you have one hell of a package. I have no idea why, but as a group, Thai bargirls have more fun than anyone that I know. And that night, at the music, Party Paul made a decision that nothing would get in his way of participating in the good times. Soon after, he had a mutual split up with his girlfriend.

Most bargirls are looking for a husband, and it would surprise people how many of them find wealthy foreigners to marry. In rural Thailand, fancy cement houses sprout from their spoils.

Party Paul did not want this type of bargirl again, and so, he started hanging around in raunchy establishments where it was less likely that he would fall in love, and the action would be uninhibited. It seemed, the seedier the place, the more fun. But fun can take a toll too.

And as I sit in my room in Tak, my mind fills with a hazy smoke and a stale smell of beer. I drift to a place where the music is loud, and the atmosphere raucous. There is an odd electricity swirling about as my thought waves travel to Bangkok with Party Paul. I might be alone in Tak, but the sounds echo through the night, and I can hear the chorus rise-up, just as he described it, as he walks through the door into his new favorite bar, two steps off the beaten path.

James Bloody Bond, The Lefty and Me

"Paul!" A voice calls out as I walk through the door of my favorite back alley Bangkok bar. The chorus will echo through the bar like "Norm!!" at Cheers. "Pawwwlll," they call out in unison.

Everyone here is "Norm!!" Well, most of us anyway. It makes us feel at home, more likely to hang out, consume another beverage, get entangled with a lovely lassie, and we're more likely to come back. "And they're always glad you came" - the theme song echoes through your subconscious.

I make my way to the back of the bar.

"Jack Coke," someone undoubtedly asks. They know your preference, habits and temperament.

"Jack Coke, OK," I call back. The girls huddle around. I have a reputation for being loose with the drinks. Lady drinks, an inclusion into my club, and a commission for the recipient. It is a rowdy bar at times. The guys get drunk and loose with their hands. Most of the girls accept it as part of the job, but it is not my style.

"Party Paul, play darts?" Someone always asks me.

"Sure," I scan the bar.

"You want to play?" I ask one of the newer girls. She flips her eyebrows, which usually means not only do I want to play, but I'll take care of you for the night.

It is late afternoon and the bar is lacking customers. Peter Popcorn is curled up in one of the booths with a girl tucked under his arm and a couple of drinks half spent on the table in front of him. He's an infrequent regular. I've seen him in here, mid-afternoon, and I figure that at his age, he's probably dead asleep by seven at night, but he likes to hang out, take a break from the mid-day heat. What could be better; lounging in the booth, munching from a bag of popcorn that he buys outside the bar somewhere, and watching whatever movie is on the big screen while quietly groping an attractive young lady fifty years his junior.

I don't know the name of the girl that he is fondling, but when I pass near she gets up, taking a break from Popcorn. She has made eyes at me before, and it always seemed like she and I could be possible, but just for a fling. She's kind of sexy in a could-be-cuddly kind of way, not the prettiest girl in the bar, but there's some flash to the eye, you know, that sparkle and glow they shoot out at you that makes you feel like a teenager at summer camp.

When I walk past, she makes small talk. Thai people have this thing about asking; "Where you been? Where are you going?" – That's personal stuff for us Westerners, but just prattle for them, but the touching my arm, in a bar like this, with a look in her eye like that, well, that's half an invite to spend the night.

Peter Popcorn leans toward her, and though she's a good two feet away in the aisle, he puts his lips together and blows noiselessly as if he were whistling. He moves his head in a slight circular motion. It takes me a minute, but then I realize; he's blowing at her ear. It would be funny, if it weren't gross. It is like some girl a long time ago told him that was sexy, or he read somewhere that if you blow in their ear they'll follow you anywhere. I can see now that is what he is working on, and I walk away because I don't want to interfere with his conquests, and besides, I don't want to puke.

We shoot for closest to the bull's-eye to see who plays first. Winning at darts is the tougher challenge in a bar like this. Getting the girl is easy, but I'm kind of square. I want a rapport. I want to at least believe the girl likes me as a person. That stuff is important to me. I don't know why, but it seems to work for the girls too. I imagine that they like that about me, you know, that I take the time to know them, even though their stories are mostly the same.

They had a couple of kids when they were young and most of them were probably drop-dead gorgeous at twenty. Then, when they were twenty-three, the husband grew tired of the scene and found a younger lady. They never see him again. There is no support financially or emotionally. When they say "all apart" they mean it. Sometimes, they'll tell you he died. Sometimes, he died for real. A lot of guys lose it in motorcycle accidents.

Now that these girls are in their 30s, well, this is it for them. They've had enough of Thai men, or so they say, and they want a Westerner to take care of them. A nice, not too drunk, older man with some change rattling around in his pocket and an ATM card.

The guys who come in here are funny. They don't like it if they get a Thai girlfriend half their age, and she likes their money. They complain that she thinks I'm an ATM machine. But, you know, it is easy to understand. When a Thai person says they have no money, they're talking fifty cents for lunch or bus fare home. Either that or they are working you for sympathy. When these guys say they have no money, the next line is always - is there an ATM machine nearby?

I hand the darts to my opponent. I've seen her around, but we've never played together. I want to ask her name, but I'm embarrassed because I probably should know. She knows mine, or maybe she just seems to because everyone yelled it out when I came in.

Drunk Darrell comes in, but nobody yells out his name. They don't have to. He's there everyday, 365. Sometimes three times a day as he repeats his rounds in the few neighborhood spots. Darrell is in his sixties, except he walks like an eighty year old. I bet Peter Popcorn could beat him in a foot race, and he's got to be 85.

Drunk Darrell is repugnant in several odd ways. Just in the slow, not sloppy, but tight, inhibited manner that he moves. He has a dark complexion and looks kind of like Mr. Potato Head with a couple of pocks, a raspberry birthmark on his forehead and a whole bunch of scars, as if he survived an explosion or something. He's droopy fat, and his stomach hangs down so far you wonder if he has to lift it up to pee. OK, I guess there is his personal brand of sloppy to it, but I think it is like a robotic, somnambulant drunk kind of thing. This guy probably hasn't had a sober day in a decade or more since he retired early. And yet, the guy has been around. I think he started in Mississippi, but worked on oil rigs all around the world. He can spout an intelligent opinion, though I don't like to get into anything with him because he doesn't stop and he's never wrong. You know the type, but like, who really cares. And if you were the kind of person who cared, would you be hanging out in a dump like this. I really do wonder what I'm doing here. Maybe I like the place because in comparison to some of the regulars, I look pretty good. I don't know, but that might be it.

My opponent steps up to the line to shoot her darts, and she's turned around backwards, a lefty. Her motions are a bumpy road. She does have nice legs, but you know, for me, its almost every lady I see in Thailand. This is a whole country full of great looking legs. Most girls have two of them, but one of the most beautiful young ladies I ever saw had only one, but that's a different story.

Her style gives new meaning to the word awkward. The way in which she lets fly from the south in a clumsy yet entrancing motion holds an odd sort of fascination for me. At first, it is difficult to watch, but like a horrible car accident, you can't look away, though this is more like a fender bender. After observing the fact that she has passable accuracy, my curiosity increases.

There is a strange double pump of her arm, a rear foot lifting in conjunction and then landing on the ground, all appearing as if in mirror image of the actual event. I am slowly being charmed. If she can do that with her left hand, I wonder what other mysterious talents she might hold.

There is something additionally exotic about that for me. I mean, not that exotic is lacking here. They all have an allure, though some to a greater extent. She looks at me flirtatiously and flips her eyebrows again.

The Lefty is subdued in comparison to some of the girls who work in the bar. She is quieter, though I know she would be ready for action if I was so inclined. A southpaw, the devils side, a touch of Lucifer, and I wonder what it might be like to be in bed with her. Would there be some odd twist or would it be uncomfortable and awkward? I guess the real question is - do I want to pay to find out?

Okay, while I have a minute, I'm going to tell you about the girl with one leg. It was at Doi Inthanon Park, up in the mountains, in the north. As I was walking toward the exit, I saw her sitting on a blanket on the ground with her one leg extended. She was wearing shorts. She was gorgeous in a real clean, fresh, just got out of the shower, innocent kind of way. She had a big wide smile that melted the money right out of people's pockets, but one leg was missing. It is not only that the leg was so gorgeous, but it was the whole package. You couldn't help but think, oh my god, what a shame, this girl is a world class beauty, and she's stuck here begging for change. Someone later told me that sometimes the parents cut a limb off the kids when they are young because it helps in their career as a beggar. That kind of made me really feel sick, and I don't even like to talk about it, cause I don't want to make you feel sick too, but man, she had one big smile that I won't forget, and I'm sorry I brought it up, but since I mentioned it before, I knew you would be curious.

Anyway, so here's what's doing -

Drunk Darrell is buying drinks for a couple of girls down the bar, and it is getting loud over there. He too is loose with the drinks, but not for the same reason. I think he feels he has to get the girls a little drunk before he could get any of them to go with him. Like, if he buys enough drinks, they owe him, I mean, he's kind of OK, but there certainly is a little creep factor working there, too many years alone on those rigs or something. I try not to watch. But, you know, I've never actually seen him take a girl out with him. I think he is always too drunk for any vigorous activity.

It's my turn to shoot next, and there is a lively song blaring on the house stereo. Fai is looking at me and dancing really sexy. She's thin and an incredible dancer. I mean when she's into it, it's not easy to take your eyes off her. She wriggles up and down, in and out; almost in a snake-like, near hypnotic, rhythmic manner that you just have to see to believe. I mean, all the girls can dance sexy, but Fai is an artist, she transcends. She sees me watching her, and smiles really wide. She laughs and when I go to take my turn at the dart board, she sneaks up behind me and gives me a knee in the butt.

The cook comes downstairs, and says hello to me. She is sixty, and nobody pays too much attention to her, but I sometimes buy her a drink. I hand her the darts, and tell her to take a turn. She resists, but I insist. I want everyone to have a good time. She tells me she has never played before, and I believe it when her first throw goes so far to the left that it lands somewhere near the desk. We all laugh.

She says, "Whatta matta you, Pawwll. I tell you never play before. Why you laugh laugh me?" And don't you know; her next shot is a dead center, flat out, red bull's eye, not the green outer ring, but dead damn center. Everybody cheers, but her next shot goes so far off to the right that it is nearly in the bathroom. It whizzes on the other side of the scorekeeper, and she gets scared because she got hit in the butt once and had to go to the hospital.

I sit down and hear loud female protesting squeals from the far end of the bar. I hear Drunk Darrell bitching out one of the girls.

"Ahh wanna see your titties. Ah baawwt you a draink, damn it, and Ah wanna see sawm teet." He has a hold of the girl's shirt, and is in a wrestling match with her trying to get his way. Man, you would think a guy his age has seen enough titties to last a lifetime, especially living in Bangkok, but this guy needs to force his will. The girl resists, but after all, she knows her place. She can be replaced in a split second, but getting customers is the tough part of running a bar. There is lots of competition in this town, and you don't want to lose a 365 alcoholic like Drunk Darrell.

She decides to give in. Darrell takes a look, indulges a squeeze, and repeats the process with the next one. You know, some things you can blame on being drunk, I mean, I've spent my share of nights wasted in Bangkok bars, but I never behaved like that. You wonder what went wrong in this guy's childhood to make him act like such an asshole.

I take my turn with the darts again, but we're not making much progress in the game. The Lefty and I are losing steam as the game is lacking in excitement, but Fai is kind of coming on to me too. I never went with her, and I'm not sure why. She is exciting to be around, but it is almost as if I already like her so much that spending the night with her might push me into some sort of obsessive involvement or relationship, which is not why I am here. I've seen too many guys fumble down that road.

About this time, you might be thinking that I love them all, and you know, I'm not sure I would disagree. These girls are fun and pretty and decent human beings with a lot of self respect and conviction. They're smart too, and nice people if you give them half a chance. I know that would surprise most people, but these girls have a degree of class that far exceeds most of the customers, but that's just my opinion – you know, it's not like they are drug addicts or something like that. They're just poor, and have babies back home, and mothers and fathers taking care of the babies. They bear a big burden, if you ask me.

I look back down the bar, and Darrell has now got hold of a newbie. She looks really young, and I don't remember seeing her around before. Age can be deceiving here, but she has that innocent 'I've never been in a bar before look.' The newbies come in and usually watch for a while before they take the leap of going home with a customer, or else they decide it is not for them. They don't have to go. None of them do. I know that would surprise some people, but they don't have to go with anyone if they don't want.

Darrell has a good grip on this little girl's wrist, and he is not letting go. You can see she is scared out of her mind, and she's fighting him off different than the other girls. She's desperate, near frantic. I hear him complain to one of the other guys down there that he bought her a drink. He isn't going to hurt her, he just wants to see her titties. She's fighting him like crazy.

And Drunk Darrell is determined, and this little girl, I mean she can't be more than 90 pounds, well, for her it's not the same as with the other girls, and he just doesn't get the distinction. She is near tears.

"Aww, OK, OK," he finally tells her. He tries to pull her in gently now, releasing the hold on her shirt. "Ah'm nawt gonna hurt yaaall," he tells her. Like I said, she is new and probably doesn't have much more in her vocabulary than "Where you from? What you name?" That's the ice breaker that the girls teach the newbies. After that, it's just flirting, the birds and bees kind of thing, wherever you want to go from there. You don't need too much language ability after that.

Drunk Darrell just wants a gentle hug now, to show her what a nice guy he is, but she doesn't understand, and she doesn't trust him. She has never seen or heard of anyone acting like this, pulling up shirts. I mean, it is a bar, but it is a public place too. Even the grossest, most down and out Thai guy would never think of behaving like that.

There are other girls and customers watching now too. It has become a side show, and she has got to be really embarrassed. There are no good options. Either she fights with a customer, or she shows her titties, which she is not going to do. There's no way on that, and Darrell has finally come to that realization now too.

He puts an arm around her in a light hug, and gently pulls her in. She half stops resisting, but is definitely braced if this is a trick. At this point, Darrell is concerned with saving face too.

"My Gawwd," he says, "she's tremblin' like a leaf." I want to yell out - no shit you fucking asshole. I mean, she was fine a minute ago. I want to rip his face off, but then I would be the bad guy for starting the fight. Still, it's tempting. Then Darrell reaches a new level of disgusting, transcending his physical appearance and horrible behavior. He starts talking about what a good guy he is – I mean, can you believe it?

"She's so scaaared. Ah'd nava do anythang to frightin her. I was just playin. All Ah wazz gonna do waz look at her titties. Ah wouldn't hurt her for anythang. Ah don't do that kinda stuff. That's nawt fun."

Man – let me tell you, now I'm really steamed. I mean there is no way this guy is going to sell himself as kind hearted and generous after that shit. He's trying to get out of this whole incident like he's a nice guy. Talk about twisting stuff around, but you know, he's buying into his own shit, and that's tough to take.

And I wonder what I am doing within a hundred yards of a guy like this. I wonder if it's contagious or something. I mean, maybe I'm on the edge of loserville myself, just by hanging out here.

You know; I'm thinking - what is it about this place for me? I'm younger and hopefully not disgusting. I don't grope. I buy drinks and play darts without putting my hands on their breasts or up their skirts. Is this just a way to make myself more attractive to a bunch of lovely girls? But, the thing is, I want to go home with them too. I wait until we are in private, where it is not socially vulgar. Sure, I pay them, but I try for some reciprocity of feeling. Damn. I don't think I can handle this anymore. I mean, I'm walking a thin line here.

Things are going nowhere with The Lefty. The atmosphere has changed, and the dart game is no longer fun. Sure, she would go with me, but I would be nothing more than a trick for her. I get the feeling that coming on to her physically would be more work than it would be worth, and I'm starting to get bummed out.

Yeah, she'd do her best to take care of me, but it would be one-sided, just a job. I don't even think she would pretend to get into it. After a while, you build up an intuition about this stuff, and that's a scary thought too. I'm feeling pretty depressed, and thinking about just going back to my hotel room and getting some sleep – alone.

Drunk Darrell keeps going on about what a good guy he is, and how if it ain't fun for her, then it wouldn't be any fun for him either. The little girl has put some distance between them and has actually thrown herself at a younger guy who is sitting further down the bar. She is embarrassed about the whole event, and doesn't want to feel out of place, so she makes an overt, and obviously uncomfortable, show of being with this other guy. And you know; this makes me even sadder.

"Ha, ha, ha," says Drunk Darrell. He doesn't actually laugh, but speaks the words. "Ha, ha, ha. Look at thhattt. Whhhy she ain't shhhy at all," he drawls out in his cool, down home, lemonade on the porch swing Mississippi accent. "She wazz jusss funnin mee, that's all. See that, she aiinn't shhhy."

He can't believe that. Can he?

"Ha, ha, ha," says Darrell too long and loud. He waggles a finger at her. I figure I could get off two or three shots before he even knew what hit him. I can picture my fist disappearing into his gut.

The evening shift is starting to arrive as the girls trickle in to work. San Diego Sam comes in, and I'm kinda glad to see him. He, at least, has an intellect. He's in his early fifties, younger than Darrell. I see them hanging out together, but they're not the same. It's not that San Diego Sam doesn't take his turn with the ladies, but I have never seen him do anything gross. Mostly, he comes in and has a drink and something to eat, then goes about his business. He's always well groomed and neat, the kind of guy who could probably get a date in the Western World, but of course, he knows that none of those ladies can hold a candle to what he has here.

San Diego Sam says hi, and the whole place takes on an air of decency just because of his presence. I mean, you know this is an interesting guy, been around Asia for a long time. He's got some class, but you have to wonder what the allure is for him here too. And you have to wonder if he is treading that same thin line to loser city.

I think about going over and joining him, but Nan beats me to it. She is not looking for a trick with him; she wants to talk about something. He's the kind of guy that I know the girls talk true to also. They go to him for advice, and that's where I want to be too someday, so, I have respect for that. And I know it is serious stuff because Nan, she's no kid. She's been around for a long time.

Nan's not bad, except she's past her days, or so you would think. And she has money, she's done it smart. She's undoubtedly been at this a long time, and you can tell when she was young, she was a definite looker; I'm talking a real killer here. Hell, even I went with her for the night, not for sex, but just because I thought she would be cuddly, and I was tired. But like I said, she's done well for herself. I heard she has a house on Phuket Island and an upper crust condo in Bangkok. She's got way more than I'll ever have, so you know, she's done fine here.

And like I said, I took her home one night just to have someone around. She's not jumpy and bouncy like the others. She's mature and calm. We watched TV and went to bed, that was it. Oh yeah, she told me a story too. You know, I don't want you to think it was like charity that I took her home. She seems to be able to get a guy any time she wants. I see her leaving with guys all the time, more so than the other girls.

Oh yeah, so here is the story that she told me. She went home with this really drunk guy one night. He was totally stitched. When she got up in the morning, she went in to the bathroom and grabbed a shower. Well, in the bar when he met her, she was all made up and dressed fine. These girls put on make-up and well, they know how to do it right, and some of them spend $1 and have this gay guy do it for them, and he can hide a lot of stuff. I mean, they come out looking like fashion models.

So, anyway, she comes out of the shower and the guy wakes up and sees her come out of the bathroom, and he screams. He pulls up the blanket around him and yells; "Who are you? What are you doing here? How did you get into my apartment?" She has got to look twenty years older without the make-up. He wants to know what she did with the young pretty girl he took out of the bar. He thinks somebody pulled a switch on him.

And you know, we both laughed, and it was great that she told me an embarrassing story like that because most girls would keep something like that to themselves. I mean, she is OK enough with who she is and trusts me. You gotta love that. Well, I do anyway. I took her again another night too.

So, she says hello, and she's sitting with San Diego Sam, and going over personal stuff with him. Like, I said, he is pretty sharp business wise, and I figure she is bouncing some financial stuff off him. I mean, I would too if I had some assets left over that I didn't blow on booze and women and having a good time.

I'm half way through my fourth jack coke now and watching the girls come in. It is five o'clock. Some come in blue jeans, and then disappear and change into something hotter, though for me, the blue jeans are pretty hot too. You know, I like that casual, take me out to the ballgame look. But I like watching the parade and the transition. I'm still tossing around the idea of giving a try with The Lefty, you know, all that exotic stuff I was talking about before.

Then Gin comes in. She has just started work here, maybe a week or two ago, and I think she has got to have the best legs in the whole bar. She's twenty-seven and trim; but those legs, they are killer legs. She sees me as she's walking through the bar and gives me a big, sigh of relief smile. She plops herself down in the seat next to me and collapses on top of me.

We've had some eye contact before, but I don't remember talking with her. A couple of smiles, sure, but you know, it's Thailand, and a smile is like change back for a dollar, everybody gets some. I don't think she's been working too long and besides, the couple of times I've been in here in the last week or two, you know, mostly I'm hanging with the darts girls, and it's like I'm their turf, so lots of the others leave me alone.

Gin has long hair, and she's got her head on my shoulder, and her hair is all over me and it's sexy, but I know those legs are down there somewhere too. But that's not the kicker. It's her skin. Having her near me is this major turn on because of her skin.

Gin has late October skin, Scorpio skin, and before you get all carried away and think that I've slept with so many women that I can tell their birth month by their skin, forget it. That's not what it is. It's just that my long time girlfriend was a mid-late month Scorpio, and when someone turns me on in that same manner, real quick like that, without hardly knowing them, well, chances are she's got that devil Scorpio in her, and I am going to be a major sucker for near everything about her. That's just how it is. And there is something different about her skin that I can't put into words. I mean, I don't want to say anything or brag or anything like that, but I'm almost always right. It's one of those things that I would bet on, even money.

I buy her a drink and another jack coke for me. I look up, and the bar has changed. It's not the same place anymore. The whole mood is different. Drunk Darrell is gone and Peter Popcorn too. I don't think he took a girl with him either. I think Popcorn has a wife waiting for him at home, but hey, for all I know he could be upstairs now on a Viagra high getting it on.

Some of the ex-pat working guys are here. They sit at the bar and the girls stand and drape themselves around them. Fai has one. But meanwhile, Gin is rubbing my leg, and she's got her legs across mine too, half sitting on my lap. The Lefty walks past and gives me a look. I still wonder what it would be like. I know how mid-October turns me on, but I don't think I've ever been with a lefty, at least not that I know of anyway.

Gin and I have made a minimum of small talk, and I figure this would be a good time to impress her. I take out a pen, and write on the back of a napkin. I debate about writing Oct 22-27, but hey, you know, sometimes you have to go for the whole ball of wax. I mean, like if it's Oct. 24th, then it just lies in the middle somewhere. But if I write Oct 24th and that's it, then I'm like this psychic guy who can do amazing things like guessing someone's birthday. So, I take a shot, but I write Oct 25th instead, and I feel pretty confident.

You know, talking about that, the great thing that these girls give you is confidence. I mean, it just feels good when a long haired, dark brown, long legged hotty plops down on you like ***she*** hit the jackpot because you're not sitting with someone else. That stuff can get to your head pretty quick. Gin takes her face out of my neck to take a slug of her jack coke. Yeah, that's right; they all drink what you do, mostly anyway.

"When's your birthday?" I ask her.

She looks at me. She doesn't quite understand. Her English is not real good, which usually means that they haven't been working too long.

"You know Happy Birthday to you," and I sing a couple of bars, and she picks up immediately at what I am after. I point and say in broken English, which I am a champion at, "Happy Birthday you, when?"

She takes my pen and writes on the napkin. I figure I have to be close on this one. I mean, I think I have got this one right on the head. When she pulls her hand back, I can't believe it. I mean, you could have knocked me over.

No. It's not only that I was wrong, or that I was way off, which I was, but her birthday is May 30th – which is my birthday too. I was stunned. I thought I was going to be right. I know mid-October skin, and she had it, but for her to share my birthday, well, that was really something. Ten percent of the population has got to be left handed, but I have certainly never been with someone who has the same birthday. This is a 1/365 shot. And you know what; I wasn't going to let it pass me by.

So, I raised my eyebrows and looked at the ceiling, and right away she nodded OK. Like I said before, you don't always need too many words here; just the intent. I know that there is a room upstairs with a big bed and a TV with a DVD. I could take her back to my hotel, but this has a feeling of immediacy, and the room upstairs is about $8 and kind of spiffy, and well, there was that immediacy factor that I was talking about. A couple of my friends get on me about how I piss my money away, buying drinks for anyone in sight, even guys sometimes, but you know, that's how I was brought up. Maybe it's this Jersey suburban ritual or something, but you can buy your buddy a drink now and again. It's not like it makes you a homosexual, and it's not like that matters over here, because in a place like Bangkok, anything goes. I mean, it's not like your everyday guy who comes here. Maybe we all have a screw loose, but this is where I'm coming on my vacations twice a year, and if I blow every last nickel – well, it's worth it. And that's the part I'm getting to now.

You see, there is this guy over at the bar, he's gotta be sixties, maybe cutting near seventy, it's not easy to tell anymore. You know, when I was young there were kids, adults and old people, but now the age brackets get broken out a lot more. Even for me, I'm thirty-nine, not yet forty, and I'm looking at that as a milestone or threshold that I'm going to cross in a couple of months. And Gin is going to cross it on the same day, except, she is going to be twenty-eight. At that age, a girl feels she's getting old here. She's too old for most Thai guys unless she wants to be a second wife, and that's no big honor here, but it does pay the bills.

So, I get up and make my way down the bar 'cause I don't want all the girls to know we are going upstairs and make all those ohhh and ummm sounds, but Fai knows anyway. She walks past me and raises an eyebrow and says "good luck" as if to say, this girl might kill you or something. The first time with someone can be a little uncomfortable, and things like that don't usually help. That is what I was trying to avoid by going down to the bartender and paying my own bill. I mean, I don't need everyone to know my business. It's bad enough the bartender has to know every time I go with a different girl because I would really like to go with her sometime, but she doesn't go. She has a boyfriend or a husband or something, and you don't see her too far from the cash register. Though sometimes, if it is real quiet, early in the afternoon, she'll shoot a game of darts, just the two of us. She is a bit rounder and cuddlier with a killer smile, but for me the attraction is partly that she doesn't go with anyone; it is the challenge. They all have killer smiles.

And while I'm waiting for my change, and my birthday girl is waiting for me, I'm standing next to this older guy, and he starts bitching out the girls in general. He's got a wife, and these girls just want to play him for a tip or a drink, and he ain't fallin' for any of their bloody shenanigans. I can hear from his accent that he is either British or

Irish, and he goes on trashing the girls. Two timers and liars, he calls them. I mean, it's like he is disgusted by them all, and I wonder what the hell he is doing coming in here in the first place, but I don't say anything. I mean, with an old crank like that, what is there to say. We both know the scene. I don't have any illusions; well, maybe I do, but if he doesn't like the girls, why come into a lady bar in Bangkok anyway? But, it's not his first time here either, and the girls know too. They don't go near him, and it's not like he's gross like Popcorn or Drunk Darrell. He has an air of being a gentleman, though I have found here that you can never really be sure.

Well, so, he looks me in the eye, and all of a sudden something clicks, like what an old crank he is being, and how I'm not pushing 70, and I'm having a good time, and he shouldn't be such an old fart. And so, for whatever reason, he softens a little, and he remembers that a long time ago, in this very bar, he used to be young too. He smiles and confesses.

"I wasn't always this way. When I first came here twenty years ago, it was great. I went through a phase. It was like I was James Bloody Bond," and a distant sparkle lights his eyes.

"Yes! That's it," I tell him. "That's it exactly! That's the phase I'm in now! I'm James Bloody Bond."

So, I head upstairs with my birthday girl, and that's usually where I would end a story like this out of respect for privacy, but this one I'm going to tell you because it's different, and I've heard a lot of stories in a lot of bars, but I've never heard this story.

When Gin collapsed on me, I figured she must have been out late and didn't sleep much, which was probably the case. And, you know, this is partly why I took the room upstairs. It was convenient, and I figured the immediacy of a good back rub was in order. So, we go upstairs, and she takes her shower and comes out in a towel. That's normal stuff, and I do the same. I tell her to lie on her stomach, and I start with a good back rub. I can give a pretty good massage, and she is really enjoying it. She looks at me with this confounded expression, and tells me that nobody ever gave her a massage before, and I extrapolate that out to the idea that she has never been treated decent by a guy. This feels like a great opportunity for me to be the different guy. You know, like I told you, I want to stand out in some way, but not like Drunk Darrell, who is an outstanding asshole.

Then we get into talking, and she tells me about her life. Now, I can't understand everything, and all the girls have a story that will tug on your heartstrings – you know, they're not working in a bar because they have a great husband who takes care of everything, or were born into a rich family, though some of them you would never know because they have really classy ways and have spent time in other countries in marriages that went bad.

So, it turns out that Gin was sold by her brother when she was fourteen to a Thai guy in Samui. Now, Samui is a beautiful tourist island, but I don't think that was the story for her. She had a couple of kids with the guy, and it sounds like she had to be more or less his slave, and then, if that wasn't bad enough, the guy dies and leaves her as a twenty year old girl with two kids to raise. And now, she is here, naked and enjoying the first back rub in her life and well, it is sort of like things have turned around for her, at least a little, because I'm here, and like I said, I'm a sucker for that kind of thing.

There are missing years in her story, and she is slipping into Thai language or maybe Laotian or Cambodian, and I can't understand too much because we're starting to get intimate, and let me tell you, it has this personal air to it now that is making it really passionate. And I'm not going to go into details, but in the middle of all this, she's moaning quietly, she furrows her brow and gives me this quizzical kind of look, as if I was actually James Bloody Bond. She explains that she has never been aroused before, she never felt anything like this. Well, that's the kind of thing that if you tell your buddies afterwards, they say, yeah, yeah, yeah, like what kind of cheese are they making the moon out of these days, but you know, being there, seeing the expression on her face; I believed it. I really did, and I still do, pretty much – in spite of what happened, which is the part of the story that I'm getting to here.

So, we get back into it, and I have to say, I am more determined than ever to show her a good time, and I am enjoying myself too. She has a great trim body to go with those beautiful legs that I told you about, and there is also this thing about having October skin and my birthday, so, things are meshing in a destiny kind of way. And the passion is rising to the top of the charts as it is feeling different for me too. I'm not sure how I can explain it, but this is rapidly turning into a memorable event.

And now, she is letting loose. She is clawing at my back and hugging me tight with those spectacular legs, and she's moaning, and she starts calling out my name, at first quietly.

"Oh Pawl," she says and it keeps building up in volume and energy level. "Ohhh Pawwwlll, Oh Pawwll!!" She is shouting really loud, louder and louder and then suddenly - nothing.

I'm with a dish rag. Her whole body goes limp like she just died of a sudden heart attack, and I might have thought that was possible with all the emotion, but that's not it either. She's sound asleep. There is a louder than gentle snore coming from her. And not only that, I couldn't wake her up. So, I let her sleep for a while, and then tried again, but nothing. I had no idea what to do, so I left her there. I mean what do you do?

On my way out, there weren't too many girls around, but The Lefty was still there. She smiled at me really seductively, and I couldn't help but wonder what she might have in store, in style, that would be different, but I think that I have had enough of different for one night. But I like that she smiled at me anyway, even though she knew I was with Gin. I mean, I'm kind of a sucker for that kind of thing, if you know what I mean.

8

My wife was edgy, an odd mood change. We were in America. That evening, she insisted on calling home to the village. She chittered nervously while I dialed. Her voice was shaking. First, the access number, then my 12 digit pin number, then the international access code, the country code, the area code, and finally, the number. I missed a digit and had to start over.

My wife was worried about Auntie. Third sister, working in Taipei, called home the same day. She knew too.

When we connect with the village, auntie is indeed not well. I tell my wife to tell Auntie to go to the hospital. She is afraid of wasting money. Tell her I have money. I will pay. She refuses to go.

That evening, we talked about Aunite. I ask about the cancer. What cancer? Her throat? The microphone attached to her larynx is not a result of cancer. Then what? – We need to go to the dictionary.

Rape.

Rape?

Yes, rape. It happened many years ago. She fought the man off, but he slit her throat. It is difficult to imagine Auntie young and attractive. The rapist ruined her chances for a husband and a family of her own.

A week later, auntie is fine.

Herman Witkowski

Herman Witkowski was at it again. His wife, Millie, rolled her eyes, bent her head, and put her hand to her brow. The upscale New York City attorney sat across from Herman, behind his all too business like desk. He didn't drum his fingers, but was deep in thought.

It was looking possible, so Herman repeated the question. It was an opportunity to reduce his legal bill by 80%. He couldn't resist.

"So, do you barter?" Herman asked.

"Well, I could use a nice wedding gift if you have anything, but I need it tonight."

"How about a chess set?"

The logistics might be difficult, but the pieces were falling into place. The wedding was on Long Island – not too far from Herman's pewter factory, but it was after hours. The place was locked tight, but for the night watchman, a tough displaced and recently homeless trucker, named Arnie, who worked there in the day and slept over at night.

"Alright," the lawyer agreed, his problem now neatly solved.

Herman Witkowski phoned the factory, but there was no answer. He explained that Arnie was most likely out to dinner, and the attorney should proceed to the factory while he continued to call ahead.

"If I can't reach Arnie, we have a secret code, and that will alert him that I sent you," Herman continued. Millie opened her eyes wide. There was no secret code; their business was profitable, but rapidly becoming a culture of the ridiculous.

The attorney, sharp in his three piece pin-stripe suit, leaned forward.

"When you get to the factory, and Arnie comes to the door, stand on one foot and jump up and down three times while saying Mickey Mouse, Mickey Mouse, Mickey Mouse."

"Mickey Mouse?" asked the attorney.

"Mickey Mouse," said Herman. "And you must say it three times."

Millie shook her head. She should have known. Even visiting an attorney to draw up a will would be laden with farce. Last week they had "funny hat" day for the accountants. Herman had purchased odd hats at a trade show, and he told them that they must wear these while working on his premises. The accountants never seemed to notice that nobody else in the factory was wearing funny hats for funny hat day, just them.

Actually, Herman thought of this new prank as a gift for Arnie. He was stoically enduring a divorce procedure and could use a laugh. And, as time passed with the attorney en route, Arnie was not answering the phone. Maybe he thought it was his ex-wife calling. Herman was beginning to worry. Arnie, was a tough mother trucker, and not the guy to get duped into giving a free chess set to anyone. Everyone knew Herman. Saying that you were a friend of Herman was not going to cut the mustard. Herman was calling frantically, but to no avail.

The attorney rang the night buzzer.

Arnie answered the door and glared.

The attorney stood on one leg and hopped up and down three times and said Mickey Mouse with each hop. "Herman said to ask you for a chess set."

A con man would never do anything so bizarre. The guy had to be under instructions from Herman. He had to be legit. Arnie's face crinkled in an unaccustomed smile.

"OK," said Arnie. "Come on in. You can take your choice."

Bruce 3

When we were kids, on occasion, we tortured our friends. I guess that is part of being a boy kid during the boring, long hot days of summer. Sometimes, we would torment each other, but mostly we teamed-up and concentrated on anyone who was near.

We played Blind Man's Bluff in Bruce's basement with Billy Stern. The first couple of games we played straight before Bruce needed to escalate the action. When Billy was the blind man, Bruce would reel him in like a fish, working a circle, making noises closer and closer, but eluding the touch that would end the turn. And each noise was a planned navigational tactic to lure Billy closer and make his lunges more desperate, until finally Bruce made a noise very close, and Billy lunged into the shock of slamming head-on into the steel pole that supported the floor.

On the next go around, having Billy suitably dazed, we instituted the dreaded silent treatment. No noise to lure him hither or yon. And, with arms outstretched, now wary of the post, Billy felt his way through the pitch darkness, listening for sounds of our breath, any slight hiccup or scurry of foot that never seemed to come because we had quietly slipped up the stairs, technically out of bounds. We would go to the shopping mall for a slice of pizza and leave Billy alone and searching around in the basement. So, we were out of bounds, we lost. Except, we were eating pizza, and he was wandering the basement in a blindfold. Winning was not always the primary issue, or maybe Bruce didn't define winning in the same terms as the rest of the world, and maybe that would eventually be his undoing.

We made up games too. On one hot day we played 'Hold On To The Garden Hose.' The object was for each of us to take a turn with the open garden hose gushing water, a useful weapon, while the two opponents tried to rip it from us; the one who holds on the longest, wins. I sprayed them down and held on for a few minutes, but Billy and Bruce were too much for me. Bruce did a good job, but there is a lot of water and the hose gets slippery. Billy and I eventually peeled it out of his hands.

But Billy, he was the champ. Or at least that was what we told him. Bruce and I had a secret plan, and nowhere embedded in this tactic was the idea of taking the hose from Billy. Instead, we would twist his arms that held the hose tight. We would turn his weapon against him and direct the water so that it would shoot into his face and mouth.

"You're incredible!" Bruce shouted. "I can't get the hose away! This guy is amazing!" Bruce would scream encouragement while holding the hose so the water went up Billy's nose. Billy gasped for breath as we damn near drowned him, but he held on tight. He wanted to win. It was all a matter of definition. We had taken the power to define the game and used it to our end. We hadn't been the first ones to think of this.

Maybe it was during those early childhood games that Bruce realized how the concept of winning drove people to endure things that were unpleasant. It led him to question and to create his own, more personal, value structures.

If you accept the rules of society and play within their guidelines, life is easier. Once you venture outside these boundaries, you are in free fall; a latticed maze-like frontier without definition, sign posts or goal lines. You are left to make your own rules and grapple with more difficult questions. When you slip outside the matrix, the freedom is intoxicating, but the chaos is a drunken sailor; a swirl of indulgences and consequences. There is not much to hold on to.

Fender Gender Bender

"Yet who the devil ain't a dreamer."

Herman Melville in a letter to Nathaniel Hawthorne - July 17, 1852

It was a strange thing to say, but I have found that a Thai woman might say anything. Where most of us have a filtration system in place, many Thai ladies seem porous in that department. I was in the midst of a conversation discussing business with Robbie Fender, when his Thai wife, who had been staring at us, interrupted my train of thought with this interesting observation in fluid, but grammatically stuttering English.

"You in love my husband."

Well, no, was my first thought. Then, well yes, was my second thought, but not the way I think she meant it. Robbie glowed like a shiny penny, and there was no doubt that he was an attractive man, in the sense that I, and everyone for that matter, was drawn to him, but not that I wanted to sleep with him. Though I am a wild and prolific daydreamer, the concept never occurred to me. In the same way that stores hire attractive sales people, his appearance was certainly a pleasant part of the Robbie Fender experience. But mostly, the attraction was that he was smart and perceptive with a quick wit and a unique outlook on life.

Robbie knew Thailand and was capable of offering advice when I could not make heads or tales of what was transpiring, which, I must admit, was a near constant state during my first month. And it is not that I am much more acute now, but that first month, it was a tornado. Even if the advice was a simple shrug of the shoulders and a 'that's just how it is here' answer; a reminder that here – was no longer there, and Iowa was more than a distance that could be measured in numbers of miles away. It was another galaxy; and being here, Bangkok, is like listening to a radio station transmitting from a previously unbeknownst frequency. But no, I most certainly did not want to be with her husband, not in a sexy way.

"That's right," I told his wife after a far too long pause. "You have found me out." It was a joke I never would have made a year ago, but then, before my recent venture, I do not think that I had ever made the acquaintance of a Thai lady. And my first year in Bangkok has been a shock to my wildest imagination, which, in retrospect, had been sometimes morbid and rather tame. I was a child of the corn with local and limited, but oft visited fantasies, bored and depressed.

A landscape of corn, planted in neat unrelenting rows, is as stiff and dull as a column of numbers that wait patiently to be added together. And with slight variations and complexities long ago become routine, I see my work as little more than that of a modern day scrivener, a copier of legal documents, a long obsolete profession, and as Melville described in Bartleby, "a very dull, wearisome and lethargic affair."

My life was melting away amidst a soporific languor and corn. With the advent of carbon paper, scriveners faded into oblivion; copy machines sealed their fate. A tedious occupation, now vanished. My work as a tax accountant one day will become equally irrelevant. The adoption of a flat tax, a tax return on a postcard - that would end my career, and for me, happily so. And as that was the talk some years ago, I made a decision to branch into international work, as if the foreign names, Paris, Rome, Nairobi, might satisfy the wanderlust that was all dream in the withering white soul of an Iowa farm boy, now turned silently into a middle-aged man. Nothing in my life fit. I was a nature lover surrounded by seemingly limitless fields, and during the day entrapped by an equally infinite flowing stream of receipts and papers filled with numbers; other people's financial affairs which they were too busy or more likely too bored, to deal with. That was my life's work.

And as Melville decried the life of a scrivener one hundred and fifty years ago, he said - "I can readily imagine that to some sanguine temperaments it would be altogether intolerable." I believe he was talking about himself and me too. And this word 'intolerable' echoed throughout my thoughts as I walked amidst the neighbor's fields. But what was I to do? Where was I to go? When your life is stationary and rooted, where is the escape hatch? What do we do when we can no longer tolerate? When boredom is the culprit, we wither in spirit, and proceed in a punch drunk haze as life trickles into old age. We daydream as the columns are added, and the hedgerows of corn grow tall and block the vision of a greater world beyond.

One day a light appeared on the horizon. A position opened in the newly formed branch office in Bangkok, a whaling ship of sorts setting out to venture the high seas. The concept was a lark at first, a step I never imagined taking as my thoughts wandered and my resume was submitted; it gradually became a reality. And having made this decision, to the surprise and acquiescence of my wife, [it was a two year assignment to be undertaken alone] the move was made and the word "life" took on a new meaning as parts of my personality formally buried as deep as Atlantis, bubbled to the fore, slowly at first, but it came about and vitality rushed forward at a new quickened pace. My demeanor was calm and unrevealing, but my heart skipped in anticipation.

It wasn't that I had a bad life. I had a nice wife. She loved to garden and make things grow, a lovely lady, but exciting, no. And I didn't expect more or less from her. She was a local lady who had no greater ambitions than the PTA, the children, and her garden, which she would not have to miss a day of tending. I would be home for a Christmas visit.

And our kids were great, genuinely nice people who were riding their own wave through university, and undoubtedly, on to prosperous careers. We didn't have problems other than making the decision of what movie video to watch that night or what to have for dinner, more precisely, what form was the meat to take that would accompany the potatoes.

We were the perfect, average American family. And I could almost hear the conversations at my oft envisioned funeral; a dark spectral vision that slipped into the dungeons of the airy castles that my mind frequented during working hours.

'We never suspected that he was unhappy. What could the problem possibly have been?' They will see a victim of that special form of unspoken existential Mid-west depression that comes from endlessly

similar landscapes of crops and the knowledge, the fear that life will lead to nothing more. '*He leaves behind; two children, a wife, a house, rows of corn, columns of numbers and a roast in the oven.*'

The accounting firm will immediately panic and check for wrong doing, a wild embezzlement scheme that went haywire and drove me over the edge. They won't find it. Such a fraud might have put excitement into my life, a sometimes visited daydream of fleeing to a tropical island with a suitcase full of hundred dollar bills, but no, just not me. At my funeral everyone will be asking why. And the answer will be simple, life is droll.

But people don't usually kill themselves from boredom. They rot slowly in a process of attrition. Bartleby, though he preferred not to work, or do anything for that matter, denied himself food. The bored have choices. Even for me, there was that embezzlement scheme that I had mentioned. Well, I worked out the particulars in my head and damned, I think I could have gotten away with it. The thing was that I didn't really need the money. What was I going to do, buy an extra hamburger or two for the Sunday barbecue? I wasn't a fancy guy. My nature was more Gulden's than Grey Poupon. Fifty-seven varieties of Heinz were far too many. I had enough, and thereby was left without wants, which resulted in the off-white translucent cloud of ennui that blanketed my life.

That was why I volunteered for the job in Thailand when it came up in the company register. I put in for it, and knew the chances were good as I had not only the qualifications, but seniority over the younger applicants who might be the ones most likely to apply. It brought with it a pay raise that I explained to my wife would help with the college years of our children. I had no idea where I was going, or what I was getting myself into, except that it would be different. It seemed like a last chance at life.

I envisioned quiet as I would not be capable of speaking the language, and the idea of lack of conversation was soothing. Talk had become inane. Of course, I would need to converse in basic ways. I went out to buy a Chinese phrasebook and met with my first experience in confusion. The young saleslady was a well-versed college student. She asked me if I wanted to learn Mandarin or Cantonese. I told her whatever they speak in Taiwan. And that was how I learned a few phrases of Chinese before I left, not realizing that Taiwan and Thailand had nothing to do with each other besides beginning with a 'T' and that they both have a couple of 'A's' in their name. And other than that, coming from Ames Iowa, there wasn't too much difference that I could see at that point.

I accepted the position with all the excitement that Herman Melville must have faced as a twenty year old youth shipping out on a whaler bound for the Pacific – I was going to Bangkok.

"Nee-ho Thailand."

Melville took his first job as a bank clerk when he was a twelve year old boy. He bounced from job to job until aged twenty, but when he shipped out on the Acushnet in 1839, I have no doubt he felt that he was leaving the dull predictable world of numbers behind. I think he feared the inevitability of how boring life can be in general, especially when one is free to pursue romantic journeys that others keep locked away in a distant 'if only' file in their minds. For most, it is more consuming and practical to yearn for the sea than to ship out.

Back in the 1840s, the work on a whaler was undoubtedly vigorous, and the long days of ocean views must have been tedious for an active creative mind such as his. Melville had a history of mutiny, from which he emerged unscathed, and with a book idea as well. Maybe the idea itself was merely a romantic way to live up to the deeds of his grandfather, a partner in the historic dumping of the King's tea into the Boston Harbor.

Melville would join a mutiny from The Acushnet, and his experiences with the natives on a South Pacific Island would lead to his first book, *Typee*. He signed on with another whaler and eventually jumped ship once more, this time in Hawaii where he took work as a bookkeeper in a general store. Four years after departing, he returned to New York where his family encouraged him to write down his tales of adventure.

And so he did. Unable to find a publisher in the USA for *Typee*, it was published in Britain and sold 6,000 copies. And he continued onward writing four more books in a five year period – *Omoo, Mardi,*

Redburn, and *White Jacket*. None received critical acclaim. Neither did *Moby Dick*. And what is an unread writer – nothing more than an unpaid scrivener.

I think Bartleby reflected the weariness that overcomes an adventurer. I think Bartleby was Melville at his core; a thirty-four year old failed novelist, a scrivener of sorts. Bartleby chose inactivity, and finally death, to the tedium of endless longhand writing. Though Melville persevered, there was a side of him which could vividly bring forth Bartleby, a weary man, too tired to live.

There are times when I think Bartleby had it right when he quit on everything. I can readily relate to the condition of weariness. It began in earnest in my third year with the firm. It was a slow, weightless, dull, yet painless existence. And just about when I felt I couldn't take it anymore, we had children. Any hope of choices disappeared. Thoughts became embroiled in their rearing, and time slipped away in an odd contradiction of hours passing slowly and years whizzing past. Twenty-one of them now with the company, a nationally known brand, where I am gaining seniority through attrition of time which others can not hold up to; I am here because I am inert. And like Bartleby, I was walking a quiet road toward non-existence.

Melville's travels slowed after his marriage in 1852. There was a trip to England, and a Mediterranean cruise, but his books were not selling, and he eventually fell into a job at the New York City Customs House, a bookkeeper once more. And where Melville had pursued adventure early in life, maybe I was tacking his track in reverse, though I don't recall thinking that as I set out for Bangkok.

Robbie Fender was a thirty-two year old kid from New York. He was an up and comer in the firm. He was full of energy, and quite an international fellow from the perspective of Ames Iowa. He had a spectacular looking Thai wife who asked me if I loved him. And though a year earlier, when he met me at the airport, I would have thought the question preposterous, after twelve months of living in Thailand, I was able to say, "That's right."

The flight from Ames had bounced me to Minneapolis and Tokyo before plunking me down in Bangkok. I slept on the plane and arrived feeling surprisingly well. Robbie was there alone to meet me on arrival. He was wearing a colorful Hawaiian-style tropical shirt which hung loosely over his blue jeans. He escorted me by taxi to a serviced apartment, which was luxurious by Ames Iowa standards. We lived outside of town in an old farmhouse. We had renovated it, and rented our corn fields to a local farmer. It added to the peace of existence, but luxurious, no.

I showered and felt refreshed. That was when Robbie suggested that we go out for a beer, and he could brief me on what was happening at the office, or we could wait. It was a Saturday, and Monday was a Buddha day, a national holiday I assumed – we had time. It wasn't so much that I was curious about work. I had a fair idea of what the job entailed, and going someplace different, well, I was looking at it as being a break from the endless computing of numbers. My heart was thumping at the prospect of seeing Bangkok. I agreed.

Well, back then, I used to say things like 'gosh' and 'holy cow'. I agree now that it is a funny, hayseed sort of expression, but that was who I was, and I only mention it now because Robbie Fender still teases me about how many times I walked around saying 'holy cow' just on that first night in Bangkok. And I have since heard that song – *One Night in Bangkok* and how the lyric says it makes a hard man humble. Well, I was in no way a hard man, so you can only imagine what it did to my doughy demeanor, but in retrospect, it is difficult to say what exactly happened to me that first night – you might say it was an acid trip without the ingestion of a hallucinogenic. Everything had a surreal carnival-like appearance, and there were no familiar places for my brain to grasp. It was like watching a film that had me as one of the characters; a bizarre circus movie with clowns and ventriloquists, dwarfs and barkers; lodged in a zone between creepy and entrancing. I couldn't believe it was me on the street in Bangkok.

Where:

Neon lights were flashing. Viewing the city from the shelter of the taxi was both comforting and confining. I wanted to be out there, on the colorful street that brimmed with excitement. Robbie talked on a little, something about going here or there, and what did I want. I didn't respond. My mind was fried by the electricity in the air.

"Why are there ladies in evening gowns sitting in the doorway?" I asked him. I think I kind of knew. I mean, I must have, right? And maybe, looking back, it was what prompted Robbie to direct our driver to a side street, crowded, but quieter than the one we turned off. Not a main thoroughfare, but quite lively. And there were several nice looking establishments with elegant ladies sitting outside, eating at roadside food vendors, a bevy of evening gowns, and Robbie was listing names of famous artists who apparently had something to do with the names of the bars. We exited the taxi in front of a place called Renoir. OK.

It's not easy to fix the moment when things began to slip into a nighttime dream-like state; where I lost control of events, as you might in a dream that swirls with non-sequiturs and unpredictable events. I think, it might go back to the airplane, and how I fell into this odd pattern of sleep - nodding naps that roosted on an edge of consciousness. Dreaming, yet nearly fully aware of my surroundings, a light sleep? A lack of clarity had taken over, not a good trait for an accountant. And when I look back, I wonder if it did not date all the way back to when I first made the decision to apply for this position, turning my life upside down in one seemingly innocent, whimsical stroke. I don't remember having an attraction for Oriental women. I didn't know any. But when I look back now, I wonder.

Robbie led me into a bar, and I felt like an Iowa farm boy who was encountering an ocean for the first time. I had heard about the ocean, seen it in movies, but to experience it was quite a thrill, and my heart skipped a beat as the spectacular young hostesses clamored around us. The high bar stools were positioned perfectly for a lady to creep in behind and massage your back as I found happening to me in an unrequested yet delicious instant. Life took on the sensation of biting into a chocolate eclair.

Robbie excused himself to use the men's room. I looked around through the misty surreal haze. Everything glowed and flickered. Robbie stopped and spoke to one of the young hostesses. He pointed to me.

She walked toward me, smiling. Though the lights were low, she seemed to glisten, as if whatever light was in the room was pulled in to her, and then reflected sparkling outward. She was a diamond, perfectly cut and formed inside an evening gown that was sailing effortlessly toward me as if propelled by a gentle breeze. Even now, I remember her as if a vision, more imaginary than real. Holy cow.

"Litchard?" she asked.

"Yes," I answered. I must have sounded uncertain because she repeated herself.

"You Litchard?"

"Yes, yes," I re-assured. "I am Richard Brock." I thought about giving her my name card and felt around for my pockets, but I had left my suit jacket in the room.

"You not sure? Maybe you not Litchard Block?" She joked with me; a stunningly perceptive jibe, which cut straight to my heart on three levels. First, I was Richard Brock, not Litchard Block. Second, in a dream, especially a daydream, as I will explain later, you are not always the person who you are. You can take on the being of another character. And third, unbeknownst to me at the time; the Richard Brock who I had been all my life had been left behind in Ames.

"Yes, I am Litchard Block," I assured, though she looked at me with a trace of disbelief. She giggled and smiled wide. In one moment, she was a spectacular looking oracle capable of penetrating my core with a glance, and in an instant transformed into a giggling childlike celestial nymph. She was gorgeous. There was an ever so slight line of wrinkle that formed next to her almond shaped eyes. Her sepia skin was smooth and alluring; her jet black hair was long and hung perfectly across her bare shoulders. Everything about her glittered, as if fairy dust had been sprinkled from above and left an angelic vision. I was entranced.

I remember Robbie's face glowing clean and fresh. I recall his boyish grin in the fringes, an elaborate border framing the pictures. Her name is Som. I saw my hand in hers. There were drinks. Cocktails and another laughing face sitting next to Robbie Fender. I didn't know any of these people a mere two hours ago. Now, they swirled in color, as I sat motionless. They were vivacious, vivid and I was stone, somewhere inside this newly created human being; this Litchard Block. Melodious words and unfamiliar sounds sang through the night. The shifting tones flashed past and swirled around me. I was drunk and dizzy. We all got in a taxi.

There was no explaining. There were left and right turns, both real and literal. Laughter was the background music mixed with the song of Thai language. We went to another bar; it was coarser than the first, smoke-filled, and the first image that struck me as I walked in was the stage in the middle of the bar with scantily clad dancers. We slipped from elegance to decadence and back out again. We were at my apartment, there were more drinks.

In the morning, I could remember the brilliant red lights on the runway when the plane landed, mixed with the neon of the bar. And a body, I recall a spectacular dark sprite with a perfect and trim frame, gyrating above me, and smiling with the knowledge that she was pleasuring me with this activity. I never imagined I would ever be with such a simply beautiful, exotic woman. She was chocked with personality in the bar, and more than a woman in bed, or actually, I think it was the living room floor where we consummated our relationship before I stumbled off to bed, waking in a half stoned haze.

She brought me coffee.

"*Shay-Shay*," I told her thank you in Chinese. And she understood. Or at least she smiled.

I had no idea what to make of my first night in Bangkok. I never, in my wildest dreams, would have imagined such an evening right off the plane. Things like last night don't happen to people like me, or at least did not before I came here. I was woozy, but the coffee seemed to be helping. Apparently my apartment had an extra bedroom, and Robbie Fender came wandering out of it not too long after my eyes began to focus. He looked surprisingly fresh, as if this sort of thing happened every night as I began to wonder what my future here was going to be like.

He went into the kitchen and both girls followed him. They spoke and laughed for a few minutes, and then they came out together. Som walked over and kissed me on the forehead, and I rested my hand on her hip as if touching a perfect sculpture, a work of art. She was no longer in the evening gown, but had changed into a very alluring pair of blue jeans, though, I think, whatever the clothing would have been, she was spectacular. She smiled flirtatiously, and then left with her friend as I sat near breathless on the couch.

"Where are they going?" I asked Robbie.

"I don't know, home probably," he told me.

"Why?"

"Because I paid them. Their job is over."

It was sinking-in, but slowly. This girl was an ahh, I couldn't bring myself to think it. I didn't want her to leave. "Then, why did you pay them," I found myself fumbling into the conversation.

Robbie laughed at my naivet . "The joke here is that we don't pay them to stay, we pay them to leave in the morning."

"But, how can such sweet girls, be ahh, you know."

Robbie laughed again. "Your not in Ames anymore," he told me, clicking his heels three times.

"Well gosh," was all I could muster. "Holy cow!"

It wasn't that my behavior of the night before was gnawing at my soul as I might have imagined. As the day wore on, I did not feel troubled by having broken my marriage vow for the first time, but on the contrary, could not wait to go out and do it again. My wife was 10,000 miles away. She would go about her day as usual. I will call, and tell her I am fine. She will be content.

And I confided my thoughts to Robbie Fender. And once more he laughed. He apologized for laughing, and then said he has been here for seven years and just doesn't see things the same way anymore.

"That's because your behavior last night was totally natural," he told me. "And in the scheme of things, it's not important. You still can love your wife, and support her, take care of her needs and security. What they seem to realize here, and have forgotten in the Western World, is that men get erections. Hey, that's nature. That's how the species is perpetuated. It's not dirty or immoral. And the society here understands that. If having an erection near a beautiful woman is a sin, well then, the whole world is screwed because that's what's going to happen. It is perfectly acceptable, and the ladies who want to satisfy that urge can make a nice living doing it. For them, it's no big deal. They're just washing the windows, checking the oil."

Well, I had never actually thought about it, but it sounded true enough. I guess every guy has some fascination with ladies of the night, but for me, the idea of consummating such a thing had previously been unthinkable. I mean, you see these sleazy guys on TV expose shows like COPS. And in San Francisco, they were talking about putting their pictures on billboards as a public shame. But here, last night, it didn't seem reprehensible in any way. When I told this to Robbie he laughed again.

He said, "If they put people's pictures on billboards here, they might end up winning elections." He told me about the concept of second and third wives. He told me guys brag about this kind of stuff.

The other surprise for me was how innocent, lovely and affectionate the girls appeared. Som was full of love. There seemed nothing coarse or dirty about it. The girls in the bar were like giggling, happy little teenage girls, though Robbie assured me they were older. When I later questioned him about the joy, "I don't know," was Robbie's response. "Go figure. Bargirls seem to be the happiest sub-set of people that I have ever encountered; easily more so than accountants."

And I could not agree more. My life was full; all the necessities you could imagine and plenty of extras, and I had been contemplating killing myself. I wasn't sure what exactly had happened last night, but it felt good. If my life had been full before, well, maybe I had been looking at things incorrectly. Something was obviously lacking. "I think I need my oil checked again," I told Robbie.

He smiled. It was not yet noon.

You might say that young Robbie Fender was conveniently my new hero. I wondered if there was any reason why the people at the firm had chosen him to act as my introduction to life in Bangkok. If it was a test of morals; I failed. If it was an opportunity to find and hold something against me; well, who cares? I certainly didn't. When you are content with the fact that it is possible to kill yourself, then anything goes, and with Robbie as my guide; it did. Robbie told me a good foot massage was luscious. I was prepared to follow him anywhere.

Numbers are logical and predictable. Dreams and fantasies are not. They inhabit a world beyond our ability to control, and once let loose, there is no forecasting the outcome. With numbers, there are no personalities or situations to deal with. Each day, they behave in the same manner. But when I look at them now, I see that there are fractions as well, and these I envision as broken off pieces of a whole; they are fragments, slices of the pie that are separated out. And we all have them, loose wires of personality buried deep inside. Others can't see them. Some are so small that we don't realize their existence until we uncover them, and once noted, in their aberration they grow so large that we can see nothing else.

At the reception desk of the fancy massage storefront, there was a young man; you might say a wolf in sheep's clothing, as he was dressed like a woman, make-up and all. I had watched enough TV to get the concept, but I had never encountered or interacted with someone this real. He tried a feminine smile, but there was no mistaking the gender thing that was going on.

He assigned me a masseuse, and she came with a basin and washed my feet. All the girls seemed quite familiar with Robbie, and in short order there was a small group gathered around us. The joking was done in Thai, and the cross dressing fellow from reception joined in. And he was considerate enough to bring me into the conversation as well, asking me in not too bad English, if I had any children.

"Yes, two boys," I answered. "Both in college." And I suddenly began feeling ancient, as I was certainly the oldest in the room.

"Are they here?" he asked.

"No, in America." And the room closed in on me, as I had, in such a short time, become un-tethered from my life back there. America was distant and unreal. Bangkok was here. It seemed like months ago that I had left, though it had been merely two days.

"Do you miss them?" he asked me.

A wistful breeze blew through the room, a soft summer zephyr which he must have noted by the expression on my face as I said nothing.

"Well, then you should adopt me." He startled me with this bizarre proposal that came so quickly. My face must have betrayed my fear. "No, no, no," he quickly responded. "It's not that bad. Just think of it this way, you adopt me, and you get both a boy and a girl." He smiled wide and nearly curtsied.

Well, I laughed, but as my foot massage went on, I found my eyes wandering over to him. He was funny, and had a lovely appealing feminine quality as well. An alluring mixture clouded my images, but I was undeniably drawn in. When the foot massage was nearing a close, my masseuse smiled sweetly and asked if I wanted to go upstairs for an oil massage. She told me there were private rooms.

She flipped her eyebrows.

Robbie Fender smiled knowingly, and nudged me with his eyes. And OK, my delightful young masseuse escorted me upstairs, and I was introduced to the wonders of baby oil, in conjunction with a spectacular twenty-two year old physique, and how the mixture of the two can produce sensations that go beyond description. And in snippets, fractions of glimpses, I felt as though I were cheating on Som. Not my wife in America, she was that far from my smoky thoughts. In a dream, faces appear clear and dominant, made more prominent by the fading of everything else – and this was surely a dream.

And, as Robbie had mentioned before my ascent, this little girl seemed to know all the places that felt best to massage, unthinkable in the USA. And my thoughts drifted back to America. If I would have a massage in America, and became aroused, I would have felt myself to be a pervert. I could imagine the masseuse fleeing in horror for the nearest phone to call the police, or maybe her lawyer – but it was a totally natural response. My young Thai masseuse giggled.

It wasn't long before I knew my way around the bars and massage venues of Bangkok. It was out in the open and accepted. And I indulged. It was the most natural thing in the world, and I came to find it amazing how the Western World had so effectively closed down the sensual delights of sex, while it exploded out from television advertisement campaigns. There existed a double standard of teasing, where sex was dangled in front of you, but you would be a horrid person if you considered engaging. Hell, even Jimmy Carter lusted in his heart. And if he were here, he could so easily satisfy that desire, and then go on about his day. Rosalind wouldn't miss him too much – twenty minutes and out, a new man would emerge with the craving wiped clean, well, as Robbie would say, like you might wash a window.

And just as my friend Bartleby, who I believe was at the heart of Melville, 'preferred not to' – well, you might say that I went head over heels in the opposite direction, 'I preferred to' indulge more times than Robbie Fender could believe. I went wild, and on this I will not elaborate, other than that the eventual consequence of my new found freedom was unexpected.

My sexual encounters often left me depressed and vacant. With my physical compulsions met, I found myself feeling lost, empty and naked with a stranger. I had nothing to want for, until the next time. My conquests organized themselves in neat columns, like numbers on a page or endless rows of corn. I found my roving thoughts magnetically drawing me to the balcony, thirty-five stories high. I would sit on the living room couch, and could feel an invisible part of me rising up and leaping over. My imagination would relentlessly draw me there. The feeling would drain from my legs as if I were standing at the edge, looking down, picturing myself in free fall. And just as in Iowa, nobody suspected my tendencies.

Each of my searches for my next experience, my next encounter, became a quest, an adventure, but eventually you learn that the result will be the same, a taming of the physical drive, and a release that set free all worldly desires. And I wonder what was it that kept Melville churning. Book after book was a failure, Moby Dick amongst them.

He lived with his lack of success until he went back to the work that sustained him. In 1862, at the age of forty-three, he returned to New York City and went to work in the U.S. Customs House. I wonder if he found himself musing at the treasures that other adventurers were sending home from overseas. It wouldn't be until after his death that they would discover *Billy Budd*. Herman Melville died in 1891, a forgotten writer.

I am sure that Melville suffered his failures as a writer, not taking comfort in the Bartleby-esque nature of what had come to be his existence. And maybe, the sweeter part of life for me was the discovery of Bangkok at an older age, when I had assumed that life had already passed me by. I was forty-three. I drank of the waters like a man dying of thirst – maybe I overdid it, but who is to judge unless he has lived his life confined to neat rows and columns?

And just as Robbie Fender had done for me, after one lascivious year in Bangkok, it fell upon my lap to escort a recent transferee to the company on his first night. A young man from Texas, somewhat macho and, as I so vividly remembered my opening night, he maintained the clarity to bring a fear into the equation. Something he carried over from the lifeless entry of a printed page. He had read about the lady boys of Bangkok and that sometimes, they were so convincing that it was difficult to tell the difference.

He said he had heard a revolting story of someone in Thailand, picking up an assumed-to-be-girl in a bar, and the next morning discovering that she was actually a man. Well, we have all heard that story often enough to not doubt the veracity, however, I wonder. How can you not know until the next day? How can you not know before? If you live in Thailand, you know. The *katoeys* are tall and trim. They act in a manner in which all the femininity of five ladies was squeezed-out like orange juice and placed inside of them. They overdo it, if you ask me.

And, back to the allure. There must be something there, because it is a big tourist attraction to go to a *Katoey* show and watch them lip sync songs dressed up in evening gowns. I have to admit, at a distance they do look beautiful, but up close, I know I am looking at a man in an evening gown. If I look in their eyes, it is a man looking back. But, I guess, if you add whiskey into the equation, well, maybe anything goes.

When I escorted Tex, I knew we were in a room full of ladies, and that his macho was a homophobic cover. I re-assured him that all was fine, and he would not have an unexpected twist to the evening. In the ensuing months, I did take to teasing him. There was something over the top in his revulsion that gave me joy in tweaking. There were newspaper photos of a cross dressing kick boxer who was devastatingly powerful, but admitted to wanting to hug and kiss her male opponents. She was really gorgeous, and I did not hesitate to point this out.

There was an article in the paper of a local doctor who was performing cut-rate sex change operations for lady boys, but only if they were psychologically fit. This would represent a Catch 22 situation in America as the mere wanting of a sex change operation was not compatible with the idea of being mentally balanced. Each time Tex would throw up his hands and scream, "Oh my god! Oh my god!" His reaction was always worth prompting, and usually provoked additional playful taunting by me.

And one day, I brought Tex along to a local bar to shoot pool. Now, I knew who was going to be there. Jill was full of life, a bouncy, tall and trim twenty-five year old with outstanding legs. And she was different in that she was born a male, but had visited a good doctor who left her with small but pleasing round silicon implants and less than nothing where something personal had previously been.

And Tex watched quietly while I joked with her familiarly. That's what a year in Bangkok will bring you; friends of all description who might not appear in your typical small Texas town, or Ames Iowa either. And it wasn't that I hadn't seen enough lady boys in my day, but Jill was different in a way you would have to see to appreciate.

It was not only that she was attractive, but when I looked into the eyes of most lady boys, as I said, I could see a man looking back at me. Not so with Jill. Her eyes had that flirtatious flash which I had proven a sucker for time and again in the lady bars of Bangkok. But, to see that same sparkle in her eyes, well, it had me thinking too. I am most definitely attracted to women and have never been attracted to any of the other lady boys I had seen, but… Jill was now technically a woman with all the parts correct. And I will admit to attraction and confusion. She had crossed genders. But -

If I went with her – what was I?

It almost frightened me how psychotically quiet Tex had been during the pool game. I was afraid I had gone too far with my little joke, and the outcome was now beyond my ability to control. He could have been contemplating murder, or been falling in love, I couldn't be sure. I was sorry that I had brought him, but after the pool game, over a reflective drink, I posed a dilemma for him.

"Tex," I asked. "If you brought home a beautiful woman and then had the absolute best sex that you ever had in your whole life, and the next day you found out it was a *katoey*; a lady boy, what would you do? If it was the best sex that you ever had; wouldn't you want to do it again?"

His eyes grew large. His mind was racing. You cannot refuse the best. The best? The worst? I stopped, afraid that I might drive him over the edge – and into high heels, if you know what I mean. But, his eyes just sort of rolled up inside his head – at least I had him thinking. And I guess, I was thinking too. What would it be like to be with Jill? I didn't think it would be all that bad, and maybe even great. Could I do it? Under the right circumstances, yes. Was I curious? Yes.

Robbie Fender has the office next to mine. The work, as it was in Ames, is monotonous, maybe more so in stark contrast to the Bangkok nights, but the mind presents an escape hatch in the form of daydreams, a lifetime habit for me, and probably most of us Bartleby's who inhabit the workplace. And as Melville said, "Who ain't a dreamer."

I sometimes wonder if lives are spent entirely in that realm, and if they are, maybe it is a more pleasant place to be. And I imagine that I am no different in that sexual pleasures play into the forefront of this fantasy world, a kind of self-satisfying foreplay that offers feats which would be unachievable on the stage of reality.

Melville was my age when he began work in the Customs House in New York City. I wonder what his day dreams were about as he stoically set about his job. He undoubtedly had brown-skinned sexual encounters in his youth, as I was now having in middle age. And my wandering thoughts traveled back to his time and forward to mine in comparison.

The beauty and variety here is overwhelming; the availability and choice unrivaled. Did Melville have so many choices? Could it have been this easy for him? I doubt it. Did Melville sit and daydream about his times of adventure while working the orderly columns of numbers, most certainly. His time working in the Customs House was called his literary silent period, but his mind had to be working.

My mind drifted to Jill. She wasn't more beautiful than any of the ladies that I have been with, just that, well, she was a man before, and a woman now, and it seemed only natural to be curious as to what that might feel like, what that experience might be. I was not homophobic, nor homosexual; rather neutral on the subject. And I do not think that Melville's fantasies could ever have imagined a beautiful female, who had once been a male, but had been surgically transformed. That is a miracle of my age, not his, and shouldn't all miracles be explored if possible, if available?

What type of person might go with someone like this? What type of man might go with a lady boy who had not been changed? These were most definitely men, exploring a new frontier. You might say the subject of gender was on my mind when it came time for our morning coffee break to interrupt my dream world.

When I walked into Robbie Fender's office and asked him what he was thinking about, this is what he told me, and this is why I would later agree with his wife when she told me that I love her husband.

"I was with two lovely girls last night," Robbie confided. "They are both trim and leggy. Nearly the same in every dimension, except one is light-skinned and the other black coffee. It was really exciting, and I have been fantasizing about taking them both away to the beach for an entire weekend."

I had never been with two women, but the fantasy had always been there, just with an unusual twist that made it entirely impossible. I knew both of the girls that Robbie was with last night. They were lovely.

"I have never been with two women," I told Robbie.

He shrugged, a 'why not' expression covering his face. Yes, I know most things are easily accomplished in this city where 'anything goes' is normal and leaving desires un-sated is strange.

"Though it has always been my desire," I told him. "I have thought about it for most of my life, and it is almost as if by fulfilling the desire, the reality could not possibly match the fantasy. But here is the twist that makes it impossible." And here I stopped, having never before offered this next thought in the audible world, "in my dreams, I am always one of the two women, and I'm not sure what to make of that."

Robbie chuckled.

I asked what.

Robbie waved me away with a nonchalant hand.

What I asked again.

"You are a lesbian trapped inside the body of a man," he told me.

As I had mentioned, on my first night, in a dream you are not always yourself. There is an inside-outside perspective that can be achieved. Am I indeed a lesbian? A lesbian would certainly fantasize about being with another woman, but would she fantasize about going with a transgender female? But the transgender female certainly did not go through a sex change operation to become a female so that she could engage in homosexual activities. Would she? There was a lot to work through here.

Actually, it sounded as plausible as anything else that I had heard or experienced in this craziest year of my life. I went back to adding columns of numbers as straight as the corn, and wondering who the real Richard Brock might be, and what I might get myself involved in tonight.

9

After reading Thailand Stories, my first novel, a friend of my mother's from Delaware hired a driver to bring her to Central Pennsylvania to meet me. With a big smile, she told me that since reading the book, she felt as though she knew me. This was an odd and unsettling thought for me at the time. It was fiction. What exactly was it that she thought she knew?

A year later, a neighbor of my parents told me the same thing. There are points of view, and pieces of our being, that color a work of writing. A part of me will surely flake off into my fiction. Richard Brock was afraid of heights, magnetically drawn to the edge, as I am too. Richard Brock had thoughts of suicide, but was not really suicidal. I have had three close friends commit suicide. It's enough to make anyone wonder.

Hot season is in full-on, radical, radiant burn, and the heat in Tak is punishing. I spend more time hibernating than checking on the progress at my house. More often, it is my wife who comes to visit me in the resort motel with the air conditioned room. I watch Fox News, even though it disappoints me. She sleeps.

The news has become partisan, too sensational and political. I am a non-voter in the same way in which I am a non-drinker. Alcohol doesn't taste good to me. It leaves me thick-tongued and cotton-mouthed. Politics and politicians don't taste good. Sorry Monica.

I was not born an abstainer. It's not that I don't care. The reasons for not voting have ripened through the years. There is no President since I have been of voting age that I would be proud to have supported.

I view politics as one might a rough spectator sport. It is a hockey match, in which, cheap shots and dirty play are part of the game. The public accepts this in politics; though my na ve assumption is that this is an arena where you might want to have a statesman, and a fine gentleman or lady, instead we nominate and elect the thug who can take the hits and dish them back harder and dirtier. Something is terribly wrong.

Ken Klein

My life has been scattered in places and events. Numbers on a calendar are not significant to me. I graduated University of Pennsylvania in 1972, and by 1974 I had fulfilled two of my career goals, and a personal objective, as well.

I had made a small, but steady, living at New York's Aqueduct and Belmont Race Tracks. The simple, conservative philosophy was to place a couple of moderate-sized place or show bets, and walk out with a $20-30 profit, thereby covering my minimal costs of living.

I studied the past performances of the horses, as well as the interactions of the trainers and jockeys in the paddock area. I would look at the intensity of conversation. Were they scanning the program, reviewing their rivals, discussing possible strategies? The human factor, intent, is of highest importance in a horse race. If all appeared right, I would place my bet. Mostly, I would watch.

My second occupational pre-occupation was to complement my love of driving with a job as a New York City taxi driver. After a short while, it became a fume infested plod of a job, but it enabled me to save enough money to pursue my real first love, travel. And through the eyes of a traveler, writer and businessman, I view the characters in my life and in my work. Melville, Bartleby, Brock – they all become filtered through my perceptions. Though they are not me, the colors I use to portray them originate from the palette of my life.

It surprises me that it was Jimmy Carter lusting in his heart who entered my mind while writing about Herman Melville and bargirls in Bangkok. I would have guessed Bill Clinton.

I Never Vote. It Only Encourages Them

Carter vs. Ford 1976

In 1976, I knew that Jimmy Carter had been a peanut farmer and that Gerry Ford bumped his head and tripped a lot. Neither was impressive.

I had a friend named Jerry, and he was clumsy too. I never knew a peanut farmer, but it harkened back to what I thought politics should be; the neighbor who was a good solid citizen, smart and capable, who should be elected to go down to DC and do a few years of public service, and then go home and tend his crops.

Jimmy Carter would be the only president in my lifetime that I could imagine enjoying as a next door neighbor. I didn't know much about him in 1976, and once more, did not vote. He was not an effective President. He has gone on to become a successful human being.

I was in the USA for Carter vs. Ford, but it did not inspire passion. I hadn't registered, and therefore, didn't vote. Ford was connected to Nixon. Carter was connected to a beer drinking brother. My vote didn't seem to matter.

In 1975, shortly after my return from travel, still under the influence of a backpacking journey through natural wonders, I visited my brother in D.C. He was living in a modest apartment, and his friends were congressman's aides and advisors.

As brothers, you would never believe that we grew up in the same household. I have heard stories of identical twins who were separated at birth, grew up in different environments and when re-united were remarkably similar. We are the flip side of that example. You would never know we had grown up in the same county.

My brother saw the ladder, and instinctively began to climb. I looked it over. It was interesting, but narrow, and held only two choices - "up" or "down". I needed a more horizontal path that I could easily wander away from, a spectrum of choices. The ladder had an element of being slippery. I walked around it, and went to the beach. My brother's pretty high up now. I had a period of being a hard working, good citizen business owner and employer. I'm back at the proverbial beach now.

My brother reached the rung of Washington Bureau Chief for Rolling Stone Magazine in 1975. I finished my first round-the-world trip in 1974. It was a year of timeless Tuesdays, Europe, Overland across the Middle East, Turkey, Iran, Afghanistan, Pakistan, India and on to Asia; Thailand, Korea, Taiwan, Japan, probably fifty countries in all. I returned walking at a far slower pace than America.

Early on, during my three day stay in DC, one of my brother's friends sat and talked with me. The subject of my non-voting was brought up. Though my track record was not long, my determination to continue the path was set. He asked why, what and who questions.

"Why" was that I saved ten dollars by not voting for McGovern. If I had used that money to vote, the difference would have been too minimal to count. George McGovern would have received 1,102,212 votes in the state of New Jersey. He would have lost by one less than the margin of 743,390 votes. New Jersey would not be his to claim along with his two small triumphs, Massachusetts and D.C. Nothing would have changed, but I still have my ten dollars.

"Who" proved to be a tougher question. It was currently a choice between a peanut farmer and a fellow with coordination problems. There just wasn't much to excite my interest. I found no one inspirational in either party.

The usual answer to the "Who" question is John F. Kennedy. His candidacy was my first political experience, and seems to be the one that inspired Americans the most. I was twelve years old. It was a blustery rainy day in October. My parents brought me along to Sunrise Highway because JFK was coming through. We waited a couple of hours in the rain. A motorcade whizzed past at 60 mph. That was it. I caught a cold and got to stay home from school the next day, but as for inspiration, not much.

The WHAT question – now that touched a note. That presented possibilities. If there was something that mattered to me personally, that I thought would directly affect me or someone I knew – then, I might vote.

He wanted to know what that 'what' might be. I couldn't imagine. Our conversation lasted about fifteen minutes, and that was it. Other than my brother, it was the last conversation I would have in DC. I could further no one's career. These were ladder guys, and a chute was more appealing to me. I could not be used as a future political or career building connection for anyone.

My brother later told me that the one fellow who talked to me was trying to learn how to reach "PEOPLE LIKE ME." Young free thinking individuals? A well traveled fellow who knew where you could get a good western breakfast in Tehran or a cheeseburger in Kabul?

No. Non-voters - the approximately 50 percent of Americans who do not vote. I think he found me unreachable. I had nothing to contribute to the important conversations going on around me. Who was invited to what party? Did you hear about the dress that some congressman's wife wore to a party? In the area of Congressional wives accessories; I was a parking lot without any cars, alone and vacant. I had no names to drop or fashionable labels to wear. Their world was cemented inside the beltway. Nothing else was of interest.

If anyone were to ask me what I did, I truly felt that I would have had to start my end of the conversation with; "Have you ever seen a tree?" – That was how out of touch I think those people were. Nobody asked.

We sat, gathered in a circle on the floor, about ten of us. They were passing a joint around. It was good stuff too. Then they passed it by me, as if I wasn't there. I had become invisible, but if these guys were the foundation of our government, I felt confident in my decision not to vote.

My redemption came the following night. We traveled to Maryland for a poker game with what proved once more to be "not" my crowd. The conversation focused on life inside the beltway trivia, and I had nothing to add.

I quickly noticed that these guys were far too bound up in their egos. Being bluffed out by someone would be considered a terrible disgrace that they might never live down. They were Kennedy at Guatanamo Bay, and were not going to let anyone force them to back down, even if it was an insignificant hand of poker, even if it meant losing their money. They would not be bluffed out, as if it might one day appear on their resume as a weakness. **He may have lost $50, but he was never ever bluffed out.** This guy has guts. He does not back down!! And so, it was the easiest money I ever made.

Mostly, I folded my cards, but when I had a good or great hand, I bet like crazy. This sudden aberrant behavior was symptomatic of a bluff, and led them to call my bets. The pots that I won were the largest of the night by far. They felt compelled to call me with mediocre cards, just in case I was bluffing. The pots I won were huge. The pots they won were normal, but mostly, I was sitting on the sideline waiting for the good hands. They cursed and bitched at the size of my bets, but rarely folded their cards. They called my bets. I won.

It wasn't long before they lost total control. They started calling me horrible names: Shithead. Slimeball. Fuckface. I hadn't said one word since I had been there, and I was being roundly assailed as Dirtbag and Asshead. They were out of control, which made the game easier. I walked away as the only winner in the game. They were writing checks at the end of the night. And these guys are influential in writing policy for our country.

After the game was finished, the host realized that I was his guest, and that he had been calling me horrible names all night. He apologized. The only time he heard me speak was after the game was over. I said, "thank you," as he wrote me a check.

I never cared for Washington, and rarely visited after that. I was so unimpressed with these "insiders" that there would be no election for a long time that would garner my interest. If you glance upwards while climbing the ladder, mostly you just see the bottoms of feet and assholes.

Jimmy Carter would win a relatively close election without me; 40,827,394 to 39,145,977.

10

I venture to the Tak night market in the early evening. I walk slowly through the lingering heat. For the price of one dollar, I purchase a coconut soup with chicken, rice and a noodle dish, more food than I can eat. In the evening, I walk around the corner to the internet shop. There are school kids who come to play games. They leave their shoes in a tangle outside the front door.

Through the mist of time, I can hear my father screaming as I stand 12,000 miles and fifty years away from my childhood. "What are you crazy?!" His voice is inside my head, forever conscious of other's foibles. "How can you leave your shoes there? Someone will trip!" In America, this would be correct. In Thailand, he would be the crazy one. His reasoning would be upside down. Thai people take off their shoes before entering a house or shop. How could you not know there were going to be shoes in front of the door?

I remember visiting Shark Fin Sammy down in Pattaya. He was up and dancing. His favorite Ad Karabou song came blasting over the radio in the backstreet restaurant where we had stopped for a snack. He couldn't resist and jumped to his feet instantly.

Sammy is a sixty-four year old retired Wells Fargo executive, smart as a whip and full of fun. He retired in Thailand, and fit right in. Sammy was boogying-up a storm and you had to wonder, if he had retired in America, would he ever have been up and dancing?

Sammy has a tall, thin thirty-five year old girlfriend, and the side dishes are unlimited. He can go-go out for a snack whenever the mood hits him. He has grown children and an ex-wife in America. For him, the beach town of Pattaya with its ex-pat bars, shopping centers, movie theatres and restaurants is paradise.

If you ask him about the magic in Thailand, he would not be able to put it into words. If you look at the expression on his face, the smile while he pumps his arms and legs without inhibition to the pounding pulse of Karabou, it is easy to see that the magic has entered inside him. He would feel lost and alone without it. In America, he would be bound by convention. Here, he can dance. Sammy signs off his emails – Sammy in Paradise.

When I had traveled as a youth, distance brought a longing for friends back home. Now, due to email, I no longer have that feeling. An hour on the internet is an hour spent with friends. I can keep in touch, and sometimes, there is a surprise visitor to my inbox.

I had written an article for my college magazine and submitted it. They accepted, and told me they would pay $500. If it was re-printed elsewhere, I had to acknowledge that they printed it first. OK, I was tickled. I had no idea they paid for this sort of thing. I had a little money trickling in from the sales of my first book. I started telling people that I now make hundreds of dollars ***a year*** as a writer. It was a rare person who got the joke. Most nodded or said wow, that's great.

People don't always listen. These are the same people who offer us advice with an equal amount of consideration, usually based on how they think they might feel in your shoes, or based on how they might feel at the moment. My mother used to tell me to put on a sweater because she was cold.

If I give advice, it is that most people don't care too much what you do, as long as you don't hurt them, or others, so, you might just as well do something that you enjoy, no matter how off-beat. Please yourself.

THE OX HERDER

The Ox Herder was first published in the Pennsylvania Gazette.

We all know the image. A small herd of powerful, neck skin drooping oxen crossing a dirt road, returning from grazing. They walk slowly with confident disdain through a timeless landscape, and are followed by a small man in a straw hat with a switch. The huge beasts are so entrancing that we seldom consider the man, what sort of life he might lead, his hopes and dreams. He appears barely significant in comparison, and does not invite the question – did he graduate from the Wharton School of Business and if so, what class was he in?

I can remember back to freshmen orientation weekend. We were presented with a list of occupations ranked according to earning potential. Doctor and lawyer were certainly at the top, though I recall being more intrigued by the lower echelon of the compilation, which closed out with fisherman [non-boat]. I might have been the only one that day who considered that an appealing option.

Bangkok is the capital city of Thailand, and the official population is about five million, though the actual figure might be as high as three times that. The discrepancy is created because people move into the city to work, but are always considered to be from their home district. This is the importance of your village. Your home will forever be the birthplace of your ancestors.

My wife, the oldest of four daughters, is from a family of hard working, land owning subsistence farmers. They own non-contiguous plots of land with fruit trees, rice paddies, a field of corn and a small plot of land that holds the family home. Her father hopes that one day they will have a large enough plot of ground to create a family compound where each of his daughters and their husbands can build homes, but land in the village is tight, not easy to find or acquire.

In one of my early meetings with my father-in-law to be, he confided the family compound concept to me, though at the time, he had more pressing issues. A failed fruit crop left him with a $500 debt that was accruing interest at a locally accepted rate of 5% per month. Though rice and vegetables are plentiful, and there is little want for food, currency is not an easily available commodity. He was having trouble sleeping and could think of nothing, but the weight of his debt. A week later, fully aware of his unspoken pride, powerful dignity and need to save face, I unceremoniously offered the cash to overcome the obstacle.

Remembering back to my first meeting with this gentle man, short of stature, but with the physique of a middleweight, there was a brief moment of uncertainty. After our introduction, he asked about my work. Any father's rightful question, for sure, but the answer was beyond my language capabilities at the time and somewhere past easy understanding. Stock markets, investments, real estate, bonds, early retirement after years of being a businessman, were probably not comprehensible for a subsistence farmer. After a too long pause, I answered that I was not currently working.

A puzzled look drifted across his face. "How do you eat?" he asked.

The apparent ease with which his debt had been re-paid brought other dreams to light during the time that transpired between visits. Surely, $3,500 was not too much to ask. Upon my return, the tending of oxen was explained, and a partnership offered. And though the deal was presented skillfully, my concerns of being seen as a banker for a family, not yet my own, led me to decline. English is a language of precision, and I stumbled through a list of business terms and alternative investments opportunities not dependent on beasts that eat or can get sick and die.

A couple of years later, after marriage made me a full fledged member of the family, I set to work on the project of acquiring land in the village for a family compound.

Khun Sak, a 62 year old recently retired government official, was a dynamo of a man. Tall and broad shouldered, neat and polite, he was engaged in several businesses. He had a granite mining concern, a roadside convenience store/gas station complex along the main highway, and was in the process of building a resort, as well as having a myriad of other ventures.

Sak was piloted around in a spanking new SUV equipped with everything but a stewardess. Years before, having purchased a large parcel of mountain land, he was currently clearing the property and selling it off in lots. This is what brought us together.

In my discussions with friends in Bangkok, Thai and foreigners alike, advice on purchasing land was freely offered. Most important, you must have a deed. Upcountry, defined as everything outside of Bangkok, is rife with land disputes. Don't be fooled by the fact that they call him *Bpee*, older brother. Everyone is *Bpee*. This I knew. You could meet someone once, and if the meeting was warm, they could be *Bpee*.

Sitting together after dinner, on the polished teak floor of the family home, we engaged in an informal family circle meeting. I asked if I could speak freely. We were considering buying into *Khun* Sak's development, but I had questions. I did not want to speak badly of Sak, as he was quite well respected. I liked him too, and felt comfortable with his fatherly demeanor. He was *Bpee* Sak.

I had concerns because there was too much that did not add up. There was no deed, but there was a story of how we would get a contract, and the deed would follow in six years. I have been in business long enough to know that a story is not a substitute for a deed. I know that government officials who retire wealthy have more than just a few tales, and the entire situation was exactly what everyone in Bangkok had warned me about. The cash to buy the land, though easily within my budget, was coming from me. And though I liked and trusted him too, *Khun* Sak had blemishes.

"What could go wrong?" the family asked me.

"He could die," I offered. Six years is a long time.

However, there seemed more right than wrong, and despite my premonition of problems, my desire to assist in the family project won out. After we signed the contract and paid a 50% deposit, father put me on the back of his motorcycle, and we went out to the land.

Thai is a language of the heart. There are probably a hundred common expressions in conjunction with the word heart. Most beautifully is "*Kao jai*" – to understand. The literal translation is "to enter the heart," as true understanding must take that route.

"*Por jai?*" literally translated as, "Is your heart full?" Satisfied, he asked me.

"Are you satisfied?" I returned the question. His smile lit the surrounding mountains.

One year later *Bpee* Sak was dead. The unwritten guarantee to bring water and electric to the property might not be upheld. His daughter, who had been left in charge of the empire that he built, did not hold his government connections. When confronted by my nervous father in law, she offered to return the money in full. I was in America at the time and when I called the village, the money was safely resting in the local bank.

As one dream may be forced into temporary remission, there are always others to take their place. We are a "castles in the air" species, forever projecting into an idyllic future. The returned deposit for the land was coincidentally $3,500, the same sum requested years ago to begin our partnership in the business of oxen. My increased involvement and continually growing respect for the family, as well as my estimated return of 44% per year, now made the venture more viable.

Thinking back once more to orientation weekend, I ponder whether or not my destiny was oddly pre-determined. Though not a fisherman, [non-boat] I can be an ox herder, [straw hat and switch] lazily sitting by the side of the road, lounging under a tree in the shade, reading a book while my livestock graze.

And if you find yourself on vacation, passing through a timeless landscape in the Central Plains of Thailand and through the window of your tour bus you see a small herd of powerful, neck skin drooping water buffalo and an insignificant tender; take a moment, consider his hopes and dreams and wave hello; it just might be me – Wharton class of 1972.

11

Before The Ox Herder appeared in The Pennsylvania Gazette, the editor made some suggestions, and I made some alterations. It was a decent process conducted with respect and courtesy. I was sent the final copy for review, and all was fine. However, somewhere between agreement and publication, both the line about fisherman [non–boat] and ox herder [straw hat and switch] – were deleted from the story without my knowledge or approval. Was it a last minute editorial decision, or a rogue typesetter with no sense of humor? I didn't really care too much. The $500 is enough to cover my electric, water and property taxes for a year, and have a couple of nights on the town left over.

When we once again found land to purchase in the village, my wife gave the seller $5,000 – 50% of the purchase price for the acre we were buying. The deed was transferred into my wife's name, but the seller, unable to read, did not follow through with the paperwork at the Land Office.

The plot of land is long and narrow, and our house was being built close to the property line. The seller became upset when she saw the house going up, and had not yet received the full amount for her land. My wife had been waiting for her to go to the land office. I chided my wife for not having a receipt for the $5,000 already tendered, and for starting to build before the government surveyed the land. I told her it was different in the USA. We had firm contracts that specified times and amounts.

When I sold my property in Pennsylvania, there were contracts that were not honored, and a deal that became screwed-up through miscommunication. The real estate agents came out fine, but a year later, the deal is still not completed. The functionality of the system depends on the decency of the people.

* * *

Ken Klein

My first time in Thailand was in 1974. After rough and dirty travel, overland through the Middle East, I had clean sheets and hot and cold running water for the first time in months. The food was good. The people were beautiful. The prices of food and lodging were reasonable. I was in backpacker heaven.

When I look back, it is difficult to pinpoint what made everything so special for me in Thailand. I didn't think about it while it was happening. I enjoyed. But after returning to America, I would hear songs on the radio that were played frequently during my month long visit. When the songs would come on, I would stop everything, and let the music carry me back. The juke box in the hotel lobby, the corner store where I had chocolate milk and cookies every day, the ornate temples where I played basketball and the smiling faces were all rolled together in a special feeling that I still experience today.

The magic is not the rabbit coming out of the hat, but the feeling of awe that it inspires. I can't believe I am here and becoming part of this place. A bowl of soup on the street with a friend or a cool breeze off the Gulf of Siam can trigger the sensation.

I try and define it. Why do I experience it so often in Thailand, and so rarely elsewhere. Could it be that there is a childlike honesty to their easy laughter? Is it the smiles that are always returned? Or could it be the non-confrontational set of manners?

Direct rebuttals are not polite. If someone wants to borrow money, "no" is not acceptable – the answer is "tomorrow"; the never ending future does not rule out possibility and softens disappointment. It is impolite to not offer an answer. If you ask for directions, a Thai person will, most likely, provide an answer. Misinformation is endemic; uncertainty is a natural result.

The first time I went to the bus station at Ekkamai, I approached a window in a parking lot that said "Tickets." Buses were parked alongside.

"Where are you going?" The lady asked the traditional Thai greeting – their equivalent of how are you.

"Rayong," I answered.

"That's lovely."

"Yes."

"Are you going for holiday?"

"Yes. I am going to the beach."

"The weather is nice now."

"Yes," and I was wondering what I was supposed to do to buy a ticket. I took out my wallet. "How much is a ticket to Rayong?"

"I think it is 90 baht."

What did she mean, I think? She isn't sure? How can she sell me a ticket if she doesn't know the price? She looked at me and smiled.

"Can I buy a ticket?" I held my money up to illustrate my sincerity.

"Yes," She responded easily.

"Well," I offered her my money.

She looked puzzled.

I looked at her puzzled. Her calm and friendliness, her devotion to being pleasant softened my feelings of frustration.

She smiled.

I smiled. What was I to do to get her to sell me a ticket? "Where can I get a ticket?"

Her face lit up. "Over there," she pointed across the small sidewalk to where the busses were lined up. She was selling tickets for the museum next door. The bus station was a few feet away. If I had experienced the same conversation in America, it would have driven me to distraction. Here it is endearing. It can be trying if you don't have the time or patience. We cannot always be in the mood for life to be a jigsaw puzzle. The trick is in an easy acceptance.

12

I grew up in the 1950s, an era of innovation, technology and possibility. There was color television and space travel. Shopping malls with air conditioning were sprouting like apple trees. A feeling was in the air that if you could dream it, you could do it.

My mother had told me that I could be anything that I wanted, do anything that I wanted to do when I grew up. I believed her. Why not? I meandered through a blissful childhood under the spell of those words. Sure, my first choice would have been to play second base for the Giants, but I wasn't unrealistic, and ruled that out by age ten. There still was everything else; I just had to figure out what I wanted to do most at that given moment. It's not as easy as it may sound. There was time spent in indecision. With so many wonderful choices, it seemed near impossible to settle on just one.

The euphoric state was so mesmerizing, that I never gave up on it. I am fifty years old and still bounce from one thing to the other, and from place to place, wondering what it is that I want to do next. I guess, at some point, I figured out that this bouncing, the constant change, is who I have become. And, for me, it is a good choice. I never feel trapped. If things go wrong, I can change. If life becomes routine and boring, I can mess with any number of variables; time, place, attitude, financial incentives, beach or mountains, hermit or city dweller, geek, businessman or butterfly; I have a lot to play with here, except, like I said, playing second base is out.

Another thing my mother told me at an early age was that someday I will find a girl who is just right for me. In my pubescent, optimistic, unknowing madness, I put my own definition to those words. I envisioned a dream. Pure as driven snow, pretty as a picture, sweet as sugar, - any clich that would fit my personal imaginings would work fine. All I had to do was relax, sit back, and wait patiently for her to come along at what would be the perfect moment.

The first time one such vision of loveliness stopped my heart was at a high school dance. She was spectacular. Our eyes met, and I filled with a desire that I did not know could exist inside a person. I saw that same longing reflected back toward me in her eyes. I later heard that she was the daughter of a diplomat, a Brazilian. We didn't speak. There was just that one moment of frozen perfection. There are flirtatious moments in my life that have stayed with me longer than some of my relationships.

The second vision came at a party in college. Through a cloud of marijuana that was traveling with me that night, I saw her. She was angelic. And she was sweet and pure, and as it turned out cultured and smart, and from a wealthy family – everything one might want, except that, under the closer examination of a few dates, she was not in the least bit sexy or exotic, and there was a touch of being obnoxious and elitist. It didn't work. Maybe if I was more normal, but probably not.

There were hormones running amok in my body, and my brain is part of my body, though at that point certainly not the neediest part, and while I was waiting, stuff happened. There were girlfriends. They were usually attractive, though not exactly the vision of perfection. There were psychological issues. They had wants and dreams too. Driven snow becomes soiled with soot and slushy; then it melts and just "crazy" remains.

I never acquired the taste for alcohol or bitters. I think it could be cool to be a drinker, a tough, two fisted kind of guy, but it's not me. There was a rare moment in a bar after college, when I had a beer induced epiphany. My mother's words came back to me, and I realized that it was her words alone that had formed this concept of perfection in my head. There was not going to be driven snow that would survive past the springtime of a relationship. I looked at the words closer through my haze. My mother never said anything about driven snow; only that there would be a special person who would be right for me; a matching piece in a jigsaw puzzle, not perfection, but someone whose neurosis would dovetail with mine, creating a screwed-up form of compatibility. I think that was the day my childhood ended, akin to the day I realized that I would not have the size or skills to play ball in the major leagues, no matter what I might want. But I maintained the idea that I could pretty much do whatever I wanted, be whoever I desired; that was too good a delusion to part with.

Being Nick Hornby

Sorry Mick Jagger, you don't make the list. It's not that you're not cool, or that I wouldn't love to prance around and sing and dance on the stage. The money must be great too. But the fame; I don't know about that. Or maybe, it is just that I like being me.

And so; here is my final, double dare, all-time list of the three people I would most like to be if I could be anyone who ever lived; past or present:

1. Me
2. Shark Fin Sammy
3. Party Paul Kinsley

The real answer is that I wouldn't want to be anyone other than me, and I understand that at the moment I'm on a semi-delusional rainbow high, even though on the surface, my life might look ordinary.

I was on my way to work at the local shopping mall in Central Pennsylvania, when a question entered my mind. I had a great life. I had rediscovered Thailand and was having a total blast there. It is a tropical paradise with lush palm trees; there is a lightly lapping Gulf of Siam and spectacular Siamese ladies with welcoming smiles.

Everywhere I went there was a party in progress. It was fun, and it had been a long time since I had fun. And maybe never quite like the fun I was having in Thailand. Life had suddenly become far more incredible than I could have ever imagined after having been pretty droll for a long time.

In addition to this, all the pebbles of life seemed to be falling out of my shoes, and I had forgotten how nice it was to walk without pain. My divorce was final, and this was definitely going to be my last year doing Christmas Season at the mall. It would be a liquidation season for me, and then, I would be free. And this kind of high doesn't come along without a love interest that makes you feel privileged to be in her company. A young exotic Thai lady in my instance, but I was in love with the whole culture, from the sweet pineapple that the ladies sell on the beach, to the spicy papaya salad made fresh to your specifications; an incredible concoction of bitter, sweet and chili peppers with tiny shrimp and tomatoes soaked in a peanut lemon sauce. And, as delicious as that is, it only ranks number five on my list of forever favorite foods that I like to eat in Thailand. And here they are:

1. *Tom Kha Gai* – The chicken, mushroom, tomato, lemon grass, chili pepper soup in a creamy coconut base. There are always things at the bottom of the bowl. I have no idea what they are.
2. *Gaeng Keow Wan* – a spicy green curry concoction with pork and what appear to be tiny eggplant, and normally I don't like eggplant, but like I said, it's a concoction.
3. *Moo Yang* – Tender fried pork, crispy on the outside.
4. *Goong* – Shrimp. At least the big four-bite ones that I get down at the fishing village, barbecued to perfection next to my table.
5. *Som Tom* - Papaya Salad.

And as I was driving along to the mall, I couldn't help but think that I had the best life that anyone ever had in the history of the world. I was number one on the life parade because I had discovered worldly joy, not a meditative, vegetative nirvana; a state which somehow seemed empty to me. Nor did I seek material wealth. While others chased recklessly after fortune and fame, not stopping to have a good time, the pursuit becoming an all consuming obsession; I was happy, glad to be alive and appreciating the earthly delights that my senses could wrap themselves around.

The goal chasing appeared a sad and losing game no matter how high up the rungs you reached, the objective might be met, but the bar was always raised higher, and in that way the triumphs became short lived and only brought on loftier ambitions.

Maybe, if it were tempered, it might be different. Maybe if each victory was met with a reward, and a chance to savor and celebrate, possibly with a month on the beach, then it would have some appeal, but most people rush forward endlessly, worker ants trapped in the constant auto payments of their existence; their lives essentially the same, only the make and model a plusher symbol of their success.

I decided on an experiment. I would take a survey in the mall and see what the other employees were thinking. The question was simple: "If you could trade lives with anyone - dead or alive, who would you choose?"

The answers were astounding.

The overweight teenage girl with the bad complexion thought for less than a minute. She could be Madonna or Margaret Thatcher, Cher or Susan B. Anthony. She could be Mike Tyson, if her fondest desire was to pummel men, but she chose to remain herself. As to my surprise, so did everyone I asked. And it wasn't just the recycled air that they pump into the mall that had warped everyone's brain. Outside, where the air was iceberg lettuce crisp and early winter clean, I met with the same results.

I wasn't unique in putting myself at the top of my list; in fact, far from it. Old people did not want to be younger people. Fat people did not want to be other people who were skinny. Nerds did not want to be the cool guy. And even I didn't want to be Party Paul or Shark Fin Sammy, even though they were my second and third choice and living in the Land of Smiles.

Well, Party Paul wasn't living there. He would come on vacations and have more fun than anyone I ever saw. He would go wild and then return home broke two weeks later; but those two weeks! Man! I never saw such fun. He would buy drinks for everyone in sight; mostly girls who worked in the bars. Sometimes eight girls at once would crowd around him. After they were all twisting-in-their-chairs drunk, he would bar fine four of them for the night.

Party Paul would then take them out bowling and to a disco. He would keep the alcohol flowing until 2 or 3 a.m. when everyone was smashed. Half the time he went home and slept alone because the girls were too drunk to come along, and then, even when a girl would go home with him, they were usually too drunk to do anything, and it was unappealing because she would be retching in the toilet for a couple of hours, after which he would call a taxi.

But, you know, during the evening, prancing around Bangkok with four hot babes; he was Mick Jagger and Don Juan all rolled into one, at least until the money ran out. I don't like to drink, and it would feel like a colossal waste of money, but he did enjoy himself more than anyone I have ever seen before or since. After his holiday, he returned to a difficult job and a treacherous life back in the States, but that two week vacation, during which time he probably had more fun than most guys ever have in a whole lifetime, well, that alone is enough to have him rate third on my list of people who I would trade lives with, even though I could do the same thing on my own, but don't. It never seems worthwhile.

Shark Fin Sammy gets second place. He is one of the brightest guys I ever met, though I would later find out that some guys called him Stupid Sammy Martelli. The nickname comes from the ex-pats who hang out in Texas Two Step, a Pattaya bar. Sammy never rid himself of his tough, Italian accent, to which he adds a few marbles in the mouth. He smiles a lot, and with a loose jowl hanging down, he looks like an oversized Bassett Hound, so the ex-pats there think he is stupid. He doesn't dispute them. He's way too smart to argue. His intellect is so far over their head that they would need binoculars to see his most common thoughts.

Stupid Sammy worked security for Wells Fargo Bank. He was a supervisor and knew his business inside and out. I once heard one of the ex-pats say that if they knew how stupid security was, that they would have robbed Wells Fargo long ago. Sammy would have nabbed him in a slick second. Being underestimated was a big advantage that he would never concede.

The draw for me in being Stupid Sammy is twofold. Stupid is a true and unique individual. He knows who he is and what he likes. Stupid likes girls. He has a hot live-in girlfriend who lets him screw around. He's a chaser, he tells me. But his philosophies always gravitate toward knowing what will make him feel best. Even on the subject of diets. He told me that when he goes on a diet, then all he does is think about when he will eat next. It wasn't an answer for him.

I don't really want to be Stupid Sammy, though he has a great life. What made him second choice on my list was that he used to go out with a girl named Ja. Now, there are plenty of beautiful Thai ladies, and you don't ever have to covet your friend's girl here, that would be a crazy masochistic waste of energy, but I met Ja after she had split up with Shark Fin Sammy, and before I met him.

Ja was certainly attractive, but what separated her out was that, if you looked in her eyes, there was a forest fire raging out of control, vastly explosive and totally entrancing. There was magic, and it was not easy to look away. Just glancing into her eyes, I damn near fell apart, and in truth, one night with her might entirely consume me, or give me a heart attack, so I declined. I could easily be manipulated any which way she wanted. But, the fact that Stupid Sammy had the experience of one full year of going out with her, and survived, well, that fact rates him second on my list.

I stopped asking the question, offering people an opportunity to trade lives. It was futile. But sometimes, when it came up in conversation, I told people of the results of my survey. And one day, several years later, a thoughtful young man named Adam Westin became the only one that I ever met to have a divergent response. He told me that he might like to trade lives with Nick Hornby.

"Who?"

"Nick Hornby, the writer."

Adam came to me through an email; a friend of a friend. I had retired to Central Thailand as planned. I had become accustomed to life there, having assimilated about knee deep [which is about the limit or as near as you can or might want to get with white skin]. I didn't think young Adam would find much of interest here.

Bangkok was spoiling with life. A visit to the beaches could be spectacular, but a small subsistence farming village in Central Thailand; there wasn't much doing. My current occupation was to oversee the construction of my house, and explain to the builder that we did not need screens on the interior doors that led from the bedroom to the hallway, but the exterior ones where the bugs were most likely to enter; things like that. Adam came anyway.

When I met Adam, he was certainly not the sort of fellow you might expect to break my neatly formed theory of changing places with other people. Things were apparently together for him. He was young, late twenties, handsome, strong, but not over-powering, unquestionably smart and learned, from a prosperous family, and he had a thick head of hair. He obviously had quite a future ahead of him no matter what he pursued, and that might have been the sticking point.

Adam was well read, and deep down in his inner heart, he would have wanted to be a screen writer, a film maker or even an actor, not the hawk businessman that he was being groomed to be. The chances of success would certainly be working against him in the highly competitive world of film making. It was certainly the practical road, and more widely accepted in his sphere, to be a businessman. That might have been the problem right there, as far as my theory goes. He was already someone else, and that person was not of his own creation.

Adam was working at adapting to a life that his family would roundly applaud, a sensible existence, New York style, and fraught with the challenges of "being somebody" as defined in the Big Apple manic-paced mentality of success through excess of production, not the way of thinking in Thailand.

New York was a different form of activity based meditation, a total absorption into progress, defined in financial terms. Money is a fine yardstick, and I am certain most Thai's would want a shot at the opportunity for wealth through hard work, but there is not much opportunity for a poor Thai person, so they loll around and chat. They joke and eat and go to the beach and, in my estimation, life passes equally or possibly more pleasantly for a poor Thai than a middle class or wealthy New Yorker. If laughter and smiles were the measuring rods, the Thai wins hands down.

Thailand can represent a serene break, an idyllic vacation from the perpetual timetable existence that is clocked in the Western World. It is a place to let your hair down, and sit on the shore in a lounge chair. You can allow the awesome leisure of having one day melt seamlessly into the next. It can be a paper umbrella stuck in your coconut cocktail existence, where you can leave the stress behind, or have a blast like Party Paul, or just flat out do nothing – recharge your batteries, indulging no personal or business accomplishments for a full two weeks.

Adam had an uneventful arrival day in Bangkok, seeing the sights and fighting off the hustlers before he came to visit me in the village, right there achieving something most vacationers never do, a visit to a small Thai village and a chance to meet with a genuine Thai family. I proceeded with him to Chiang Mai where he took a one day tour of hilltribe villages, and a one day cooking course before heading to Phuket. There he spent a week helping out in a tsunami flattened village.

This is all well and fine – good work indeed to be roundly applauded, but not really a holiday. It was an experience, and almost read to me like a resume builder, something to have achieved, and which could be recited to his friends and mentors back home, an elaborate answer to the inevitable, 'What did you do on your vacation?' question.

I am an ex-New Yorker, and I understand that there is a little of that need to be productive lingering beneath my own fragile surface too. I was unable to come to Thailand and just hang out on the beach and relax. I had to find something satisfying to fill my time, and so, I began to write, which fortunately is a pursuit that I enjoy [a disease of choice, as if picked from a menu] and can be transferred via laptop to the sea or mountains as I like.

I am unable to overindulge like Stupid Sammy Martelli and Party Paul Kinsley, which is why they make my list. They have entirely detached from the expectations of others. They have a rare ability to luxuriate in uncompromised hedonistic delight, while I still need to sometimes obsess over work and other times speckle my thoughts with random mental notes, hoping to achieve a literary quest for a comprehensible sentence with the commas properly placed.

Adam Westin might be in the clutches of what others want him to be, and that was why on the bus to Chiang Mai, when I told him of my informal survey, he broke the mold. That was when, after a moments thought, he said he might like to be Nick Hornby.

The second-hand bookstores in Chiang Mai have Hornby well represented. Adam offered me his definite and final, all time favorite list of Nick Hornby books:

1. High Fidelity
2. Fever Pitch
3. About A Boy

Therefore, he chose *High Fidelity* as a good place for me to start. And it was – I loved it and have enjoyed other Hornby books too. But, would I want to be him, well, not really.

* * *

Thirty years ago, at five a.m. my dog nudged me with her nose. An aging dog can have bladder problems, and you best rise to the occasion. I was living in Greenwich Village, in New York City at the time, and the Sunday morning sidewalks devoid of people hold only sparks of the energy leftover from the crowds of the night before. The quiet is misty and surreal as if it didn't belong there. Walking through the dream-like silence, on an otherwise vacant West Fourth Street, were my dog, myself, Mick Jagger and a couple of Rolling Stones who were window shopping. I ignored them, figuring that they preferred it that way, and were entitled to a few minutes of not being a celebrity.

That is why Mick doesn't make my top ten all-time list of people who I would want to be. Mick Jagger could not go out in public without being mobbed, and so, he had to content himself with window shopping at 5 a.m. Stupid Sammy and Party Paul can go out when they want. My dog with the bladder problem had more freedom than that. Being Mick Jagger would have an element to it of being in jail. I couldn't do it.

But – being Nick Hornby? Well, that was a thought. He is probably only recognized on the street by a handful of fine, literate people, and football hooligans who can finish a novel. A reasonable amount of recognition like that might be fun. Affirmation for his work must be wonderful; the big bucks would be great.

And the odd truth is that Nick and I, and a battalion of others who write for fun or profit, probably have oddly similar ways in which we spend the vast majority of our time. I assume that even when not doing the dance of the chicken beak at the computer, he walks about the world observing and formulating ideas in his head, be it a turn of phrase, a plot twist or a realization about the human condition. Right or wrong, insightful or not, it is an interesting perspective, and that opportunity to view life from the outside, as a novel, is a good part of what makes being a writer fun. Certainly, he spends time doing interviews and promotional work which also looks to be fun.

And so, maybe, in a small percent sort of way, my life is already a little bit like being Nick Hornby, in that we spend some of our time in a similar fashion. And if, in that way, we have similar lives, then what separates us out is what we do when not pecking away. And I wonder; how good can the papaya salad be in London? How fresh is the pineapple?

* * *

I have had many enjoyable moments bobbing around in The Gulf of Siam. The waves are soft and lapping, not powerful and threatening. I have had many wonderful conversations with friends, thirty yards out. I don't remember what we talked about, other than it was a particularly pleasant place to interact in that manner, to be in the Gulf of Siam bouncing with the waves and discussing plans and dreams.

And in my breaks from writing, that's where I go. I celebrate with down time at the beach. There is no pressure on me to perform a next book or anything for that matter. I can write for the sheer joy of doing it. And as I bounce in the warm waters, my eyes slightly salty and filled with the view of coconut palms along the shoreline, I wonder what it would be like to have Nick Hornby here with me now. I wonder what he might answer if asked the question; - Is there anyone, past or present, with whom you would trade lives?

And together, we could bob around and discuss this and other meaningless, hypothetical questions. I'll bet he could use a good laugh too, but then maybe that applies to everyone. I would present to him a list of my all time favorite, funny English language signs that I have seen in Thailand.

3.] "**Thai Food**" – a sign in front of a restaurant in Chiang Mai where there seem to be more Westerners than Thai people and local cuisine has become a novelty in the tourist zones.

2.] "**Toilet – For People**" – a sign along the road in a restaurant near Nakhon Sawan. It took me a while to figure this one out. It is a unisex toilet. Not for Men or Women, but for people.

1.] And finally, my all time favorite sign that I have ever seen anywhere in the whole wide world. This too was found in the tourist zone of Chiang Mai. It simply said – "**Bungee Jump – Nobody Die**."

After our swim in the gulf, we could sit in the lounge chairs on the beach and wait for the ladies to come by selling plates full of mussels for a dollar and bags of fresh mango and pineapple for twenty five cents. This is great, we would tell each other. This is great.

13

Adam Westin noticed her as soon as he walked on my property. She must have seemed exotic; the youthful, thin-frame clad in blue jeans and topped with a baseball cap, the glowing smile that stood out from the gaggle of construction ladies. She noticed him too. He took pictures of the construction, and wandered around my land. The exterior cement walls were mostly up. The tiled roof was on. The inside was beginning to be carved from the outside world. Adam noticed that she noticed him and smiled.

I cannot imagine how or what he thought of my world, but his presence brought New York to me. The phrases "rat race" and "escape" pounded vividly in my head, and it was odd for me to re-visit the hurried atmosphere of New York while standing amidst the timeless fields of rice, far from the concrete maze of queer customs.

I had been at a business meeting in New York City. My early inheritance [my father is still alive] is a limited partnership in a Tribeca building. It was being converted to condominiums – slowly. There were problems with the majority partner. My parents were there, as well as my brother and my Thai wife.

After the meeting, we gathered in small groups. The conversation was pleasant. My brother said that he had an hour to kill before his next appointment. I said I better make a run for it before the traffic clogged the tunnel. While I waved goodbye to everyone, my brother said – I have to go and rushed out the door.

If I left before him, would I have been considered more important? To whom? I didn't know all the rules of cool anymore; last to show up, first to leave, a silly musical chairs of hierarchy.

For me, expatriating was a gradual process begun years before. A slow process of detachment and drifting away unnoticed. There was no sudden adjustment to living in Thailand. The greater change was from large city Bangkok to small town Tak, to the off the map village of Mer Nam Noy. During my days as a businessman, I would joke that I wanted to disappear. Oddly, even here, that feeling has not left me.

The reasons for leaving are a continuous saga of wrongs, lies and deceit – refusal to take responsibility by the government that collects taxes, and then will not behave honorably toward its own citizenry. The USA, this great, most powerful country on earth, always talking as if on the moral high ground; I expected more from them. It was the government's direct actions toward me that was the biggest cause for upset.

Our local Pennsylvania Department of Transportation graded the highway that ran near my house. They forgot to clean the drains. When a sudden torrent of summer rain fell straight and powerful, water rushed down my mountain road, over the clogged drains, and turned our local dirt road into a river which veered and flowed through my garage, and into the gardens that my first wife had been laboring over for years. When it receded, it left ruination in my garage, and a coating of gravel on an acre of manicured gardens.

Before I could explain on the phone to Penn Dot management, they denied responsibility and hung up. The workers admitted that they had clogged the drains, but were afraid to come forward – afraid to lose their jobs – afraid to tell the truth to their employer, my government. The damage was several thousand dollars; their mistake, my dollars.

And the incidents piled on top of each other through the years, none large enough to necessitate an escape, but the weight grew, and the pace of events quickened. My first wife, working at getting a new life together after our divorce, was in her car when a landscaping truck, that had more than likely been working for the township a few blocks away, made a left turn from the right lane crushing her car, landing her in the hospital, and setting her back months with trauma, back pain, and a concussion from the side view mirror shattering the window, flying through the car and knocking her dizzy. The landscaping truck fled the scene. There were witnesses. They had the bumper of the truck, and knew the make and model. They had 4 out of 5 digits of the license plate number. They had the shape of the logo. The case went unsolved.

A few years later, that same police force gave me a parking ticket for being 20 inches from the curb, when the legal limit is 18 inches. The officer was arrogant, aggressive and a liar. He told me that he measured, and the distance was more than two feet. When I requested he re-measure, an act done with his shoes, it was less than two feet, but still two inches over the limit. My police force could find 2 inches, and charge me $15, but in the name of justice, with nothing in it for them but the satisfaction of upholding the law, they could not find a landscaping truck.

The police act as a fund raising crew for local and state government. As the federal government bankrupts itself in Iraq, it will get worse. They hide in the bushes with radar guns blazing. When the students are rushing back from holidays, the police are out in force. I always wonder: Is this what they expected to be doing when they enrolled to become cops?

While I was selling off assets, the government was constructing a new road which necessitated blasting. I owned a rental house that had previously served as headquarters for my business. I had a contract to sell it. The blasting shook the building so badly that the foundation caved in. Three neighbor's homes in a row had damage. The disturbances were so dramatic that it left children crying, afraid to stay in their homes. The culprit again was The Pennsylvania Department of Transportation. I pursued half heartedly. I knew that they were not going to take responsibility for their actions. They eventually assured me that the ground never shook.

There is nothing within reason that you can do. It was the same when the telephone company out and out cheated me, and when the rebate on my computer was not as advertised. I lost the pep and vigor to fight for my money, my principles and sense of fairness. The war was not winnable, and my struggle against larger forces was meek and laughable. If I could get customer service on the phone, they didn't care. The answer offered from friends - that's how it is these days.

These things didn't happen all at once – it was a ten year accumulation accelerating in pace with the blasting damage of $20,000 being the kick as the door was closing. The war in Iraq, the war on terror, the fraud and waste, corruption, local, state and federal governments are going to be increasingly strapped for cash, - we the people will pay for it with two income families, untended kids and cash; $150 for a speeding ticket that will reverberate through your insurance bill, and echo down the roads of stress and tension that nag and pull at relations of all sorts. Uptight! Me! You're damn straight!

Most everyone knows the feeling of having had enough, the fury of the trap, the punch-drunk boggle of wondering how can I go on, where do I go to surrender. Is this the country I was raised in? Ho Ho say can't you see? I no longer feel privileged or special. I feel stressed, stepped on and out of step.

What are those rules of cool that I cannot fully understand? Come late and leave early. Not having time as a measure of status. Having less time to enjoy a good time was better. Being too busy to talk, to relate, to relax was the measure of importance. This is a great party, but I have to go, to run, get things done - - - Who made these crazy rules? When did not having something become cool? TIME is the most precious and limited commodity in our lives. How can not having any be cool? Something is askew.

Wouldn't the opposite be more compelling; to be able to say that - I have time to come early, stay late, have another coffee, relax and philosophize – that's how together I have it. I can savor. In the rush to accomplish the most, to use their valuable time well, people are missing so much.

Surely some of this busy-ness compulsion is bound up in the bill paying and maintenance slice of existence. The more work, the more money, the less need for worry. This mindset turns to first one out the door gets the story, or the cheese, as life becomes a frantic rush. The speed of movement, the need for accomplishment makes the clock blanch to provide so few minutes in a day, a week. There is the forever of never getting ahead, or far enough ahead or so far ahead that you forget there are others, or why you were running in the first place – why – to get ahead – a head – get head. And the ones you want to impress with this performance, they missed it, you missed them - so you better do it over, bigger and faster, higher and harder – nip a corner, step on a toe, a face – just don't stop, don't look around. You are losing distance, you are wasting time.

Adam Westin saw that curl up in the hootch with me and forget about time smile. I think I saw a momentary glint of question in his eyes - what would happen if he never went back? But for him, it wasn't an option.

My brother does not know that I write. My mother became concerned that he would find out, someone would refer to my book. She wanted to tell him. I told her that she didn't have to say anything. If he asked about me, what was I doing – she could tell him I was writing. He hasn't asked about me in twenty-five years.

And when I was back in the USA to visit my parents, I answered their phone. It was a surprised brother. How are you? Fine, I told him. It had been so many years since he asked, fine indeed; he was now exhausted with the subject of me, and proceeded to talk for five minutes. His voiced cracked. I represent a threat. He complained about his school taxes at $45,000 a year, and the school district was so bad that he had to send his children to private school.

My acre of land in Thailand was $10,000, and there is plenty of room to share with family. I will have a 2,500 square foot home with air conditioning and flush toilets, parquet wood floors and a kitchen of granite for the same $45,000. Property taxes will be between $5 and $10 a year. My wife isn't sure.

Fantastic and self absorbed, powerful, bullying and frighteningly dysfunctional, it was not easy to relate to my family or country, more so as my return trips became shorter in duration. There was no suddenness to expatriation, an incident here and there, a loosening of shackles and a chipping away at chains, a change in perspective, and the hope that maybe I could do something about it.

The word "home" has always been elusive for me. Home base suits better. The long, gray Pennsylvania winters are replaced by gallons of direct Thai sunlight; so much of it that you forget that it is different elsewhere. Even the rainy season is mostly sunny. The Thai smiles reflect the warmth. They glow with possibility and radiate contagion. Yes, Adam Westin probably caught a flicker, but the tides of his world will whisk him back and swirl him around. He'll get ahead. I'll root for him to succeed while I indulge in another sweet-tart mango.

Ping and Duff

It was mid-afternoon and burning sunshine when they ventured out to explore. Duff wanted to walk to the strip of restaurants, which looked to be about a half mile down the beach, but Ping looked at him as though his sanity might be in question. Mid-afternoon heat and walking were not compatible concepts. She started a conversation with a motorcycle taxi driver, and then beckoned Duff to hop on.

"Go restaurant. He know good restaurant."

Duff shrugged, and they both climbed on. In Bangkok, motorcycle taxis cannot put three on a bike, but Cha'am is a friendly town without big city police. They blew through town and made a right turn, away from the beach. After another half mile, they stopped at what was little more than a roadside stand. They had an ordinary meal of fried rice with chicken, nothing special.

"Must be restaurant of sister," Duff told Ping after lunch.

"Maybe," she said, smiling in agreement.

When they finished the meal, Duff wanted to walk back to the main road.

"Wait here, get taxi," Ping told him. The road was quiet; not much traffic, and there was little chance of finding a motorcycle taxi this far from the tourist centers.

"We walk." He motioned with his head in the direction of the main road.

"We wait." For her, walking two blocks was a major accomplishment, let alone a half-mile.

"Come, we walk," Duff pressed on. "In America, sometimes people walk all day in the forest, just for fun." This did not impress her.

"Wait here for taxi, *dee gwah*," better, Ping insisted.

"Ping, what the Thai word for lazy?"

"Kee kiat," she told him, thinking it was another in a series of language lessons.

"OK, we walk," he answered.

"We wait!"

"Ping, what's the Thai word for lazy?" Duff repeated, trying to sound puzzled.

"OK," she nodded; picking up on his game. He was calling her lazy, but if he wanted to play games, Ping was ready.

Duff misread her pause, and thought it was over. She was lazy, and he had her dead to rights. Duff thought she was conceding defeat as she nodded knowingly, her eyes penetrating deep and disgruntled, grinding into his. But Duff was wrong. It was an ever so brief, Ping-style, pause to add drama before launching her response, "OK," she conceded. "Maybe I lazy for walking, BUT YOU ARE LAZY FOR WAITING," she pointed an index finger in his direction and concluded with assurance. She folded her arms, content with having taught him a lesson, satisfied to have turned the tables.

She was right, Duff realized. Impatient; he was being impatient. This is Thailand, and it was his western mind in a hurry that was out of step with the suffocating blanket of afternoon heat and awe inspiring humidity. And in a hurry to do what, to sit in lounge chairs? He was in a race to return to the lounge chairs, whereas Ping existed in a lounge chair.

She got him. He had no answer. They waited for ten minutes until a stray motorcycle taxi found them and ferried them back to the hotel.

Herman 2

Herman Witkowski viewed his employees as an extension of family, and there are certain times when a family must come together. Sarah Rosen was one of his first employees. She started as a bookkeeper, and became an integral part of the business. When her mother died, Herman Witkowski insisted that all twenty-two, some rough and scraggly, of his employees must attend the wake.

They arrived together at the funeral hall, looking more like the Jets from West Side Story, than grieving kin. A sign for the 'Rosen' funeral pointed up the stairs and with Herman in the lead, the nearly washed herd followed obediently behind. They entered and filled a not too large mourning room. There were two other family members already there, but Sarah had not yet arrived.

Herman sat. The group sat. They held their heads low in respect. There were no sounds, little movement – just an occasional knowing glance of sympathy that Herman would offer the two seated elderly ladies. He had known Sarah for many years, but he did not know the two family members who were present. Herman's intimidating horde sat quietly on their best behavior for twenty minutes until one of the ladies in mourning mustered the courage to ask Herman – "Excuse me, who are you people?"

In an instant, it all came clear. Rosen was Sarah's married name. Her mother wouldn't be Rosen. They were at the wrong wake. They were now too late to attend the wake for Sarah's mother, Mrs. Hershorn. It was over.

Bruce 4

Bruce was a runt in high school, at least in terms of the basketball team. He was fast as hell, he could shoot, rebound, pass and steal the ball from the opponents hands before they knew what happened. And for a little guy, he could really jump too. In his junior year, he was the star of the team.

One warm late fall afternoon, I found Bruce shooting hoops alone down at the elementary school on the outdoor courts; a place for pick-up games, not all county all-stars like Bruce.

"I quit." He told me.

I didn't get it. He was a celebrity in high school, a bona fide potential scholarship star. How could he quit?

"It just isn't fun anymore," he told me. The implications were obvious. He didn't need to say more, too much pressure. The practices were long and hard. And for what? Winning just didn't mean all that much to him, and his attitude drove the coach wild. "I just like to play ball," Bruce told me.

About this time you might be thinking that Bruce and I are quitters. And I wouldn't dispute that with you. It's just, what is so wrong with being a quitter? If something sucks, isn't it better to quit than stick it out? Is the opposite of quitting a masochistic, societally inflicted compulsion to endure, right or wrong, bad or good? That's how people end up in dead end jobs and boring careers; they don't quit. Who made these rules?

Nobody benefits from a bad marriage or a job they hate. Bruce figured that out early in life, miles ahead of the pack. During high school and early university years, we worked summer jobs and quit at the slightest injustice. We were champion quitters.

We had a job distributing flyers door to door. The boss was to meet us at the local diner. We showed up on time, at 9 a.m. He arrived at 10 a.m., and told us we would be paid from 10 o'clock as our starting time. I was pissed off, and felt cheated out of an hours pay. I told Bruce we should deliver to every other house. If we skipped an entire street, the boss would know, but every other house would lead him to think that some people had picked their flyers up already.

Bruce wanted to work it straight. He wanted to deliver to every house on the block. I was not into it. This guy was docking my pay because he came late. Maybe, just to be contrary or maybe because he had a burst of energy, Bruce ran to the other side of the street.

"Let's race," he yelled out the challenge, and we were off and running. Leaping bicycles strewn on patios, crossing manicured lawns, plunging over and through hedges, we whipped out that block in no time. Bruce finished first, and when I arrived moments later, he was laughing, hands on his knees, gasping for air. The boss drove by and yelled out the window for him to stop loafing, or he would dock his salary. Loafing? We had just set a record for flyer delivery to one block in less than five minutes. We didn't miss a house.

I could see the fury flash in Bruce's eyes.

"OK," Bruce yelled back and waved, straightening up as the boss drove off. Bruce reached for my pile of flyers, and I handed them to him with a knowing glance. He walked over to the sewer and tossed them in. "Let's go to the schoolyard and shoot some hoops," he said.

I don't think it was so much that we were quitters, but that we were always looking for something better to do.

A Perfect Spring Day

Billy Wilson's fastball had a sense of humor. It would jump and dance, burp and giggle, mocking the hitters, most of whom swung weakly having barely started the process when they heard the ultimate whack of the ball exploding into the catcher's mitt of Big Bull Barton. It was a major league fastball rocketing toward terrified high school boys who barely caught a glimpse of the streaking comet that whizzed past. They never had a chance.

Bull was an essential part of the equation. There were not many catchers of high school age who could corral the bolt of lightning that flashed toward home plate. Billy would look in for the sign, his piercing ocean blue eyes overflowing with energy, and there they would meet the flat-brown eyes of Bull. The Sahara Desert stretched for generations inside his pupils. There was no emotion. And yet, Bull's reflexes were amazingly fast, his big mitt moving easily to meet the ball. The hitters weren't much of a challenge for Billy. What he really wanted was to be able to throw the ball faster than Bull could react. He wanted to knock Bull's head off, and Bull knew it.

Coach McCracken, standing in the dugout, was as thick in the cranium as they come. At some point the fluids in his brain had coagulated leaving no direct path for thought to travel. New ideas had to bore through the old hardwood. They needed time to penetrate, to affirm, and once they did, they became fact; hard, indisputable data that solidified and joined the granite mass of tissue inside his head. Coach McCracken liked Bull Barton. He did not particularly care for Billy Wilson whose cranial fluids flowed free, undisciplined, windswept and wild. Billy was as out of control as his fastball, which seemingly had a mind of its own after it left his hand on its uncharted journey, each one different from the last.

There was no way to handle Billy Wilson and McCracken never tried. Maybe it never occurred to him that he could or should try. That was the job of the catcher, and for his money, there was no one more capable on the team, in the county, than Big Bull. He wouldn't trade

Big Bull for any three players from another school. Though Billy had a rare natural gift, McCracken would have gladly given him away, especially when Billy's father came to the game and yelled obscenities from the stands.

Everyone tried not to notice. They had heard that he was in the Korean War and didn't come back quite right in the head. There were rumors of medals and heroic acts; however a perennially stiff leg and a distant look that emanated from a frozen mountain lake was all that remained. Exceptions were made when he bellowed words that had their roots in another era, a tougher, colder, more confusing time. He launched nonsensical gibberish, shouted at odd intervals, often during quiet moments when there was little doing and everyone could hear. The opposing pitcher might be kicking dirt around or the second baseman wiping diamond dust from his eyes.

"A cold day in hell mother...!" Edward Wilson would yell from the stands. "A cold day, yes sir." And then, he would stand quietly while the heavy snows swelled to blizzard and the large white flakes swirled through his mind, transporting him down the slippery trails of memory.

North Korea. The winter of 1950 clawed his skin, cold as hell. No place to fight a war. Edward Wilson unzipped his trousers, sifted through a couple of layers of underwear and urinated on the movement of his M-1 rifle, and then on the more complex Browning automatic of his buddy Tony Galante, the Brooklyn Dodger fan. That was what he learned to do when the mechanism froze solid in the below zero temperatures. Warm urine would keep it in operating condition for a while. Dug deep into the snow, they shared the night watch, guarding the left flank. Tony would return the favor later on.

They talked in brief whispers through the night. The Bums. The Giants. The Polo Grounds and Ebbetts Field. Tony had been to live major league baseball games, so Edward mostly listened, yielding to his worldly expertise. Tony saw Jackie Robinson when he first came up, had seen him steal home. The Duke. Roy Campanella. Carl Furillo.

"I know Joey Boley," added Edward. "The shortstop. The old timer. He comes from my town in Pennsylvania."

Tony drained wistfully, lapsing into thoughts of home. He had a wife and kids now. Boy three years, girl one. Sure, baseball was important, but his interest was fading under the weight of a new family. The wife and kids, ball and chain he called them with unconcealed love and an obvious yearning. He took out the black and white Polaroid's now creased and worn that he kept in his helmet.

"There's a photo of me on the mantle, my wedding picture. That's probably all they'll ever have to remember their father."

Somehow the Bums and Giants didn't seem too important anymore. The season was over. Philadelphia won the pennant before losing the series four straight to the Yankees. It was too cold for anything to have meaning beyond numb.

Tony and Edward huddled together for warmth and watched the night. The Chinese preferred method was to attack at night. First, they would probe the lines for the weak spots, the South Korean units, and then later come in waves. Edward and Tony could hear sporadic fire from the center of the lines, but could see nothing through the blue black moonless night.

"I'm not gonna make it back," Tony said with the resolve of a death row convict, a statement of fact that he had accepted and learned to live with. Edward believed him. There were guys dying all over the place.

"A cold day in hell. Yes Sir."

Billy heard the familiar chant from the stands. Damn. His old man was there. Why today? Why now?

The newspapers were out in force. There was a rumor that the Orioles were sending a scout. Billy was being touted as a pro prospect. That was what the paper said last week after he pitched a near perfect game against the cross-town rivals, the Steelestown Eagles. It was not just his fastball, and not only that he had found control, but the curve ball his father had taught him to throw was snapping and breaking at phenomenal angles causing hitters to swing upward toward the sky at balls that were landing in the dirt.

The papers were forecasting this game as the real test. The game of the year against the heavy hitting Newcastle Ravens come down from

Perry County. They were big burly farm boys. Dumb as spit, tough as nails. Like his idiot catcher, thought Billy with disdain, and yet, he could not help but take them seriously. In practice, Bull Barton was the only one on the team who could touch him, pound him even, swinging easily and driving his fastball toward the bleachers. It was as if having caught so many of them, he knew their secret path and could track them effortlessly.

Billy was cool, but there was definitely an adrenaline factor as his first pitch flew way outside with Bull jumping out to meet it. Bull shook the ball at him, a warning, before throwing it back. Billy smiled. The second pitch sent the batter diving for his life. He found the strike zone once before the next two pitches sailed way outside. Ball four.

Here we go. Control problems. Bull shaking the ball as if that might propose an answer. Ball four. First and second.

"You're throwin' like a girl," Edward Wilson shouted from the stands shattering the concerned silence.

Ball Four, bases loaded and out comes Bull to the mound. Billy turned away, leaving his glove outstretched behind him for Bull to deposit the ball. It wasn't going to be that easy, and Billy knew it, but he was in no mood to have another inane conversation with Bull Head, Big Bull No Brains Barton.

"Whatsa matta?"

"I don't know. Just give me the ball."

"Whatsa matta?"

"Give me the ball."

"I'm not gonna give ya the ball until you tell me whatsa matta."

Billy glared at Bull.

"Give me the ball," he demanded more forcefully.

"Whatsa matta?" Bull queried again as if for the first time.

Bull had far more patience than Billy for this type of conversation. Steam was venting, pissing out of Billy's ears. He took off his cap, wiped his hand through his cropped blonde hair and noticed McCracken walking toward the mound. He stood his ground, and at six foot two, a long thin straw, he looked down at the stub of McCracken who approached calmly.

"Whatsa Matta?" McCracken asked directing the question at Billy.

Billy flared his eyes.

McCracken exchanged glances with Bull before proposing a possible answer. "You got a new chick in the stands, and you can't get the ball over the plate?"

Ahhh, Allison Purcell. Billy floated dreamlike at the thought; as blonde and blue as he, an all American beauty; Allison Purcell with her vanilla milkshake complexion. The crisp breeze of first autumnal air was woven through her sharp demeanor. Touch, don't touch.

The long patchwork skirts and baggy peasant shirts could not hide the truth of youthful perfection blossoming in her recently formed figure. Heaven sent long, fine, straight, nearly platinum blonde hair flowed to her waist and flirted with each caressing breeze causing drivers of all ages to slam on the brakes the instant she dropped her thumb along the side of the road. A shoe-in for the hitchhikers' hall of fame, if that was her chosen path. The roadways were transformed into her own private taxi network with lifts willing to drive out of their way to drop her at the door of her destination. Dream laden drivers hoped, but were too shy to ask, while she sat quietly, leaking a smile from Athena. She was out of their league.

Her road wound different, expanded. She was bookish, intellectual, revolutionary and rebellious. Not the cheerleader type, a flower in her hair hippie, and Billy's thoughts drifted to the possibility that he might get laid tonight.

"And your old man is here too," McCracken added, breaking the moment of silence and snapping Billy's attention back to the game. These conversations on the mound never went quickly.

"And not only that," Billy added with feigned emotion. "Bull won't give me the ball."

McCracken turned slowly to Bull.

"He won't tell me whatsa matter."

McCracken turned back to Billy and looked at him with his usual calm. The question sounded reasonable enough. "OK, whatsa matta?"

"Just tell Bull to give me the damn ball."

Both Bull and McCracken hardened their expressions. Damn was only a half step from God damn. They were not going to let the heathen blaspheme and get away with it.

"Hey. Whatcha language," Bull took a challenging step forward.

Billy stood his ground.

"Alright. Never mind." McCracken took the ball from Bull. He signaled to Mel Martin to start warming up and gave the ball back to Billy. He knew this was not going to be Billy's day.

"OK," he said, and gave Billy an obligatory pat on the butt. "Forget the chick and your old man, and keep your head in the game." He walked pensively back to the sideline as though something important had just taken place on the mound, a correction in delivery or the angle of trajectory, serious baseball stuff. When did it stop being a game? Billy wondered, drifting back through the years.

Billy Wilson is holding a rubber ball tight in his hand. It is a Spalding, and it has a lot of hop to it, he thinks. Today is his ninth birthday, and he is playing alone in front of the house, throwing the ball against the garage door, pretending he is somewhere else, imagining he is someone else, projecting himself into the future, bouncing off the recent past.

"Bo Belinsky on the mound," he speaks to himself. Billy Wilson is transformed, pitching for a professional baseball team while he mimics the announcer from the television. He takes on the shape and form of Bo Belinsky, and the voice and mind of the radio announcer. It is a complicated function to be both characters at the same moment in time while remaining Billy Wilson, the nine-year old boy, but he accomplishes this feat with minimal effort and natural ease.

Bo Belinsky is not a very good pitcher, but Billy likes the sound of his name. It bubbles and tickles as it trips off his tongue. There is no mound, there are no runners on base, but he looks around and checks anyway, as if there were others in the game, and he was not home alone waiting for his parents to return from work. "He checks the runners," Billy continues.

"Bo Belinsky looks in for the sign. Bo Belinsky goes into his stretch, here's the wind-up and the pitch." He pumps his arms and kicks his leg as he throws the ball with remarkable velocity for a young boy. He follows through bringing his leg around square with the garage. He can hear his father's voice yelling, "follow through" almost as if his dad were hovering in the sky, watching his every move.

The ball strikes the garage door handle and pops into the air. "Fly ball to right field, Roberto Clemente waits underneath," the announcer cries out, though once more it is Billy Wilson assuming the part. "He's out!" he shouts when he catches the ball.

After a while he becomes bored with the game and sits on the stoop waiting for his mother or father to return home from work. The evening breeze blows cool. He is anticipating the presents his parents will bring to celebrate his birthday.

Edward Wilson arrives home first. He has a brand new baseball glove for his son. Tonight, Edward will teach Billy the proper way to break-in a new glove, how to rub it down with linseed oil, position two hardballs, one in the webbing and one in the pocket before clamping it together with rubber bands and letting it sit for the night. The smell of cow leather and linseed oil will bring dreams of playing in the big leagues with Roberto Clemente, Jim Bunning and the Pittsburgh Pirates. Someday.

As his father gets out of the car Billy runs toward him, knowing there will be a present waiting, but not knowing it will be the brand new baseball glove. It is much larger and more professional looking than his old mitt that is falling apart, the stitching coming undone, the fingers and webbing short, designed for a young boy. His heart jumps and pounds when he sees the glove. It is so like a big league glove that, at first, he thinks it is not for him, but that his father has mistakenly bought a present for himself.

Edward says, "Go ahead, try it on," and then brings out a catcher's mitt that he has purchased for himself. Patricia Wilson arrives home minutes later and proceeds inside the house to make dinner. There are no special foods, meat and potatoes as always, but there is a store bought birthday cake that has Happy Birthday Billy written in green colored frosting. There will be no party.

Billy barely notices Mom's arrival as he puts on the mitt and pounds his hand into the pocket like he has seen the pros do on television. The mitt is large compared to his hand. Edward tosses him a brand new hard ball. It is shiny, clean and slippery. The seams are bright red and add texture. It is heavier than the Spalding, but Billy likes the heft. He snags the ball easily in his brand new glove as Edward walks across the lawn and drops into a catcher's squat. He holds his bull's eye shaped mitt up to be used as a target, round and pillowy, facing toward Billy.

"Lets see what ya' got," he calls out. There is enthusiasm in his voice and Billy is so excited that he forgets to go into a wind-up and just lets one fly.

"Go into your wind-up like I showed you," Edward tosses the ball back.

"Bo Belinsky on the mound," Billy slides back into his announcer tone as he begins to swing his arms.

Why Bo Belinsky thinks Edward shaking his head? Why not Koufax, Bunning, or Warren Spahn? Bo Belinsky? The screwball with a screwball. Came up to the big leagues some years ago and had promise. He pitched a no hitter in his first month, but then his career fizzled. He changed teams as many times as he changed movie star girlfriends, Ann Margaret, Mamie Van Doren, Tina Louise. The boy could pretend to be Koufax, but he chooses Bo Belinsky. The boy is weird, Edward thinks.

"OK, Bo, let's see what you got. Give me your fastball." Edward drops back onto his haunches and puts down one finger signaling for the pitch. Just like in the big leagues, Billy thinks. There in front of him is a real catcher with a professional catcher's mitt. He imagines himself in the stadium. There is a sell-out crowd cheering wildly.

"Willie Mays at the plate, the count is even," Billy windmills his arms to begin his wind-up with increased excitement now because Dad is into the game. It adds an air of validity. He uncorks a powerful fastball right down the middle creating an exhilarating popping sound as it whomps into the big catcher's mitt.

"Strike Three! He struck him out!" Billy calls out as Edward jumps up to celebrate, losing himself in the moment. But, for Edward, it is not the moment at hand. He has fallen backwards to 1953.

Edward's leg is aching, but it still has the power of youth and his arm is as strong as ever. The Korean War is winding down in stalemate. No longer fit for action, he has been reassigned to the States. They are playing a pick-up game as they sometimes do in the warm Virginia afternoon at Fort Eustis. There are a few pro ballplayers sitting out the war there, including the highly touted and talented young budding superstar, Willie Mays.

Edward had pitched in high school and shown promise. The retired shortstop from the Philadelphia Athletics, Joey Boley had told him so. He told Edward that if he keeps improving that he would call Connie Mack and get him a try-out. Edward thought he was joking or being kind. Everyone knew Joey Boley was a great guy.

Edward did not usually play in the pick-up games at Fort Eustis. He was gimpy and supposed to be disabled. He did not want to be sent back to the war. He'd had enough. He watched with interest though, especially the pros, Vernon Law, the young fireballer Johnny Antonelli and the phenom, Willie Mays. The glider Edward would call him as he flew around the field with exceptional grace.

Willie was an energetic kid with lots of power and raw talent as well as an easy going smile. Before the games he relished in leading the calisthenics, and then would go out and field fly balls, easily gliding to grab each one, working on a funny new style where he would catch the ball near his stomach, just a tad to the side and in one fluid motion come up throwing. Edward did note that if he had any flaw at all, he was too aggressive at the plate. Joey Boley had taught Edward to be patient.

It was a perfect spring day and Edward could not help but volunteer as the supply of available pitchers was running short. It would just be one inning and there was an itch that getting in the game just might satisfy. He got the first two hitters to ground out and then using slow looping curve balls and a change-up, he struck out Willie Mays to end the game.

Now, sixteen years later, and what seemed a lifetime after the fact, Edward wondered whether he might have had a chance in the pros, if things had been different. How did things get so screwed up? He thought about telling Billy about striking out Willie Mays for real, but the time wasn't right. The boy was too young to understand. The story could wait for an imagined perfect time that would never come. Right times are a rarity Edward mused as Billy jumped around as if he had actually struck out the real Willie Mays himself.

The un-muffled sound of a VW hippie van can be heard pulling into the neighbor's driveway. There is a peace sign painted in day glow neon colors on one side. It has a bumper sticker protesting the Viet Nam War. It says, "Make Love, Not War" as if there was a choice, and if you decided to get laid the commies would stop their aggression.

The neighbor's son gets out of the front seat, driver's side. He has long hair that curls down to his shoulders. His pants are ironically navy style bellbottoms, and he is wearing a tie-dye shirt. He looks like a bizarre transvestite clown, and Edward feels a compelling need to inform him of this.

"You look like a girl. Why don't you cut your hair?"

"Get lost, you old psycho," the boy yells back. Edward suddenly begins to feel childish, standing on his front lawn with a catcher's mitt, playing an imaginary game with a nine-year old boy, and trading barbs with a teenager who looks like he has just arrived from outer space.

"I've got a gun. You want to see my gun. I can blow your brains all over the lawn," Edward tosses down his mitt and beats a retreat inside the house to return with the proper equipment for the job. At least, he would scare the hell out of the boy next door, maybe even shoot off a round or two and teach the boy a lesson.

The baseball action is halted. Game called on account of the neighbor's son coming home. Billy drops his shoulders. The neighbor's son shrugs and dismisses Edward with a wave of his hand. The enthralling taste of victory that had glittered in Billy's mouth moments before, now smacks of a dry bitter aftertaste. The game is over.

Billy walks inside with his new baseball glove. He shows it to his mother. "That's nice," she tells him and pats his head, brushing his sandy blonde hair off his forehead. He is going to be handsome, just like her father. The girls will go crazy for him. I hope he can handle it, she thinks, knowing that she doesn't have a vague idea of how to teach him a proper way to do so.

After dinner, Edward will lead Billy to the fireplace mantle. He will slip back into thoughts of the war in Korea, and see his friend Tony Galante. He will remember being dug in together in a foxhole in the snow. Tony had lifted his head as a shot rang out, and then crumbled like a sack of flour on top of Edward providing cover. The Chinese scurried around above and then left.

Edward can recall vague frozen conversations about The Bums and Phillies, but Tony's voice echoed through the years, and he would repeat the words for his son though they had no meaning in the current context.

"You see this photo," he said to Billy. "Someday I'll be gone and that's all you'll have to remember your father."

"Concentrate!" McCracken yelled from the sideline.

Taking a deep breath, Billy wound up slowly, deliberately and took aim at Bull's head. He released a fastball more vengeful than any he had ever thrown. It had more ferocity than humor, carrying rage, bottomless fury, frustration and venom. It also had height and distance as Bull leaped but could only wave as it disappeared over his head.

Sprinting to the backstop, Bull retrieved the ball, but not before all the runners advanced, including the first run of the game which easily crossed home plate. Billy dropped his arms in disgust. Bull, having regained control of the ball was slowly walking out to the mound again. Not another discussion. Billy would have none of it.

Billy flared his eyes at Bull, and once more was met straight on by nothing. Billy needed to see something, to elicit life, passion, now, so he slapped Bull flush across the face with the back of his mitt. It was not much of a sucker punch, more an indulgent whim; a symbolic attempt at what Billy wanted in the first place, a shot at knocking Bull Barton's head off.

Bull grabbed Billy under the left armpit, and easily threw him to the ground, landing full force on top. The air whooshed from Billy's stomach and lungs...

The clouds were white and billowy, the sky was a wind-swept icy spearmint blue, the sun spitting soft, dusty-yellow rays. It was a glorious springtime day complete with the freedom that comes with knowing there are endless possibilities, a bigger world beyond Newcastle versus Harrisburg. Surely there must be something better to do on such a glorious day than to try and keep hold of Bull Barton's arms so that he didn't get pummeled to death.

The entire team rushed off the bench to stop the fight. The Newcastle runners circled the bases and were allowed to score as the agitated umpire ruled that time out had not been called. Allison Purcell did not know much about baseball, but something inside her flickered at Billy Wilson's spunk. She was pretty sure that Billy had never smoked marijuana, and figured this would probably be a good night to introduce him to it. He'd be a natural she thought and a wisp of a smile slid from the edges of her mouth.

Edward Wilson shook his head in disgust as he walked out of the bleachers. He would have been a fool to expect any different. The boy was out of control, mentally disturbed. He marched down the sideline, distracted, before almost colliding with Bull Barton's father who was standing as still and solid as a hundred year old oak. Edward looked up and offered not quite an apology, more an explanation.

"I taught the boy everything I know and he still knows nothin'."

Billy Wilson never again threw another fastball; however, that night in the back seat of Allison's car, he felt the warmth of sweet smoke filling his lungs. His capacity was extraordinary, and he dragged hard, sucking in all he could, trying to pull the most out of the ganja that it, that life, could offer. And that night, as his baseball career came to an end, there was a new beginning with much more potential, the challenge of inhaling as much weed, as much life as he possibly could.

Allison and Billy tumbled around in the back seat of the car. There was so much to do, to learn, to experience, to taste, sense and touch. This was more fun than baseball and spring was just starting to bloom golden and warm in Central Pennsylvania.

14

Youngest sister has been a person of concern for a long time. She is living with a Burmese man who works construction in the never-ending projects of Bangkok. He is paid less than a Thai worker. They inhabit a ramshackle, slum-style, corrugated tin shack, not a whisper away from the connecting hovels of the other workers.

The first time I met her, she had turned the front of the shack into a convenience store, selling necessities to the other, mostly Burmese, workers. I saw her as being in difficult straits, but enterprising. She went out of business because everyone bought on credit, and rarely paid their bills.

Father and mother are worried. They don't want their daughter living with a Burmese man. History is a tale of constant neighboring invasions. It is the conflicts between Greece and Turkey, Hutu and Tutsi, New York and New Jersey, all rolled into one. Father and mother are not concerned about history. They worry for her future. The Burmese boyfriend is an illegal alien, and is not free to travel in Thailand. He can be deported at any time. The police can harass him. Younger sister has been with him for several years. This is not a good match.

When younger sister returns to the village, she cries all weekend. Father is angry; he will not speak to her. Mother and second sister will pound her with logic and reason, but it collides with her world in Bangkok. It makes her head spin. She doesn't know what is right or wrong as her cloth of life is ripped apart, so she cries.

My wife also did not marry a Thai man, and this does not escape the eye of youngest sister. There are differences. I am free. I am here legally. I tell my wife that everyone must not treat her like that. They must accept her choices, or she will not come back to the village. If she cries all the time, and it is unpleasant, she won't come home. This is true in America. We are not in America.

My wife nods in agreement though she knows that what I said is ridiculous. She wonders how I can be smart in my head with numbers like a hand calculator, and not understand anything about a family.

* * *

We have a friend, Toom, who is a bargirl. She works in a freelance bar where girls hang out, looking for customers. They are not bound to or salaried by the bar. They come and go as they please. When Toom walks into the bar, her long hair flowing, her face angelic and aglow, all heads turn her way.

Some guys go there because they save money by not paying bar fines. Others go for the illusion that they are not going with a prostitute, but someone who works part-time, or is looking to supplement their income, or is a first timer and not really a working girl. Most everything that happens in Bangkok between foreign men and Thai ladies happens inside the head of the customer.

We met Toom through a friend. Bargirls are accepted for who they are deep inside, not necessarily discriminated against for their occupation, and not excluded from normal company. We had dinner together. Dressed to kill, with glitter in her hair, she was entrancing. I couldn't take my eyes off her. Her laughter rolled easily and resonated with joy and truth.

A few days later, we would cruise the Chao Paya River together on a day trip to Nonthaburi. Toom's English is self taught and near perfect. Though most Thai ladies are happy in Thailand, Toom harbors a dream of going to America.

We talked about life in America and about families in Thailand. My friend had briefed me that Toom's family relentlessly pressured her for money. I think America represented an escape for her, and she eventually found a rotund older fellow to bring her in on a fianc visa. Sometimes our dreams are nightmares. She called us from Cleveland. She hated it.

As we sat at the temple in Nonthaburi, she explained the commitment to her family in the most concise of terms. There is

Buddha, and then there is your mother and father. Without your mother and father, you do not exist. The implication is obedience.

Some fathers send their daughters out to work in the bars. My family has no such pressure. Father has four attractive daughters. He could be a wealthy man. None of his daughters has ever worked in a bar. This is not a family that you don't return to because of a well-intentioned spat initiated out of concern for your welfare. When I voice my opinion about younger sister not coming back to the village, my wife must think I am crazy. From her point of view, maybe I am.

The Monk On The Mountain

My husband, he good man, but sometime, he crazy too much. He no understand. I tell him ghost come to village, but he no believe. I call home and talk with Father. Father tell me every night one man die. Seven night. Seven men die. Young man, strong man too. He die. He go to bed, he fine. Morning, not get up.

Husband, no believe. He say people not die like that. He say maybe water bad, and have something like a bacteria. But father live in village. He know. He say, one week, moon not come out. Every night, village dog barking. Bark bark all night. My cousin die too. Only thirty five.

I talk him in night have noise from road, same like people drink too much. Father hear sound, like wagon wheel on road, and hear people singing and drag chain on ground, and like that. Husband, he think children make big mischief, make noise for scare everyone, but I know about village. Nobody do like that. Everybody afraid too much. Nobody leave house in dark. Husband look for the logic, but there is no the logic, there are ghosts, and no way the logic can explain about people die like that.

This is what my wife was telling me when she got off the phone with her father in the village. I let her tell me the story of what was happening in her village, and then felt a need for a reflective midnight moment alone. I stepped into the cool Pennsylvania night air, and my life was changed forever.

It was a coming of age moment, but not in the usual sense of the phrase. Not a transition from adolescence to manhood, more a snap of the fingers stumble affording a glimpse of the unimaginable, old age; a startlingly shadowy vista, a sullen faced vision that even the elderly rarely admit to seeing.

The mountain stream that cascades through my Pennsylvania woods is spring fed and diamond studded clean. Softly flowing waters sound an unexpected Gregorian chant of mystic bass notes as they tumble over and gurgle under dramatic, randomly dropped ice-age boulders.

I ponder whether or not the crystalline quality of the natural setting brings clarity as the issues of my life unravel.

As midnight approached, I wandered onto one of the larger boulders, bent down to pick up a stick, stumbled and went head under heels, somersaulting forward over the edge. Wracked and dazed, in amazingly sharp pain, I looked up at the night sky from the jagged rocks along the waters edge.

The result was severe nerve damage. The doctors could offer only an x-ray revealing no broken bones, and a statistic that claimed ninety percent with similar injuries recover in six weeks. It was three weeks before I could elevate my legs enough to enter a car or lie in a bed. I slept sitting up, and lived in constant fear that a minor movement would trigger a dramatic knifing stab. A sneeze or cough was unfathomable.

Two months later, I was well enough to travel. The razor sharp stabs had subsided to a million pinpricks that sparked uncomfortably, unprovoked. However, those first three weeks of non-movement had allowed time for existential angst to meld with physical pain, leaving behind pertinent questions as to whether, and for how long, a life of immobility and hurt would be worth living. But my mind wanders backwards. This is not the picture I wish to paint, merely the backdrop; the primer on the canvas.

My wife is from a small farming village in the North Central Plains of Thailand. Life there goes on nearly untouched by the outside world, evoking a time before "back to nature" was a hippie mantra. The week-long rampage of ghosts is now six months in the past and relegated to lore. A visitor would never know that such a thing ever happened and might find the village eternally peaceful and sublimely meditative, but for me, after one full day of hanging-out, restlessness floods my mood. After an early dinner, I decide to take a walk and soon realize that I am being tailed by my ten year old nephew and his friend. I stop.

"*Pie nai*?" Where are you going they ask?

"*Dern len*," I answer, literally translated as 'walk play' or just taking a stroll for the fun of it. "*Pie nai*?" I return their question which also can translate as – hey, whaddaya doin'.

"Watching you take a walk," is their innocent reply.

In a distant serene village, if someone goes out for a walk, watching them take that walk is something to do, especially if that person is a pale-skinned foreigner. For them, it is a whimsy to pursue.

The following day, my wife, sensitive to my restless nature, scheduled an outing to nearby Bhumibol Dam, the impressive structure that backs up the Ping River, and undoubtedly produces billions of watts of electricity. It is the largest Dam in Asia, and the eighth largest in the world, but the main attraction lies upstream in the lake created by the Ping River.

At the Dam, we boarded a long-tail motorized boat which troddled steadily north along placid waters, winding through mountain passes. Thirty minutes later, far enough upstream to almost officially qualify as having disappeared, a small helmet-shaped island, about the size of a football field, rose from the river. Atop the helmet was a terraced Buddhist Wat.

Comfortable in the solitude of my self-attained exile, I sat quietly for a long time. I wondered if I was absorbing the absolute tranquility of my surroundings, or if it was, more likely, consuming me. My worldly concerns were dissolving with each breath. It was not so much that life was explained, but a realization that all was distant, nothing mattered.

After a while, a septuagenarian, shaven white-haired, orange-robed monk came and sat with me. We spoke casually. He had been living alone in the Wat for ten years, and the peacefulness of his existence radiated in kind, tender waves from his content, confident demeanor. He noticed my discomfort, and asked about my back.

Eliminating the parts about cascading mountain streams and Gregorian bass notes, I told him that I fell on some rocks and suffered nerve damage. His career had been that of a doctor before becoming a full time monk. I explained to him that the pain, which had initially emanated from my lower back, had spread upward. He requested that I kneel on all fours, and using a handful of what appeared to resemble chopsticks and tremendous strength, he went to work pressing the point of the sticks into my back.

The jabbing pain brought tears to my eyes. When I was no longer sure that I could endure, he would pause and more splash than sprinkle holy water on me while invoking a prayer. The treatment was interesting, but not fun, and I was seriously questioning the wisdom of allowing the procedure, which went on for over an hour. When he stopped, the pain blasted powerful and pulsating.

I thanked him and made a donation to the Wat. He invited me to come back any time, stay and live there if I wanted. He offered to teach me Pali, the language of the monks.

The following day my wife and I ventured across the mountains to Mae Sot where I walked across the border into Burma and returned to renew my Thai visa. My back was sore and ached like crazy for three days. Though the lower part of my back still tinges with electrical flashes, the center of my back, the parts he worked on, never hurt again.

And now, a week later, on the bus trip back to Bangkok, I contemplate my family in the village, and how they came to be part of my life. I didn't discount their beliefs and the ghost stories, but wondered how much was a figment of impressionable imaginations. Strong men died, but did they perish from a collective fear that riddled their attempts at sleep? Are we not all, to some extent, figments of our imagination? Do we need to bend and warp our lives to make it more palatable? I look out the window of the bus as we cruise through the central plains. I wonder what alternative options I have to traipse through my days.

It is both a relief and an oppression to be back in Bangkok. Distance from the isolation of the village represents a return to the realities of my life. Email, where good news and bad can linger in a timeless cyber world, patiently awaits my arrival. An hour in the internet caf whisks me into another dimension that is the equivalent of an hour back home talking with family and friends.

Our neighborhood storefront is fresh, newly opened by a couple of savvy young Thai men, air-con icy, more internet than caf , and a comfortable oasis from the heat, humidity and crush of humanity that is Bangkok. I lose myself in the world of email buddies, until my bladder makes a demand. Proceeding through the shop to the back room that serves as a kitchen and foyer for the owners, I push against the door to the bathroom, which budges, but does not open. Not locked – obstructed maybe?

"The bathroom door is blocked," I tell the owner as I re-enter the shop.

He smiles knowingly. "It's OK. Just push your way in."

I wrinkle a brow of miscomprehension.

"My friend. He sleeping."

"On the toilet?" I ask, picturing the broom closet-sized room.

"Yes."

"Why does he sleep on the toilet?"

"I don't know," he answers with a shrug. It is strange, but it is a question he has never pondered. The answer he offers is delightfully obvious. "He like to sleep there."

I decide to postpone my bodily function, and return to my internet portal. There, sitting next to me, is an egg-shaped polished dome of a new neighbor. He has a white head, and a semi-circular shag carpet, Bozo the Clown hair-do, which protrudes outward. His clothing is disheveled through sloppy habit, not expense. A missed button exposes a blubbery hairless chest; food glongs on his tailored pants, but his kind face and pleasant smile transcend his rumpled appearance.

We make small talk sharing an East Coast sensibility, and draw easy familiarity in both being Americans in Thailand. There is an odd comfort gained by conversing with someone who knows that the K in KFC stands for Kentucky. I soon learn that his brilliance transcends the ordinary.

Spewing facts and figures easily, without intent to impress, he has me awed; medicine, physics, history, stock market, politics; this guy is smart and informed. A real computer brain if I have ever seen one. We even get down to the Miracle Mets of 1969.

"Kranepool, Seaver, Cleon Jones, Hot Rod Kanehl," I say their names drooping my shoulders in a relaxed posture evoked by a more innocent period of my life, a youthful nostalgia.

"Kanehl was earlier," he tells me. "He played three years in the mid sixties, before '69."

"Ohhh," I accept easily. He is machine-like in his ease of recalling information. Interpretations of stock charts and the voting records of politicians tripped off his tongue with certainty and familiarity.

Pleased to be once more communicating in English, I invite my new friend out to the sidewalk tables where the caf part of the operation is located. Next to us, there is a thriving noodle soup operation and a young lady with bright red lipstick barbecuing pork *satays* on a hibachi. A 7-11 is behind her. KFC is across the street. Thai people teem past, chasing their daily activities.

My new friend's name is Martin Sternberg, age 58, retired, financially comfortable, and he has been bouncing through South East Asia for several months looking for a new home. Japan was OK. He likes Bangkok; similar to New York City. We chat like old pals as personal details flow naturally, rippling through the current of conversation. What to do, where to go next, seem to be the subject on his mind, a dilemma that I easily relate to.

I tell him that I love Thailand, but haven't yet found my place; like a dog who circles and scratches, seeking his spot. Beaches, mountains, my wife loves Bangkok, we could live in the village; compromises; choices; too many to list.

Suddenly, Martin slumps, bringing his hands to his face and rolling his head as if the muscles in his neck have suddenly given out and he speaks wearily, "It's different for you. They're not after you."

Uh oh. Oh no. My mind re-visits his rumpled appearance. The miss-buttoned shirt and the food caked on his pants are not likely a one time occurrence. This is his look. His eyes are kind, but a devilish wild flare squeaks out from beneath the exhaustion.

"The CIA," he confides. "I have proof of government fraud that dates back twenty years. I have a website exposing them." He went on to tell me that they were after him, and he had to change hotels every third day. They confronted him in the lobby. There was a melee. He made a run for it.

I could only imagine an innocent Thai desk clerk having no idea what the crazy white guy was doing. I search for a polite way out of this. "So, how did you like Japan?"

"It was OK." He rolled his head in weariness once more. He was not going to let my simple ruse to change the subject get in his way. There was no outsmarting him. "Last night was terrible. At three a.m. they started pumping gas into my room through the air conditioner. My testicles were swollen to twice their normal size."

What could I say? Continuing the conversation would be an oppressive contact high as we soared through a disconnected array of sentences that sent me swirling along with him. I felt bad, but did not want to visit the fantastic crevices of his mind. A mental image of him clutching his balls in a hotel room at 3 a.m. was not where I wanted to spend my afternoon.

He said he trusted me, and asked for my advice. Do I offer a possible diagnosis? Do I tell him that they have pills for schizophrenic delusions? He would most likely reject it. There must have been a diagnosis in the past and pills not taken. Was this mind created delusional tempest a means to a more exciting life? To be tracked through Asia by the CIA would be a far more enthralling existence than being a rumpled retired guy nearing sixty with no family or friends and food glonged on his pants.

"So, how 'bout them Mets?" I asked. "Do you still keep up with baseball?"

My husband, he good man, but he crazy too much. He talk talk everybody like he politician or something like that. He always find crazy people he tell me. He say not know why. They come to him like magnet. I think he like that. I think he crazy too.

I talk him on phone. I tell him Momma not well. He good man. He tell me not worry for money. Go doctor. He say he pay everything. I tell him we go already. Doctor in village, not hospital, she have clinic. Momma complain, her stomach hurt. Doctor say of course stomach hurt – you old lady – you go home.

"She's like a witch doctor," I tell my wife when she calls. "Don't go to the clinic in the village. Take your mother to the hospital in town."

"We go which doctor? At clinic. In village."

"Not good doctor. Same like witch doctor."

"Not have which doctor. No have choice. Clinic have one doctor. What you talking like that?"

"Go into the city."

"Momma not go. She sick. She worry for money."

"Tell her not to worry. I pay. I need to go back to the hotel now," I tell my wife. "I have to get some sleep. I have a headache."

"Ohhhh, you go do the re-lacks. Not do thinking too much. Every day same. You think too much you get headache."

It's a simple approach, but how do you not think? How do I look around and not observe the quirks of other people's mind? This is the road I have chosen, not the path of most, which is to consume their mind in work so that they don't have to notice the suffering around them. Ghosts and monks with magical cures exist as surely as nine to five jobs present a method of avoiding awareness of these types of phenomenon and offer a fast paced, but dull, reliable path to oblivion.

Maybe my wife has the right idea. I can remove myself into a smaller, less complicated world without crazy people and schizophrenics. I should learn to relax, keep to myself, and not think so much. Westerners don't know much about relaxing. We have been taught that production is positive, no matter what we produce. It is our nature.

I ponder this as I wander toward the hotel. I pass an Italian Restaurant, and that seems a nice place to satisfy my hunger. I think how fortunate I am that I can indulge in excellent cuisine on occasion. I enter, take a seat and open an English language magazine that was left on a table nearby. I am determined to enjoy my solitude, not engage in conversation.

A young, foreign couple, maybe Japanese, is sitting across the room. A young American couple with a baby plunk themselves down next to me. The baby is quietly sleeping in a stroller. A man with a shaven head is sitting alone to my left. He is nibbling a pastry, just finishing up. I wonder what he is eating. He sips a cup of tea and looks up at me.

"Where you from?" I ask.

He do like that. He not know man, and he ask where you from. He talk talk everybody. All day. He talk people, he don't know who they are.

They could be axe killer or like that, and he talk them. I no understand why he do like that. Then he complain me; he get headache.

When husband in America on rock outside, I think ghost from village come push him. Maybe want kill him too because he say he no believe, but in America they not have power same like in village. He lucky not die too. He get up from rock, and he dizzy from pain. Cannot walk stair. Cannot sleep bed. I worry too much him when he hurt bad like that. I bring pillow, sleep on floor near him. He talk me, go sleep up stair in bed. He no understand that in the village we sleep on hard floor. He good man, but he lucky ghost only play with him. Not kill him too. I think ghost laughing him, like play a game.

The man with the shaven head talks a little, but he pays his bill and leaves. I go back to my magazine. The couple sitting next to me; look only at each other, occasionally glancing at the stroller. I could reach over and touch them, but they have no cognizance of my existence. I am invisible to them, not on their radar. I sit back and enjoy the vicarious nature of my fly on the wall presence. If I talk, I will not be heard and so I listen.

"Four hundred degrees is four hundred degrees," he informs her.

"But it's not the same," she counters.

"Four hundred degrees is four hundred degrees."

"But they have a pizza oven. We have a regular oven. It heats differently."

"Heat is heat."

"But a pizza oven is not the same as a regular oven."

"They can both cook at four hundred degrees."

"But they have a pizza oven."

"Four hundred degrees is four hundred degrees."

They don't seem bothered by the inanity and repetitiveness of their conversation. They are young and haven't realized how conversations like this wear you down. In ten years, they will sit at this same table and not speak, bored to silence through years of silly chatter. Or, more likely, they will have parted ways.

"A regular oven is not a pizza oven."

"Heat is heat."

I can't believe they can continue this way for so long. I don't want to ask them where they are from. It is not a place that I would ever want to visit.

"A pizza oven heats more evenly."

"Four hundred degrees is four hundred degrees."

I consider throwing my magazine at them and screaming, but they can't see or hear me, and the intrusion might upset an already fragile cosmic balance. There is a quiet learning that is available in invisibility; an act of witnessing without a need to partake. All I can do is wince and consider that this type of conversation violates any meaningful answer as to why we exist.

People ask me about not having the same native language as my wife. They ask me how we communicate our deepest feelings. I smile; it's not a problem I tell them. And it is not so much that we cannot communicate these ideas, or whether any other couple can, it's just that for us, we don't trouble over it. It's not a problem.

Be it quantum physics, the stock market or secret CIA experiments, the temperature inside an oven does not seem to matter any more or less. Life, for some, is at its best when they give in to whatever unusual quirks make them feel good, more important, interesting or unique, and maybe that's why the fellow at the internet café is sleeping on the toilet.

Bruce 5

College wasn't a great fit for either one of us, but I managed to muddle through. My roommate got on my nerves. I threw text books at him when he talked too much, but Bruce took it to the next step. He threatened to kill his roommate, which was how he ended up in the psychiatrist's office for the first time.

His first visit to the shrink was un-enlightening. The doctor spoke little, other than to prod Bruce to speak, and then would respond with "Do you think so?" This did not seem helpful and Bruce, after giving it a shot, stopped talking. What exactly was the point if the answer was that predictable?

At the end of the session, the shrink told Bruce he should come three times a week. "So, I will see you on Tuesday," the psychiatrist said noting an appointment time in his register.

"Do you think so?" Bruce mimicked.

He never went back, but there would be other shrinks after he dropped out of school and relegated his life to part time jobs well below his intellect. Gas stations, house painting, lawn care, Bruce always strove for outdoor work that would quickly prove to be unfulfilling. That became the story of his work history and life.

A chemical imbalance was identified, but knowledge was limited. His dad was a pharmacist, and various anti-depressants were prescribed, which Bruce hated. They left him stiff and robotic, unable to work and barely alive; he slept away large portions of the day. The inactivity was particularly difficult for an athlete who was born to run.

I had grown stronger through high school and became a much better athlete, though never reaching the caliber of Bruce. But, just as when I learned to run like Willie Mays from watching Bruce, I learned something else too. He was fast, but he always had an inner reserve that he could reach down and tap into, an extra burst of acceleration when needed. I learned how to use that extra something, not only for athletics, but I found ways to apply it to other aspects of my life as well. It's not something that you can teach or explain – it's there if you are aware and can reach inside and find it.

After finishing college, I started to travel. My assortment of odd jobs led to savings, which led to an exploration of Europe. Bruce decided to meet me in Crete. Maybe, if it were during the era of email, things would have turned out differently. I had no idea he was coming, and left for the Middle East and on to Asia.

While I circled the globe, Bruce proceeded to Matala, Crete, where I had been camping out the month before. He wandered into the mountains. There was no connection to the outside world, and in his head, the war between good and evil was waged, the fate of the world at stake. In his delusional state, he waved signals to the good ships at sea and spied on the bad ones. He raced back into the mountains and hid until hunger got the best of him.

Was there marijuana involved?

Had someone given him acid?

Did any of it actually happen?

Where was the reality amidst the blur of fact and fiction? Does anybody really know the truth beyond their perceived notions? There are countless tests of surprised classrooms and staged events. The responses afterwards, when asked to recount the events that they witnessed mere moments before, are as windblown and varied as a blustery autumn afternoon.

When I returned a year later, having circled the globe, he told me about his flight home. He stood on his seat the entire time in a karate stance. Back then, you might have been able to get away with that. Or maybe, he slept and dreamed it. I don't know, but the paranoia was there and strong. If someone were talking on a cell phone, a rare person then, they were FBI, tracking him.

The doctors experimented with anti-depressants. The chemistry was not advanced. They couldn't put him back in balance, and possibly made things worse. It became difficult to spend time with him. I saw Bruce less often. My life was moving in a different direction. The Star Spangled Banner was no longer funny.

Willie

"We'd play football against the white kids. And we thought nothing of it, neither the blacks nor the whites. It was the grownups who got upset ..."

Say Hey : The Autobiography of Willie Mays (1988)

Toward the end of his career, the reporters were saying that he was over the hill. He couldn't get the bat around. I thought he could still play. I think I remember a pinch hit home run. Baseball was fading as part of my life – professional sports had become less interesting.

I played alongside my brother for a while on the Rolling Stone softball team. I was the centerfielder. I hustled like crazy – made running grabs – pretended to be Willie Mays. There was purity in Willie's love of the game that was not easy to find in the rest of our lives.

I took to travel. There was something in movement that called out - tomorrow will be different. You never know what will happen around the next bend. It was an intoxicant that I have not recovered from to this day.

I lived in a cave on Crete for a month. It cost me a dollar a day. I calculated at current interest rates what it would cost me to live on Crete for a dollar a day for the rest of my life. The numbers have changed through time. The concept has remained the same.

My life, later on, as a businessman held challenge. Growth was exhilarating, having Herman Witkowski as a mentor was fun. The money was a measure of progress, never the sole purpose, but still, time became money. The trade off was odd, but worthwhile. I made money. I lived frugally.

I solved my dislike of confrontation by offering full refunds for returned merchandise, wholesale or retail. My favorite was a returned T-shirt at my shop in the mall. It was several years old, and not only well-worn, but ripped to shreds and full of holes. The customer told my employee that she only washed it once. "In battery acid," my worker inquired.

People like to get over. One guy took the turquoise stones out of an American Indian ring before returning it. He said the stones went down the drain. Employees stole. Wholesale and retail customers wrote bad checks and pulled scams, but my percent of loss was far below the industry average. I never had a lawsuit or a worker's compensation claim. There were many wonderful customers and employees.

Willie Mays would hit 660 homeruns in his career. He would win twelve gold gloves and two MVP awards. He would play in 24 All Star games. He would be the most exciting player ever to wear a baseball uniform. Bruce and I were twenty-two when he retired. We had never known a day in our lives when we weren't concerned with how Willie did. It was time to grow up, but neither of us was ready.

In 1979, Willie would be inducted into the hall of fame. In 1980, Bruce would decide that life was not going to come together. The neighborhood was no longer filled with kids to play with, and being a grown-up was not working out.

I Never Vote. It Only Encourages Them

1980 Reagan vs. Carter

Ronald Reagan lost to Gerry Ford in the '76 primary – I dismissed him as a loser, but he turned out to be a Nixon-style loser – one who gets beaten-up and re-appears stronger.

It was 1986 when I would see one of the most impressive sights of my life. My first wife, an American, and I were pursuing a business life as importers that made more sense than dollars. It guaranteed travel. After making purchases in Kathmandu, Nepal, we ventured by car through the foothills of the Himalayas, and out to the western part of Nepal, to a town called Pokhara.

Annapurna, the fifth highest peak in the world towered above. It was across a lake and what appeared to be a short plateau. It was enormous. You could reach out and touch it. The fact that multiplied the phantasm of this sight was that Annapurna was 90 miles away from where we stood, about the same distance from New York to Philadelphia.

We sat on a bluff across the lake. Sound was oddly muted; distance warped and hazy. All my senses were snared in a surreal vision, as if in a faded dream. I could see ladies washing clothes along the side of the lake. They were far away, but I could clearly hear the razor snap of fabric flicking against stone. There was a full second difference as I saw the act before hearing the sound.

There was a hotel on an island in the lake. We stopped for lunch, and were told that Jimmy Carter had stayed there. He had viewed Annapurna, as I was viewing it then. Though separated by a couple of years, a sneeze in the handkerchiefs of time, we were nearly there together, sharing the awe.

After his presidency, Jimmy would become a peace negotiator. He would build homes for the needy. The biggest problem during his term was that in a world of professional politicians, the good guy is not necessarily going to get much done.

Jimmy will be a Rutherford Hayes or a Millard Fillmore, a difficult name for schoolchildren to remember, and not easy to place in history. But he can live next to me in the woods anytime.

As a foreigner and business traveler during the Reagan years, especially during the second term, it was a time of embarrassment. Reagan was portrayed as a tough talking cowboy and ridiculed by travelers from a multitude of countries as a mental light-weight.

Reagan did get results by spending us into massive debt. The cold war was over. Walls were literally coming down. No, I did not like him. Yes, he did get some results. Was I tempted to vote? No. It would have been the same story. I would have been voting against someone, not for an inspiration. It would have been a negative act, not positive. And once more it would not have affected the vote in either case.

But 2004 was different friends were telling me. There was a tangible evil; a man who led us into an unprovoked war. We could no longer keep any illusion that we were the good guys in the world.

Bruce 6

Bruce filled the house with flowers. He was thirty years old, and his ventures in and out of the country had led nowhere. There was time spent camping-out in Florida. At best, he had become a drifter, at worst, he was a non-functional lump, pumped with sedatives and existing in his parent's basement, sleeping most of the day.

There was a dose of pleasure in music. Not much. Life held little enjoyment, and if the future was to be anything like the last ten years, well, it wasn't much of a decision.

With his father being a pharmacist, and his mom assisting during the day, Bruce had the house to himself and the availability of a ton of pharmacological products. A huge stockpile and vast assortment of pills cascaded through a kaleidoscope of color. Bruce ingested them all. He swallowed every pill in the house. He got in his car, and drove to the State Park. He sat by the lake and waited.

His mother and father returned from work to find the shock of a house full of flowers, and a bathroom strewn with empty pill bottles. There was a suicide note, but no body. Bruce was missing and alone. They called the police who searched, but could not find him.

At 11 p.m. Bruce walked in the door. He waved off any conversation, and said he was going to bed. Ten minutes later, they could hear him gagging. At 11:20 p.m., Bruce died in the ambulance on the way to the hospital.

I wasn't surprised when I got the call. Everyone expected it would happen one day.

I Never Vote. It Only Encourages Them

Mondale vs. Reagan 1984

My lasting image of the '84 campaign is the Reagan joke during the debate. The one about not letting his opponent's youth and inexperience be a factor in the election, thereby turning around the all too prophetic question about his aging. There are some who say that Alzheimer's disease was already beginning to take effect during his second term.

I can't remember any jokes from Robin Williams or Buddy Hackett or Eddie Murphy. Reagan was not funny to me, but I remember that quip. Mondale was fated to failure. Democratic Vice Presidents - Humphrey, Mondale and Gore – all run a history of being losers. It is Republican Vice Presidents and defeated heroes who get a bounce.

I was living on top of a mountain in upstate New York at the time of Reagan vs. Carter and working as an antique dealer. New York voted for Reagan by a margin of 165,459, a relatively close contest that once more my one vote would not have changed. The victory over Mondale was accomplished with equal ease and by a larger margin.

15

I was alone in Bangkok for a couple of days. I lay on my back in bed, shirt off, contemplating sit ups, an easier task than actually doing them. As I rose up a little, an enormous bulge appeared in my stomach. A gargantuan tumor? I had no idea other than this looked neither normal nor healthy. I rarely get sick, but any physical or health problems lead me to wonder if they might be the first step in a progression leading to the final act? Death's doorstep is my neighbor and friend. It scared me at first, but I have been there before.

I wrote a note with my name and a contact number, if I were not to make it through the night. I laughed. When I was young there was a story about my mother's cousin. The burglar alarm in her house was not working. She took all her valuables, furs, jewelry and cash and left them in the front vestibule with a note. "This is all we have. Please take it and leave us alone." I slept peacefully, but I did leave the note. Months later, I would learn that the bulge in my stomach was a hernia.

My leg hurts due to a hamstring injury from twenty years earlier. I take one pill daily to eliminate stomach acid, which has eaten away part of my esophagus. I am prone to migraine headaches, especially in the heat. My back is achy, my feet often hurt, and I have become overweight. I need reading glasses for small print.

The part in the story about falling on the rocks and suffering nerve damage was fact. I sat for three weeks unable to raise my legs. My feet became dangerously swollen. I did wonder how long I could endure, how close I had come to ending life as I knew it. I am not suicidal, but I am concerned with the quality of whatever time remains. I don't fear death. I fear immobility and aging.

My entire back had been stressed from that midnight fall on the rocks, and the tension had spread throughout. It was the tightening of nerve and muscle that the monk eliminated from my back. I would later learn that the technique he used was called "covering the pain." My nerves still spark an uneasy reminder. On bad days, I fear a recurrence. My back has not been in good shape for many years.

I have scars from a cancer scare operation where they removed a piece of my rib and a scar on my face from a skin cancer also removed. These are inconsequential.

My blood pressure is fine. My heart is strong. The issue for me is that these annoyances are not going to get better. They will continue to degenerate as I get older. And yet, if you ask, I would tell you that I am quite healthy, that I feel like a kid.

16

Father wants me to come with him. There is an old teak house that is being torn down, and the owner's are selling the lumber. Teak is a hardwood and prized for being resistant to the tropical climate. We climb aboard his motorcycle. My wife rides with her uncle.

The house is large. He does not measure the board feet. He knows it is a good deal. The next few days are spent doing whatever he can to raise the cash. I expect that he will come to me for a loan, but he does not.

Two years earlier, at my wedding, I had paid a bride price of $5,000. My wife told me that I could pay $2,500. She also told me that one of the neighbors had recently received $5,000. I told my wife, I too would pay $5,000. It is a gift to her parents for rearing a lovely daughter.

Our wedding had been a simple affair for family and friends, about 150 people. The ladies had gathered the day before and prepared food. Before the ceremony, I was told to wait in the house of second sister next door. I showered and changed into my electric-blue silk shirt with gold brocade. An older lady came for me at the exact, pre-determined, lucky time of 1:12 p.m. She led me to Father's house as all the ladies whooped cat calls. She loudly alerted the family that I was coming to call. She negotiated permission for me to enter, and then washed my feet. I gave her an envelope with 50 cents. At the top of the stairs, two of my soon to be nieces held a string barring the way. I gave them each an envelope, and they let me pass into the house where I was seated across from the family.

A village elder presented the money with great fanfare. It was a moment of pride. The family accepted, and I then was permitted to sit with them, next to my wife. The guests sat while the elder chanted. My wife and I sat with our wrists resting next to each other on an ornate pillow. He anointed our foreheads with a decorative paste like substance and tied string around each of our wrists. Father and mother did the same. The guests formed a line that snaked through the house and down the stairs into the yard. In turn, each guest walked up to us, greeted us and draped a string across both of our wrists.

* * *

Father and mother sold their gold and scraped their savings account to the bone to buy the wood from the teak house. There was frantic activity for a couple of days. This was an important transaction. It was for youngest daughter, the same daughter who father would not speak to a month before.

He wanted the teak so that he could build her a house in the village. No matter how angry he was, he wanted her to have the security of a home. If her Burmese boyfriend would not be able to provide for her, then her father would. This is what I did not know about my Thai family. Though upset and disappointed with her choices, they would do anything in their power to help secure their youngest daughter's future. In a Thai family, everyone helps out.

Father had paid nearly $3,000 for the wood. Second sister gave $500. Third sister, who had worked overseas for three years, chipped in $2,500, most of her savings. They were still short $2,000. My wife proposed that we provide the shortfall. $700 would be a gift and $1,300 would be considered a loan to be re-paid when the money was available

I was in the process of selling my home in America. I could no longer afford to keep it. My savings account had been drained by the limited partnership that was part of my inheritance. My house in America was an idyllic cottage in the woods. It was twenty minutes from a lovely college town. There was a rushing mountain stream that cascaded down waterfalls in my backyard just as I described in the story about the monk on the mountain.

There is no village where my family lives and returns to. It is a collection of countries and provinces, states and counties where my ancestors lived for a while before moving on. I have no homeland.

17

The old men sit in the lobby of the Nana Hotel in Bangkok's foreign district. There are multitudes of international restaurants within easy walking distance. There are girls.

Abe is 76 years old and retired. He lives in the Nana Hotel. He tells me that, years ago, he would take a girl to his room for the night, then just short time, now not at all. He likes to sit in the lobby and watch the parade. There is always something doing in the lobby of the Nana Hotel. Abe watches CNN and talks about politics. He likes to tell me what he thinks because he knows my brother is a political commentator. I listen because I like Abe.

I never had a grandfather. I have a long history of finding little old Jewish men and taking them on outings, often to the racetrack. They had interesting philosophies of life. They all had stories about making a fortune, and then losing it. I vowed if I ever made money, I would be sure to hold on to it.

Sam is 80. He no longer has family in America. He is kind and round, but mostly he is sad. He is alone, and the easy chatter with lobby acquaintances cannot fill his void. I am sure his original draw to Bangkok was the girls, but that is probably many years in his past. He doesn't care much about politics. When I talk with him in the lobby, melancholy overflows, and he cries. I think he is somewhat like Richard Brock from my story. I think that he feels both emptiness and full of love at the same time. The love has nowhere to go. It overflows in tears. Whenever I meet him walking in the street, he cries.

After not seeing Sam for a long time, I ask Abe of his whereabouts. Sam went back to America for a visit and never returned. Abe thinks he died. I wonder where people go when they die. Wherever we go, I hope it is friendlier and less competitive. I hope I'll see my dog again from my younger days. I hope I'll see my friends, and they won't be so tormented. They have suffered enough. I hope there is a place beyond the pain where only kindness exists.

People are hurt and frightened. They do bad things and suffer for them when it is obvious that good deeds make us feel better. Has the commercialism made it so that people want so much, so badly that they believe they can't be happy without whatever "thing" is the latest rage? How many useless plastic items do people need to buy to feel better? Most of the time I find that when I do indulge in a purchase, I am shortly thereafter disappointed with being its owner. Things rarely live up to my expectations. Simple things are often most satisfying.

Before I leave Bangkok, I see Abe walking down the street. He has a big smile and a quickened pace. He is undeniably joyful. I just took a great dump he tells me.

I Never Vote. It Only Encourages Them

1988 Dukakis vs. Bush

It was too bad about Gary Hart. He seemed like a fresh young Kennedy-esque type; a handsome, free-thinking kind of guy, though I cannot remember one policy initiative or clever thing he said. He was of my generation, nearly. I kind of liked him, though I can't say why. He had lost to Mondale in the '84 primaries after coming out of nowhere, and then being mocked through an imitation of a Wendy's commercial when Mondale inquired, "Where's the Beef?" This was in response to his campaign of "new ideas."

Where was the beef? I'm not sure, other than that he proved himself to be one of the most ridiculous political figures of my time. He jumped out to an early lead in the '88 primaries, well ahead of Dukakis. Rumors began of an affair.

Hart, formerly Hartpence, challenged the press to follow him around. He didn't care. He told the press - if anyone wants to put a tail on me, go ahead. They'd be very bored. He bluffed.

A couple of days after Donna Rice was spotted leaving his DC townhouse early in the morning, he cited that the press was only watching the front door, and since there was a backdoor, nobody could really be certain of her arrival time. Ha ha. He was quite the card.

The press is persistent. They represent their own crusade, of sorts, when it comes to pursuing and unraveling political entities. Shortly after this near miss, Hart and Rice were found on a private yacht named "Monkey Business" [could it get any funnier?] visiting Bimini. There was a photo of her sitting on his lap.

He committed political suicide in about as dumb a way as imaginable. It was enough to start me wondering. Would I have voted for him? – I doubt it, but lots of people did in the primaries. And the point I am making is; what did I know? How can I really know much of anything about a politician based on a campaign?

Did I like him because of his presumed Kennedy-esque appeal? Was that just a matter of appearance? Does a politician have to be handsome to be compared to a Kennedy? Maybe, since he went through all the effort, what he should have done was to change his name to the one that he really wanted; Kennedy. He could have been Gary Kennedypence. In November of 2003, Gary Hart said this:

"John Kennedy restored to our country's national discourse the idea of citizen's duty, the nobility of service and the virtue of participation in our nation's life."

John Kennedy was before my time. I was too young. And yet, he has cast a huge spectral shadow on American politics. I remember the family playing touch football on the White House lawn. I was twelve. I could relate to that.

George Bush Sr. issued a vision of 1000 points of light, volunteers helping all across the country. But I didn't get a warm, emotional response from this. I felt like he was urging us to do the work of the government because he and Reagan had bankrupted the country. From him, the concept of volunteerism came across as disingenuous after the Reagan administration presided over the S&L scandal, the biggest bank heist in history.

Was it all a matter of delivery? Was it any less sincere than the Kennedy proposal? The lasting images from the '88 campaign were from the vice presidential debate. Lloyd Bentsen, who appeared more presidential than all of the candidates, caught Dan Quayle comparing himself to JFK, a Democrat of all people, of all unlikely comparisons.

What was he thinking? Or maybe, more accurately, what had he been told? I think politicians are so insulated from the real world that they have no idea of what is going on. Just as the guys in the poker game that I played in Washington had no concept of the world outside of the beltway, it must be more so for the higher-ups. Somebody must have told him that he was handsome, like John Kennedy; but Kennedy had charisma and Quayle had less personality than a potato.

The campaign of 1988 was an affair of negative charisma, with Bentsen the only star on the night when he told Quayle that he knew John Kennedy and Senator, you are no John Kennedy. That was great.

It was on the news forever. It might have been enough to influence the campaign, but Dukakis seemed hell bent on not winning. I really believe he did not want to win. I would feel the same way about Gore in 2000. It was as if a quelling survival instinct, deep in their subconscious, was propelling them to lose. It is all too easy to understand why someone would not want the job. My lasting image is Dukakis riding around in a tank, with a hat that screamed goofy, while setting Willie Horton free on a weekend pass. Ah, the power of the press.

During Quayle's reign as Vice President, I happened to be in Indonesia buying jewelry for my business at the same time as his visit there. It is impolite to be late in Indonesia. Dan Quayle, on an Asian swing, was having too much fun scuba diving off the coast of Australia to stop. He came late, thereby insulting President Suharto, who was awaiting his arrival. Surely, Quayle had no idea.

It's amazing to me how uninformed politicians can be and how embarrassing it was to be an American citizen in Indonesia that day. He went scuba diving, we took the flack. However, the field is wide open. Anyone can run for office. That's one of the great things about America. Right?

18

The trim construction worker with the terrific smile and baseball cap is not the teenager I had thought. She is sitting with her husband when I arrive at my house that is nearing completion. My pattern has become to visit the project after the workers have gone. The nonsensical banter and forever requests for whiskey wear thin.

The Wonder, I nickname her due to her teenage appearance, is actually twenty-eight years old, and has two children. Up close, I can see that she is more mature than I had thought, but not much. The cap, the blue jeans, the trim legs and petite figure give her the appearance of youth. Her eyes are kick-ass on fire, hot and sexy.

When she works on the large cement houses being built by foreigners with Thai wives who maintain ownership of these homes, does she consider if it could have been, still could be her? Foreign husbands seem to be popping up everywhere, but so difficult to find. Sometimes it seems everyone wants one.

At a Bank in Bangkok, as we waited on line, a woman asked my wife where she found her husband. She wants a *farang* too. Whether I go into Seven-Eleven or the supermarket, the conversation with the cashier is the same as she asks; How come you can speak Thai? Where do you live? Do you live alone? There is no age barrier.

Thai ladies have a knack for making you feel special. If you are old, they like old men, more mature, fat is lovely, young is handsome, so is old. Everyone is handsome. As a foreigner, you pretty much can't lose – though there are serious losers here. They too prosper. Money talks; nobody walks.

The game for foreigners is played out in the bars. I think part of the allure is that not every girl will go with just any customer, and this creates a challenge for the customer and an air of courtship. Bargirls are free and can be picky.

There is undiscriminating prostitution, but this is in massage parlors or fish bowls as they are called. The lady sits in a glassed-in room with a number on her shirt. The customer chooses from the other side.

To me, these places are horrible. I don't feel the same way about a bar, where there is interaction, and personality comes into play. The girls have choice.

Many foreigners come for vacation and leave feeling sorry for the girls. They go home and send them money. It represents a veritable adopt a bargirl program with letters of love from your own personal bargirl. Some will text message daily. It is Save the Children with extra-curricular activities, often extramarital, but the monthly check is all that matters.

Most foreign men have their first experience with Thai people in a bar. The girls know charming snippets of English, and how to relate to a clumsy visitor who does not understand language or custom. Some choose wives who will return to their foreign culture. They both compromise, glossing over the differences in language and ways of thought.

Duff had met Ping in a bar, though the setting was not typical for either one. They fell into something that was more real, at least for a while. And sometimes, reality can be quite a challenge.

Mae Hon Son

Ping and Duff arrived in the afternoon. The one-hour flight from Bangkok to Chiang Mai was smooth, but a long time for Ping to sit in one place. There had been a forty minute layover in the airport before the thirty-minute flight around the mountains and into Mae Hon Son.

They checked into the Holiday Inn, which used to be Rook's hotel. The rooms were comfortable, but worn. Duff wanted a peaceful vacation after the hectic pace of Bangkok, but this was not an option with Ping as a companion. She immediately settled in at a bamboo bar down the street from the hotel and became instant friends with the proprietor, a young lady named Bpah. While Duff nursed a wine cooler, the two ladies worked out the evening's plan.

It was not until returning to the states and reading "Chasing the Dragon," by Christopher R. Cox, that Duff learned something of the area. Local legend holds that an 1831 elephant hunt, begun in Chiang Mai, ended in the jungle near Burma. Unwilling to drive the elephants back, they built a kraal which grew into a town.

Cox went on to say, "Mae Hon Son became Thailand's tropical equivalent of Siberia, a favored internal exile for provocateurs, criminals and scandal tainted government officials. Their legacy lingered still, an unsavory current beneath the town's paradissiacal facade."

He described the surrounding mountains that stretch into Burma and the Shan State, calling them, "... a petri dish for disease, yaws, polio, hepatitis, cholera, yellow fever, blackwater fever, dengue fever, leprosy, scabies, amoebic dysentery, Japanese encephalitis, meningitis and typhoid," all being common to the region.

"I like too much Mae Hon Son," said Ping, brimming with enthusiasm as they walked up the hill into town after finishing their drinks at Bpah's bar. "We go eat Mae Hon Son food," Ping suggested.

The late afternoon heat pounded and bounced off the concrete sidewalks as they plodded along in search of a place to eat, passing one restaurant after the next.

"How about here?" Duff asked. Ping strongly shook her head, no.

"This one," he said, stopping in front of a large, nicely appointed eatery.

"Want Mae Hon Son food!" Ping stomped her foot.

"Ping, this Mae Hon Son, everything Mae Hon Son food."

"NOT SAME, NOT SAME!" She threw her arms about wildly, too frustrated with the search to take the time to explain.

They trekked onward finally arriving at a curbside stand that looked to be the extended kitchen of the ramshackle shack next to it. Two stools were positioned in front of a makeshift table, which consisted of a board stretched across a pile of crates. A small, round lady with a baby at her side was wok-cooking vegetables and brewing a pot of soup. It looked a bit gamey for Duff.

"Order for you only," he told Ping.

Moments later the food arrived. "What?" He asked Ping.

"Fried pa pa ya," she answered pointing at the vegetable and motioning to him to take a taste while she sipped at the soup.

He picked at the papaya and then decided to attempt a thimble-full of the soup.

"Phet nid noy." A little spicy Ping warned.

"Ahhhyyyy! Hooooo!" Duff exclaimed suddenly ablaze. He could feel the blood rushing to his face. Fearful of the likely bacteria-laden water in the glass in front of him, he stuffed a large piece of papaya in his mouth and held it there hoping to smother the explosion of flames that were blazing through him. His eyes welled tears, and his nose ran as sweat rained like a sprinkler system. His body summoned moisture from every pore and possible reservoir. Ping watched amused.

"Phet mahk." Very spicy, Duff finally choked out the words. Ping smiled wide as the valley, enjoying this immensely. For some reason, this seems to transcends cultures, Duff thought. My getting hurt, hitting my head on the way out of a car, minor burns and abrasions, seem to be a delightful source of humor for the opposite sex.

"For me, not hot," she answered trying to sound apologetic, but unable to hold back the laughter. He continued to pick at the papaya while Ping finished the soup and then asked the lady how much they owed.

"Sib baht," ten baht, about twenty five cents, the cook told her.

"SIB BAHT! SIB BAHT!!" Ping made sure everyone heard the exciting news. She gestured wildly as they walked away after paying the bill.

"Can eat Mae Hon Son, *sib baht*," she told Duff again. "Wait until we go Bangkok. I tell everyone. Can eat Mae Hon Son *sib baht*! They don't believe, shure."

The two companions never ate that cheap again. They always settled on larger, cleaner looking establishments where Duff could eat too. They chose well. After three days in Mae Hon Son, both left in good health.

They walked about, exploring the small town after their dining experience. The mountains framed the town, but did not give a fishbowl appearance to the valley. It seemed distant, protected, forgotten.

"Tomorrow we rent motorbike. Go mountains," Ping suggested.

Duff could envision the headlines in the Bangkok Post when they eventually recovered the bodies. It would read, "STUPID FOREIGNER KILLED IN MOTORBIKE ACCIDENT." It would go on to describe the scene. "Forty kilo lady driver with Seventy kilo American man riding on back..." He said nothing, but Ping read the silence.

"Can drive, can!" she insisted. "Don't believe!" She challenged his continued quiet. "Can drive shure," she continued calmer now, trying to be reassuring.

"HUUUGGH!" Duff grunted, imitating her noise from the night before. He figured the rough translation was, NO WAY IN HELL!

"CAN SHURE!" Ping insisted with renewed stress.

"Hoo a jai wai." Heart attack, he responded gripping his chest. Duff found the word in his translation book and was trying it out for the first time.

"How you know that word?" she snapped in surprise. Duff shrugged not feeling like talking about his habit of studying Thai language in the bathroom.

"Osmosis shure," she concluded puffing out her lower lip and nodding.

"How you know that word!?" He snapped right back at her.

Both smiled and looked deeper, penetrating and curious.

That night they went with Bpah to the Baiyoke Chalet to listen to Mae Hon Son music. It turned out to be an eclectic assortment of Santana, Thai up-country pop and Loso, the current most popular Thai rock group. The simple chord progressions and catchy melodies made the Loso songs easy to recognize and fun to listen to. Ping's obvious favorites were the Thai-Issan-style rock, and what she called country music of Kallawan and Karabou.

"Nah Kallawan! Nah Kallawan song!" she would gush with pride as she pointed each one out. "Issan person, Nah, he my friend. I like too much Nah Kallawan."

They were back in the room by midnight, much too early for sleep time. For Ping, it was still work time. Duff was not tired either, starting to function on bargirl time as well. They went outside to the balcony adjoining the room. They sat with feet propped up and stared through the clear dark endless sky, entranced by the stars.

"You know, I crazy sometimes," Ping finally spoke. "I go crazy hospital many time." She interpreted his silence as disbelief. "You can ask girls in Nook's bar, they tell you shure, they know."

Duff put an arm around her for comfort, wondering why the crazies always found him, or was it the other way around? Maybe the problem was that everyone was crazy. In this world, where man could walk the face of the moon, but not inner city streets at night, maybe there was no such thing as sanity.

"Not crazy," he told her. "Just not have good job."

"You know, I not same. Not like other girls in Nook's bar."

"I know."

"Not same shure," Ping stressed.

"I know, sure." And he did know it was true. She was not a bargirl. She was not capable of the condescending, wait-on-your-man, servile-type behavior. "You know, I'm different too," Duff told her. "Not same like other customers."

Duff remembered Eddy telling him that he went wild when he first came to Thailand, a different girl every night, maybe two hundred different girls the first year. It sounded like fun, but in reality, for Duff, it would not be. The definition of fun varies.

"I know," she said softly, but with certainty.

There were a few minutes of silence.

"I think," she stuttered, searching for thoughts and words, "maybe... you... me... a little bit same."

And that night, they watched the stars in the clear sky until sleep time. They sat quietly, calm and content, at peace and comfortable in their surroundings, and in themselves. They were at home with each other, with the world. And that night, they didn't just have sex, for the first time, Duff and Ping truly made love.

The morning broke slowly as the two lingered, softly hugging and dozing in bed. It proceeded at a not unusual, typically Thai, possum-like pace. They had plans to tour the countryside with Bpah, and Duff knew that if they did not get going soon, the day would be gone. It had happened often enough. The days slip through your fingers; Thailand, the land of smiles; Thailand, the land of time pissed away. Americans would never accept or tolerate it. They would find ways to measure and regulate it. They would invent a time pissed away index and chart the value in conjunction with increased or decreased productivity. Duff lay in bed wondering if a middle ground were possible; a combination of cultures, knowing it was not.

Bpah, in addition to running her bar, was a tour guide, and late in the morning came to search them out in the hotel. She had arranged for a long boat to transport them downstream to a Paduang village, a relaxed thirty-minute trip.

The village was home to about fifteen longneck Karen hilltribe families, or as they are known, Paduang. Their fame comes from the spiraling brass rings worn around the necks of the ladies. Grass huts lined either side of the exceedingly clean dirt road that led up an incline to a schoolhouse at the top of the hill. The tribespeople welcomed the few tourists they received. They had handcrafted dolls and woven fabrics for sale. A set of neck rings was available to hold and feel the heaviness of weight.

According to Cox, the century's old custom was begun by Paduang men, hoping the disfigurement would discourage lowland Burmese from carrying off their women. At the early age of five, brass coils are permanently placed around the neck and rings are added annually. The rings are heavy and x-rays have revealed that longneck is not a proper description. The downward pressure from the weight of the rings displaces the collarbone and ribs. Neck muscles atrophy and the rings become indispensable. Removal is a death sentence by suffocation. As it turns out, it is also a convenient penalty for adultery.

Duff and Ping talked with the ladies, took photos, watched them spin thread and hung out in the village. The candy they brought for the children was shared with the adults as well. Ping wandered the village with Bpah. Duff sat and watched, absorbing and appreciating the exotic nature of the setting. Ping was dressed in a tan blazer borrowed from Bpah and capped by a round, rice-paddy style straw hat that he bought for two dollars to protect her from the sun. In her trim, tight blue jeans, Ping looked exquisite. Maybe it was because they were out of Bangkok where there were so many strikingly beautiful women, or because she was particularly happy, or maybe something inside him crashed and imploded, but Ping was spectacular and Duff's eyes followed her through the village. She had her own unique style, grace and personality imprinted in every gesture, every step.

When they returned to the boat dock in Mae Hon Son, a driver was waiting to take them on a scenic ride through winding passes high into the surrounding mountains. After an hour's drive, they arrived at a Hmong hilltribe village perched near the top of a mountain with sweeping panoramic views. As much as Duff enjoyed the drive, he was delightfully content to quietly sit next to Ping, holding her hand. Having her next to him was a sexually stimulating experience. He could not remember the last time so little provocation brought such a powerful response. Duff felt young, vital.

They wandered around the Hmong village, and Ping stood out, being taller than the tribe people in her two inch heels, and as trim as she was, she looked un-characteristically fashion-model elegant. The children ran to her as she distributed the remainder of the candies, which she carefully meted out while smiling and laughing. When it was gone, she looked up the hill and smiled at Duff. Walking towards him, watching him watch her, her smile grew larger. She threw both her hands to one side, then snapped her fingers and threw them to the other side, marching to the music in her head.

When they arrived back at the hotel, Ping initiated afternoon delight. They napped, showered and returned to Bpah Bar, as Ping had come to call it. They relaxed over wine coolers, and talked with Bpah about life in Mae Hon Son.

"Nice house with furniture, just walk in with suitcase, seventy-five dollars one month," Bpah told them. Then an idea came to her. She spoke to Ping in Thai and then said to Duff, "We go now."

The three of them climbed onto her motorcycle and off they went. There was an entire guesthouse for rent. The owner was tired of running it; ten rooms, one hundred fifty dollars a month for the whole place. There were large teak wood porches and decks that overlooked the lake and provided a dining area for the guests. It was only a five minute walk from the center of town and ideal in many ways, except the rooms and bathrooms were Thai style and not suitable for higher paying foreigners. The potential was there and the temptation too.

Ping wandered with Duff back into town, and they stopped at the Fern Restaurant for dinner. It was one of the few nicer eateries in town and set-up to cater to Westerners. Duff was trying to imagine living in Mae Hon Son. What would he do here? The guesthouse could be fun but it was not perfect. After dinner, he was longing for something sweet. The thought of a Ben and Jerry's ice cream popped into his head. Would I be able to duplicate the taste in Thailand? He daydreamed as he waited for Ping to finish her meal.

"I always want open ice cream shop in Bangkok," Ping said and Duff looked up surprised. "Same like ice cream store in Kolat, my home." She paused, knowing she was talking to a businessman. *"Bangkok mais mee."* No have.

Duff looked at her, but did not say anything. There was some sort of E.S.P. working. He had noticed little things with Ping. He would think something, and she would say it, but they were more normal, everyday things. Thirsty? Hungry? Tired? He was not a regular ice cream eater, and neither was she. What unseen form of communication was created so that their thought patterns could cross in that manner?

Duff had once met a crazy Dutchman who told this story:

"When I was home in Amsterdam, I had long hair and a full beard. One day I shaved everything, shaved my head too. I went into my neighborhood bar. I go there everyday. I walked in and sat down next to my best friend. Nobody knew who I was."

"Then, I go back to Thailand, and go to my favorite bar," he continued. "There everybody knows who I am." He paused for emphasis and looked Duff in the eye, and then finished with a pointed flourish. "Thai people, they look you in the eye and see inside you." There is an old Thai saying – *Mawng dtah, lu jai* - look in the eye and know the heart.

Understanding the process of intuition was not easy for Duff. It was like trying to reach into a cloud and pull down a solid. He could see the cloud, but could not pull any of it away. He was finding deficiencies in the language and wondered as to the correlation. Was the intuition a result of a shortage of words? I like you, *chorbp mahk*; I am wild about you, *chorbp mahk*; I am so crazy about you that my head is spinning and I am about to explode, *chorbp mahk mahk*. Duff would later learn how rich in words Thai language could be, having many words that English cannot easily define. He would also later learn that most Thai people are gifted with a unique sixth sense, though their modesty keeps this ability unbeknownst to most foreigners.

Duff did not mention his ice cream cone thoughts to Ping; he just looked at her amazed, confused.

"Maybe I don't go back work Nook's bar," she said.

"Mais chorbp?" Don't like? Duff asked.

Ping made a face full of contempt and disgust, then spat the words more than spoke them, "Nook's husband, he want to use me too much."

Duff knew the guy. Jimmy, he never said much. He was a big burly Englishman who looked full of himself. Thoughts darted through Duff's head in fragments... petite Ping... sweaty Jimmy... shithead... asshole... don't get jealous... that bastard... she is a bargirl... tell her not to go back... that is her job... do I want the responsibility of paying for her life? Anybody's life? He want to use me too much... little Ping... hairy, fat, arrogant Jimmy...

Duff could hear the words of his experienced friend, Eddy, "They tell you they quit so that you send them money, and then they go back to work. Don't ever..." That asshole Jimmy... Ping... He want to use me too much, use me too much... use me.

The food came and they ate quietly, while Duff's mind continued to race. He would not allow himself to get upset, to be possessive of person or thing ever again. He would not be imprisoned. This is life, and it is not always pretty. His newly self-created job was to have a good time, and share it with the people around him. He was surprised how quickly his mind settled down. It was dusk, and the air was still, heavy and warm. That ice cream would have been nice.

The crossing of thoughts about the ice cream store could have been coincidence, but it was not. He felt so close to Ping. His feelings for her had developed through some unseen process. Sitting with her at Fern Restaurant, he felt as though he had known her for years, maybe all his life. And now, he was concerned, unsettled, as she told him about Jimmy, that gorilla of a sub-human being; he wanted to use her too much!

"What Nook say?" Duff asked calmly, having trained himself to dull any negative emotions. "She don't mind that Jimmy want to use you?"

Ping looked up puzzled.

"She don't mind he use you for sex?" Duff asked now unsure.

"HHuuuuuGHH!!" Ping grunted long and hard, expelling more air than he would have thought her lungs could hold. "Go store. Get coffee. Get newspaper!!" she exclaimed excitedly flaring her eyes more than wide.

"Speak English," she continued the explanation. "Other girls not speak," she added. She relaxed and then smiled as the full meaning of the misunderstanding took hold. With a glint in her eye she added, "Nook kill him shure," in answer to the original question.

"Ahhh," was about all Duff could think of to say. How could they communicate so deeply one minute and so poorly the next? The problems went beyond simple language translations. There was a different way of thinking; a Thai way of thinking that he realized might take years for him to fully understand.

Duff sat back in his chair and drifted dreamlike and relaxed. This is vacation, enjoy every minute. That is all we have, the minutes, piled one on top of the other, they add up. They become life.

"EEEm." Full, said Ping, looking up and smiling. Duff paid the bill, and they walked slowly back to Bpah Bar. They had wine coolers. Ping and Bpah chattered away, and Duff made no attempt to follow their conversation. He gazed at the surroundings; bamboo bar; thatched roof; Ping, my girlfriend; Bpah, my friend; Mae Hon Son rimmed with lush forested mountains. This is all right.

The next thing he knew, Bpah was once again motioning for him to hop on the back of her motorcycle. Ping pushed him up close to Bpah so that she could climb on behind. He put his hand on Bpah's shoulders, and Ping wrapped her arms around his waist. As the three of them rode off together through the Mae Hon Son night, Duff could feel Ping lean her head against his back as her arms hugged tighter.

They rode past a couple of Westerners. There were not many foreigners in town. Duff looked at them, and they looked surprised to see a farang, sandwiched between two Thai ladies. And, for just a moment, he fell outside himself and looked with them; a split second, a snapshot. There he was on the motorcycle in a remote mountain town of Northwestern Thailand. Who would have ever believed his life would lead to this moment? He was at peace with his situation, surroundings and himself, because whatever else had happened to him in this crazy life, it had led to this moment.

Duff's first trip alone to a foreign country was Italy. On the bus from the airport to Rome, a young American traveler conversed freely and easily in Italian with obvious strangers.

"How did you learn to speak Italian so well?" Duff asked in awe.

"Oh," he smiled. "I have a girlfriend."

He was a part of the place, and that was so cool.

And now, as they rode three on the motorcycle, past the Westerners on the street, he was the white guy riding past. He could imagine them thinking. Who is he? How long has he been here? Who is the pretty girl hugging him? How did he come to be a part of this place?

Once again, they were at Baiyoke Chalet for music. Loso, now easily recognizable, was mixed with the Issan music Ping loved too much.

"This Ad Karabou song," she told him and attempted a rough translation of the lyrics. "This Nah Kallawan. Nah Kallawan very good friend for me," she swelled with pride.

The music was starting to sink in. Duff was starting to recognize songs and particularly liked the catchy chorus of a song called Super Highway. *"Bin Pie."* Plane go. *"Bin bin bin - bin pie - bin pie bin pie moo jai dee..."*

"Nah Kallawan," Ping reminded him, "He called Bob Dylan of Thailand."

Once more, they were back in their room before midnight. It was not yet "sleep" time, and they sat on the balcony ensconced in the night, illuminated by a bright nearly full moon.

"Ping, I want to write a book about Thailand," Duff told her. "You know Amerigah don't have bargirls. I want to tell people about Thailand. I want you to help me understand better."

Duff wanted a quick, easy explanation, as if bargirls could be lumped into some neat, pre-packaged definition that could be easily understood like a math formula. He needed more than Eddy's colored input, more than his own muddled senses could provide. He wanted the inside scoop, from an inside point of view, as if it were all one and the same.

"Do you remember when I was with Bpun and her boyfriend come? She jump up, you come and hold my hand?" Duff asked.

"Remember," Ping replied. "Remember everything. Remember first time you walk in bar."

"When Bpun leave, how come you run to me so fast?" He asked.

Ping stared straight ahead. He could see her thinking. He could feel a chasm being created between them as her eyes were growing wide. Direct questions are not always polite in Thailand, but he wanted her help. He wanted to understand. Duff pushed his luck.

"Did Bpun talk to you after she come with me?" When he saw the look in her eyes, he did not wait for an answer. "What she say?"

The fuse had already been lit. Her thoughts were exploding inside her like a boiling kettle. The steam had to go somewhere. "HOOOOO!!" came screaming out of every pore in her body.

Ping was up on her feet pacing rapidly back and forth, barely constricted by the walls. A boomerang on uppers, a cartoon pinball machine out of control; her arms flew wild as if not connected to a body.

"MAIS POOT THAI!! MAIS POOT ENGLISH!!" Do not speak Thai, do not speak English, she shouted over and again during the exhales. When she eventually calmed, he took her hand and looked her in the eye.

"Why *mais dai*?" Why no can?

"Cannot speak. Bargirl secret." She left him to wonder.

For the second time that day, they made love. He enjoyed the hugging and the ease of whirling her around. Ping was eighty-eight pounds of pure energy. Her emotional flame was on high, and the kettle was once more boiling over.

"Oh Peetuur, Oh Peetuur, ruk (love) Peetuur, ruk Peetuur," she spewed wildly as they thrashed and rolled about, entangled in the sheets. "OH, OH, OH, RUK PEETUUR, RUK PEETUUR!"

Eddy's voice spiraled through Duff's head, "If the act is good, who cares?" It seemed pretty real. Maybe too real. It was more emotion than Duff could handle, and certainly more than he was capable of returning. He was hoping the decibel level would not bother anyone in the neighboring rooms. Ping sensed his distance, and paused.

"Mais ruk Ping?" Don't love?

"*Ruk* Ping, *ruk* Ping," he answered calmly, saying the words that would not usually flow easily. He knew he would have to explain later. He lay quietly, propped up by two pillows, and Ping calmed down and rested her head on his chest.

"Why you *ruk* Ping?" she asked as he was drifting past the edge of consciousness.

"Funny girl," he mumbled through his sleep. "Funny girl, crazy girl."

Duff could feel her head nodding approval on his chest as if this made perfect sense. "Funny girl, crazy girl," she repeated, quietly pleased, recognizing the image of herself in the mirror of his words.

Mae Hon Son had been fun, but exhausting, not the restful couple of days that he had hoped. He was not sure that relaxation would be possible with Ping in the picture. When she was ready to go out to the market, he gave her money to buy food for her friends in Bangkok, and remained behind alone to rest and write letters in the room. "My el like too much Mae Hon Son food," Ping informed.

"What mean, el?" He asked after a moment to ponder.

"EL, EL!!" Ping snapped at his lack of comprehension. "You know El," she insisted.

Duff thought a moment, mentally scanning his Thai words, and then switched brain waves trying to locate a similar sound in English. He soon quit. "Ping, what language el?" he asked in resignation.

"Hooo! How come you don't know el?" she popped back quickly, then paused, scanning her memory as well. "Mother, have sister," she explained. "What name for sister of mother?"

"Aunt!" he informed her. "You mean aunt."

She threw her head back in realization, and then looked at him with eyes wide. "Not smart girl," she said in the form of an apology.

"Smart girl," he corrected. "Maybe too smart."

When Ping returned from the market, Duff was deep in the comforts of an afternoon nap. He was sailing on light breezes through his subconscious, through scenic mountains, Paduang villages and back down to a *soi* splashed with neon. He drifted ghostlike through and above cameos of his recent past.

The rustling of grocery bags roused him as the glass door leading to the balcony was sliding open. He heard Ping speaking in fluent Thai before she noticed his eyes start to open and then heard her saying, "I think you don't mind I bring him back," she said pointing to the young man sitting on the balcony. "I think for you, no problem."

"No problem," Duff confirmed through his slumber.

"He very nice boy. His mother, I buy many many thing from her in market, she tell me, OK, he take you wherever you want to go. He take me all around Mae Hon Son," she finished.

Duff knew why this was important, and did not mind. The girl at the photo center had improperly loaded Ping's camera. All her film had been ruined. The images of Paduang ladies and Hmong children were gone. All the Mae Hon Son pictures were going to be left to the distortions of her mind without the solid proof of photos, and he knew how special the trip had been for her. He was disappointed too.

"He take me all around town to take new photo. He good boy. Ooo Mae Hon Son people very nice people," Ping told Duff while fishing a beer from the mini bar. After a short while on the balcony, Ping arranged to have him pick them up later, and he left.

Ping lay down beside Duff in an attempt to join his afternoon nap, but her mind was racing too fast to sleep.

"Is it cold now in America?"

"Maybe a little, for you, but hot season soon. Not cold for me."

"Everything *paing mahk*?" Very expensive?

"Yeah, but not same. You make more money." Duff pondered the idea of trying to explain minimum wage, insurance, taxes, mortgages, unemployment insurance, and decided to hold off. "OK, you come with me Amerigah," he taunted, imagining her awe, an endless stream of silly and perceptive questions.

"Huuh," she grunted a short strong no.

"Why no?" he asked.

"Gloo-a, gloo-a." Afraid.

"Why *gloo-a*?"

"You sell me, shure."

"Sell you?" Duff was stunned, unsure if she was serious. "Cannot sell you. How I sell you?"

"CAN! CAN!!" she insisted. "*Farang* sell Thai lady. Happen many time."

"Don't worry," he reassured. "Cannot sell you. Spend too much money on you already. I sell you, I lose money sure."

"Huuugh!" she grunted.

* * *

Whiskey, weak Mekong, poured over ice and mixed with water, another new music guide, Bpah worn out, but replaced by Chai, still on loan from his mother. A new bar/restaurant/club along the edge of the man-made lake, a different Thai singer, "Karabou, Kallawan, he from my town, the Bob Dylan of Thailand," Ping informed as the waitress stood next to the table and kept their whiskey and his cola flowing. A deaf mute massaged his back, his hands strong. They paid him in glasses of whiskey; he laughed heartily with unselfconscious honesty having never heard the sound of his own laughter. Duff walked alone around the lake where groups sat with guitars and invited him to join, couples sat alone. When he came back, Ping was invited on stage to sing. Through the whiskey, her voice was sweet and musical, higher pitched than normal. The place closed at midnight, but Ping was energized with the thrill of performing. Duff asked the few other *farang* customers to clap loudly. He was falling-through-the-floor tired and so was the boy. Three on a motorcycle, once more riding back-roads, but the hotel was the other way, he thought. The outskirts, the edge of the jungle, what felt like the edge of civilization, another bar? Oh no, more whiskey, more Kallawan songs, a plugged-in Ping with two worn out companions.

"Ping, I think Chai is tired."

"Not tired." She refused to see that his head was drooping.

"He work in market with mother, start early morning."

"Not tired."

There was no moving her, so Duff leaned back and watched, removing himself instead, fading into the dark, well after midnight, in who the hell knew where. An open air bar; lanterns strung loosely, swaying in the gentle early morning breeze; thatched roof; lots of bamboo, personal detachment, here, not here, Kallawan songs, and the crowd of twenty or so fumbling through late night conversations, the last ones still awake in this sleepy mountain town, maybe the last awake in the whole world. Chai looked at him pleadingly; he shrugged. What could he do? Duff sat back, inhaled deep, tried to relax.

"Ping, Chai tired." He told her again ten minutes later.

"Not tired."

Duff decided on a new approach and switched from cola to whiskey. When the Mekhong was gone, the night would be over. Chai understood and drank more too. Weak whiskey poured over ice and mixed with water. Thirty minutes later and a wobbly Chai scooted through a night he would remember for a long time. Three on a motorcycle arrived back at Rook's Hotel. Chai dropped them off and disappeared through the mist of mountain morning.

Through sleepy weary arms, Duff and Ping made love again. He rolled over, more than halfway to sleep and Ping dropped her head on his chest and again, as if able to view his thoughts, Ping said, "Duff, you not customer, you *fairn*." Boyfriend.

"Frien or *fairn*?" he asked playing with the pronunciation. Thai people frequently drop the last consonant leaving 'friend' to be spoken as fren, very similar to *fairn*.

"Frairn," said Ping, softly combining the words with a smile, picking up on the game before becoming serious.

"Duff, why you don't *ruk* me?" Ping asked.

This was amazing. In one day they had gone from why do you love me, to why don't you love me? It had been a long night, and Duff was too tired to deal with this, not now.

"Funny girl, crazy girl," He said reverting to what worked before. "Ping, sleep time," he told her, and in seconds, she was out.

"LOOK, LOOK!!" Ping shouted the next morning, waving a Thai newspaper in his direction. "*Farang* sell Thai lady!"

All Duff could make out was a photo of officials leading a *farang* away in handcuffs. "How much he get for her?" He asked with a businessman's curiosity, not expecting an answer.

Ping settled in and read further into the article, then looked up at him surprised. "Forty thousand."

"Dollars?"

"Dollar," she told him. "*Jing jing*, true," she added. "Forty Thousand Dollar!"

"OK!! We go Amerigah, I sell you, sure!" Duff informed her without hesitation. Ping nodded and said nothing, as though she were willing to accept her fate in polite Thai style. He waited a moment, then added with feigned disgust, "Cannot sell you. Don't want angry customer. One week, customer want money back, sure."

Ping seemed to like that. She knew she was not easy, and was more flattered than insulted when he shook his head and added, "Difficult girl."

"Dif fee cult girl," she repeated enjoying the rhythm of the broken syllables, nodding along.

"*Bin, bin, bin, bin pie*." Plane go. Duff sang the Nah Kallawan song to Ping as they packed for the return to Bangkok.

"Ping, you can work at hotel, here," he told her as they checked out. "The people at the desk do not speak English well."

"Cannot." she told him with an air of finality.

"You speak better than they do," he pointed out, nodding toward the desk.

"Cannot!" she stomped.

"Can," he insisted. "Can!"

Ping shook her head violently, understanding more about Thai culture than she cared to explain. These jobs were for recent graduates, and though young by Western standards, in Thailand, nearing thirty, she was old.

Duff went to the post office when they arrived at the airport in Bangkok. He entertained an ill-conceived hope that being near the planes might put some jump in the process of mail delivery, which can take several weeks from Thailand. He bought the appropriate stamps, and began to lick and apply.

Ping pointed at the dish with the wet sponge on the counter. Duff nodded and continued to lick the stamps. He preferred to lick his stamps rather than dab. Ping began pulling on his sleeve in disbelief and pointing frantically at the dish.

When Duff shook his head, no, Ping put her head down even with the counter, next to the dish with the wet sponge. With eyes wide, she opened her mouth and stuck her tongue out as far as it would go. She pointed at her tongue while still pulling on his sleeve. She looked ridiculous, and Duff wrinkled his forehead to let her know that he did not understand what the hell she was doing.

Ping pointed to her tongue, then the stamps. "New job for me," she said, sticking her tongue out again and pointing to the stamps, and then pointing back to her tongue. "One baht."

There, Duff stood in the Bangkok airport, standing next to a clown; big eyes wide and tongue extended to the limit with her head next to a dish with a wet sponge and her finger pointing to her tongue, Ping was beckoning for work.

"OK, I get it," he told her wondering if he would always be her straight man? "OH, LUCY!!"

"What that mean?"

"It mean," he paused, but soon realized that any explanation might only inspire her further. "Never mind."

"OK, never mind," she bobbed her smiling head rather pleased with herself. "Never mind. Never mind."

Excerpted and adapted from Butterflies of the Night

I Never Vote. It Only Encourages Them

1992 - Bush - Clinton – Perot

In the year 1992, I would cast my first vote. I slipped up. I heard Ross Perot on NPR. I was sold. I loved this guy, who had previously been not more than a mysterious name, an eccentric billionaire. The stump speech was a masterpiece. Hell yes. Let's clean out the barn.

He was smart and logical. He was practical, not elitist. He had facts and figures to back up his positions. I could not listen to him without vigorously nodding my head yes! Yes! That's how easy it is to mess with the minds of the voters. One good speech and I was sold.

He would have brought excitement to the presidency. He was certainly something different, an outsider, a businessman. Wow. It was too bad he turned out to be Howard Hughes without the germs. And as the vault opened, it could be argued that he was the consummate insider, having made a fortune on government contracts.

After he unraveled, he still made more sense than the other candidates. In the debates, he was the most amusing. He had this to say in regards to a question about experience:

"Well, they've got a point. I don't have any experience in running up a four trillion dollar debt. I don't have any experience in gridlock government where nobody takes responsibility for anything and everybody blames everybody else. I don't have any experience in creating the worst school system in the industrialized world, but I do have a lot of experience in getting things done."

Perot was put on the ballot by the people. This had grass roots appeal. It was great stuff, and if nothing else, it would be a change. It was his choice of James Stockdale as a Vice Presidential running mate that provided the nail in the coffin for me. I have no doubts that Stockdale was a fine human being, but as a second in charge, it didn't work; a good "yes" man, but not a good idea for Vice President.

When he nervously began the Vice Presidential debates by posing the questions; "Who am I? And why am I here?" There was a flutter to his voice, and a Don Quixote-esque look on his face. I wasn't certain that he knew the answers.

These are great questions. They raise issues that I query of my inner self on a regular basis. Pokhara, Nepal? A small village in Central Thailand? Wow. Sure. Good questions indeed - Who am I? Why am I here? But my questions are spoken in times of awe or disillusion, not nationally televised debates.

Would this be Perot's track through government? Finding devoted corporate style clones. And what would happen if Perot went down for the count, could James Stockdale lead the country? The media beat heavily on Perot's paranoia.

Maybe it was the same way in which they kept showing Dukakis wearing the dumb helmet in the tank. They didn't have to show that picture over and again. It wasn't newsworthy. It was a moment of Dukakis looking like a doof. I bet if you followed any one of us around with a camera all day there would be more than enough instances of us looking like doofs.

Ross Perot spent $55 million of his own money. He put on a great show and ended up with a phenomenal 19% of the vote, though he did not win one state which illustrates to me that his popularity was well spread around. My guess is that many of his followers were previously non-voters.

What would have happened if he hadn't dropped out and then re-entered the race? What would have happened if he spent $100 million or $200 million or more? Could he have bought the whole thing if he played his cards a little closer to the vest and opened the purse strings wider? I think so. But it was not Ross Perot who I voted for in '92. It would be Bill Clinton – and here is why. It dates back to my trip to DC. The one fellow who spoke with me during my three day stay? I had told him that I would vote if it would affect me directly.

Though by this time, I rarely saw or spoke to my busy brother, he had early on hitched his star to Governor Clinton. They were buddies. He told me how smart Clinton was, a phenomenal memory and a true concern for ordinary people; a music aficionado. He told me Bill Clinton knew what was on the flip side.

Clinton had shook hands with JFK. He *was* John F. Kennedy. My brother was in love. And I voted for Clinton because he was my brother's buddy. This was something that would affect if not me, at least a family member. I think Clinton made a good president. He wiped out the deficit and amazingly, he brought in a surplus. I can't remember such fiscal responsibility.

What I never understood was that Republicans, who campaign on fiscal responsibility, always brand Democrats as tax and spend liberals, and then when they get elected run-up enormous deficits. I don't understand why Republicans don't hate fellow Republicans like Reagan and George W. who have squandered trillions. They should all become Democrats. This would force the Democrats to become something else, because it seems they don't want anything to do with Republicans or vice versa. The Democrats currently look pretty void. Maybe they could start anew.

Clinton should be a hero of Republicans, and yet they hated him with a passion that went beyond reason; the same spectacular intensity of hatred with which democrats and liberals would hold for W. before the 2004 election, and that my brother held for me. I had no idea why. We had little contact.

My brother wore fake glasses with a big nose and moustache attached when he held his press conference to come forward as Anonymous. The press corps crucified him. The headline on the evening news was that my brother was a liar. These were pretty rough days, but he dealt with it. What I didn't know was that there had been something far worse in his life. He later told me that the worst day in his whole life was when they brought me home from the hospital. He was 3 years old.

Jan

The second love of my life was never consummated, and it was better that way. My around the world adventure in 1974 left me intellectually intoxicated and unprepared for life in the USA. I became an antique dealer, fascinated with the history and enamored by the stuff. I settled in to a shop on a street in an Italian neighborhood. The rent was cheap, and there were living quarters creatively installed in the back. Across the street was a general store. One of the young girls working there was Jan.

I spent my time plunked in a rocker, deposited on the sidewalk. There wasn't much business. I was more interested in Dostoyevsky than dollars. Jan asked what I was reading. The other girls who worked in the general store could barely make change without a manual and a consultation with the boss. Jan had read Dostoyevsky.

At the time, I didn't know that she was older than I or from out of town. She looked fifteen. I was twenty-five. I would know her for twenty years, and never know her birthday or year. In our wide open whirlwind conversations, this only was off limits.

Jan was from Illinois, and came to the neighborhood via her uncle. At least, that was who I thought he was, until that unraveled too. He was forty and looked sixty. She was 30 and looked fifteen. When I found out they lived together, uncle was a good assumption. I think everyone in the neighborhood thought that. Neither one of them fit the provincial world of our odd mixed community. There were more than a handful of us 'out of towners' drawn together by this in-distinction.

We hung out at Elias' Lebanese restaurant and ate hummus and falafel. Elias did not fit with either the Italians or the hippie fringe, drawn by one-step from the action Greenwich Village pricing. As we would pair up, split up, re-pair, Elias was left in the cold. He didn't get it.

"Why she fuck for you, not fuck for me?" he would protest loudly. Then he would throw the question at one of the females. "Why you fuck for him, not fuck for me?" He was dismayed and not charming. We soon left the place empty.

My store became a hang out for out of work actors, designers and artists. I would place rocking chairs on the sidewalk, and we would chat. The only regular hours that I kept were Saturday afternoons. Otherwise, I was open when I was home. I hung a sign on the front door that read: **Closed – For No Particular Reason**.

On one of those early Saturdays, Jane Davis came to my store. She had been recently released from a mental institution and needed furniture. She was smart and funky, and we became friends.

Jane worked in brain research, smoked marijuana, did pills and went in and out of mental facilities where she would meet and marry psychotic guys. She had a penchant for blaming her hardships on her parents. The injustices that she related never seemed that bad. I have a photo of Jane and Jan sitting together at a party; one photo with two future suicide victims.

Jan's live in, Lou, was an interesting guy, but we didn't see much of him. Eventually they would split up, and though Jan and I flirted with the idea, and spent long hours in conversation on the deepest of philosophical issues, I think we both knew it would be a dangerous match. Some friendships are too good to ruin.

Though it has been years since her suicide, there is one place in my life that suffers her void. After moving out of New York, we kept in touch. Jan was the one person that I knew who was always awake early in the morning. When my dreams went sour or my enthusiasm for a new idea radiated, I could call her at 6 am. There is no longer a close friend available at the break of dawn. There is no longer Jan available at any time. I miss her.

I look back at our choices. Though we both spent years living alone, Jan chose to live with Lou, the older fellow who I originally thought was her uncle. In my first book, I wrote a short vignette about him. Lou still holds a strong image in my mind. Here's what I wrote.

Oh, The Black

His name was Lou. He didn't have many friends. He wasn't what you would call a social guy. Mostly, he stayed in his apartment and went to work.

I had known him for years, but only to say hello and nod when we passed in the street. He wasn't the type to stop and shoot the shit like the others on our friendly little New York City neighborhood block.

Lou was short and stocky. He had the build and look of a cigar butt that had been stubbed out. His perpetually unshaven face with the irregular stubble looked like the strands of tobacco hanging from the end of the butt. His eyes, forever bloodshot, were the embers of fire that once kept it lit. The only reason that I got to know Lou at all, was because I was friendly with his live-in girlfriend. She was sociable though, like Lou, she had a reclusive side. She was perceptive, intelligent and very well read.

Lou, too, was particularly smart, maybe the most brilliant man I ever met. He could recite pages and pages of Shakespeare from memory. Lou worked as a subway messenger. He carried packages for a publishing company through the dirty, piss smelling underground tunnels of New York City. He prided himself on his knowledge of the tubular tangle of routes, and his ability to deliver the packages with the utmost speed. It was a low paying job that carried little respect, but for Lou, it was perfect. He could sit on the train and read all day, unnoticed.

I remember going out socially with him only once. We went to a bar with some friends from the neighborhood, and we all got pissed drunk. It was New Year's Eve. The normally reclusive Lou was the life of the party; a funny, falling down, word slurring drunken performance. We left the bar with him draped between two of us.

As we walked down Sixth Avenue and turned onto Bleeker Street, a nicely dressed, preppy, young man approached us. His wallet had been stolen, he needed cab fare to get home, back to his Upper East Side probably upper crust abode. We were all pretty broke and on the edge back then. Lou reached for his wallet.

"No," we told him. "Come on, that's the oldest ruse in the world!"

"It's a con!"

"No way!"

When you live in New York City, you get to learn all the cons. If a stranger starts to talk, you know it's probably a con. We continued to drag Lou onwards when he stopped suddenly, planted his feet.

His round red face lit up. His eyes went wide with enlightenment. He turned to face the young man now several feet behind us.

"Spectacular!" he shouted raising an arm theatrically, finger pointing toward the sky. "Bravo!" He turned to plead with us to let him go. "I take the subway, and he wants **me** to give **him** money for a taxi!"

We had to drag Lou away because he wanted to give the kid all of his remaining money. We didn't exactly see the brilliance, and we figured Lou would not feel the same way about it in the morning, so we pulled him away, and half carried him home.

That was the only time I remember going out with Lou. He was a carnival act, a one man show, but that was on a good day. I knew there was a flip side. There is always a flip side, and it can be equally extreme.

One evening, he walked past me on the street. He didn't see me. His attention was elsewhere. His focus was on his live-in girlfriend who was half way up the block. His face drooped with total despair. His entire demeanor matched his face. You could almost see the dark ominous storm clouds that hung above and covered him alone. The pain was far greater than one person could hold for themselves alone. He had to be hurting for all of mankind, lamenting the misery of the human condition.

Jan walked toward him, and they met a few feet from where I was standing. I could see his shoulders droop, feel his demeanor sink. He spoke to her in something between a cry and a soft wail, but he only said three words and that told the whole story. It was the flip side of the comedy routine that we saw in the bar. It was the reality of a subway messenger.

"Oh, the black," he told Jan with the tears not on his face, but cloistered inside the sound of his voice. That was all he said. That was all he needed to say. She lived with him. She'd seen it before.

If you saw his face, heard his voice, you could see the depths of the abyss that he had fallen into, how far from the light he was. "Oh, the black," pretty much said it all.

* * *

Jan withdrew to a greater extent with each passing year. She would walk her dogs early in the morning and late at night. She had told me that she wanted to see her dogs through their lifetimes, and after that, she didn't have much interest in going on. She had told me that she always imagined herself becoming a hermit, but never envisioned it being in a five story walk up in Manhattan.

After her dogs passed along, she moved back to Illinois. I had no phone contact. She sent a rare rambling post card often difficult to decipher. Her mother, a rotund lady, was in a nursing home. Jan tried to help the nurse with her mothers care. Her mother slapped Jan across the face. That was it. Here is the end of the story that I wrote about Lou:

Lou died young a few years later, emphysema restricting the oxygen in his lungs. Someone at the publishing company had figured out how smart he was and promoted him. He worked the last couple of years as an editor. He could no longer walk the streets and ride the subways all day. My guess is that was when and why he let them know how smart he was, so he could work inside. It was no accident that he was working for a publisher. He ended up in a plush office with piles of manuscripts scattered about the floor, a secretary and a subway messenger at his disposal.

He died in a New York City hospital after a two week stay. Jan lasted another ten years, and then killed herself in the garage of her mother's home. She cleaned her mother's house, left everything neat and tidy, then went into the car, draped a blanket around herself and turned on the engine. It was night. She died in a monoxide sleep, deep in her own abyss. Sometimes, the flip side gets too far away, and it feels like the sun will never come out again, and you will never overcome the darkness inside your soul. Oh, the black.

Here's what I didn't find out about Jan until after her death. Jan was born on August 6th 1945. This is why she never talked about her age or celebrated her birthday.

Hiroshima – August 6, 1945

At 7:09 a.m. an air raid alert sounded. A lone plane was sighted far above the ground.

At 7:31 the alert was lifted. It was Monday morning, and people were starting off to work. The skies were clear and bright. The sun was beginning to heat the air.

At 8:15 a B-29 Bomber named the Enola Gay passed over Hiroshima. They had named their payload "Little Boy."

Many reported seeing a bright light, a second sun. The atomic bomb exploded 580 meters in the air above Shima Hospital. The temperature at the point of explosion was over 1,000,000 degrees centigrade. Intense heat rays ignited a rage of fire. Radiation was released in all directions.

There was a wind of phenomenal force. The wind knocked people off their feet and blasted them through the air. The wind damaged most houses and buildings within one and a half miles of the explosion. The wind slammed into the mountain outside of the city and bounced back again increasing the rage of the firestorm.

More than 4 square miles of Hiroshima were instantly and totally devastated by the combination of wind, heat and fire.

It seemed as though everything was on fire or already melted. People rushed to the narrow bridges to escape the fires. Their flesh was melting and hung from their arms. It was high tide, and the rivers were filled with burning logs. Anyone who fell in died.

More than 66,000 people died from the initial explosion. 140,000 people died slowly from injuries. It is estimated that more than 200,000 people died by the end of the year. Radiation would cause a host of disorders, birth defects and disease. In 1960, fifteen years after the blast, there were increased rates of thyroid cancer, breast cancer, lung cancer and salivary gland cancer.

Paul Tibbets, the pilot of the Enola Gay wrote that a bright light filled the plane.
Robert Lewis, the co-pilot of the Enola Gay wrote in his journal, "My God. What have we done?"

During this day of horror, while people died, while the living screamed and cried in pain, and mourning, while the streets of Hiroshima were transformed into the chaos of fire and devastation, lost children and broken families, somewhere, in the prairies of Illinois, Jan was born. She felt her birthday was the blackest day in the history of mankind. She carried this burden daily.

19

I have three close friends who have killed themselves. I don't know any Thai people who have committed suicide. There was a story in the newspaper that created a stir. A lady, upset with her husband's drunken philandering, killed herself by jumping into the pit at the Crocodile Farm in Samut Prakran.

My wife has a friend whose husband can be charming. He earns 10,000 baht a month, and blows it all within three days on whiskey and gambling. She earns 3,000 baht a month, [$75] and this is what they live on. He is controlling and crazy jealous. My wife is younger than he, and cannot take him to task for his behavior. It would not be polite.

He called to ask if we would like to accompany them to the Crocodile Farm. My well mannered wife replies, making tangential reference to her friend's difficult plight, "No thanks. We'll stay home, and read about it in tomorrow's newspaper."

As my wife learns English, we have greater communication problems. I am sometimes not sure if she is using a Thai word that I am not familiar with, or mispronouncing an English word. We rarely use the dictionary, but when we do, it is incorrect about 10% of the time and often outdated.

In Thai language, the word for "put on" as in to put on clothing - is *Sai*. If you put on cream, it is a different word, *Tah.* Both should be translated into English as "put on." The dictionary lists *Tah* as besmear. I have done a little besmirching, but I can't remember the last time I besmeared.

Both my wife and I enjoy learning our new languages. She loves to say 'traffic jam,' as though it were derived from Strawberry Jam. When the traffic loosens up a bit, I tell her we call this traffic jelly.

My Thai is self taught, and sometimes incorrect. I used to call the refrigerator *Tua yen* which means 'cool beans' as opposed to the correct pronunciation of *tu yen*. My wife never corrected me because she knew what I meant. Nobody else did.

I have never studied the tones. I think of it as the difference between signing a **contract,** and the possibility that you might **contract** a disease. The pronunciation is ever so slightly different, but if used in context, it would never create a problem. I think of the tones as being part of the song of the language. My conversations are fluid with a hint of a New York accent.

At the bank:

"Where did you get that bag?" a lady asked admiring my hand woven tote.

"Ecuador."

"How much was it?"

"Two dollars."

"I want it."

"It's not for sale."

"I didn't say I wanted to buy it. I want you to give it to me."

A direct no is impolite, and I watch my manners.

"If I give you the bag, what will I tell my wife when I get home?"

"Tell her you gave me the bag."

In our village produce store:

"*Gloo-a farang, gloo-a farang,*" a lady spoke over and again to her infant. It means be afraid of the foreigner. It touched a raw nerve because my nephews, who now come to Uncle for snacks and comfort and outings in my car, would at first run and cry when they saw me. "*gloo-a farang,*" they would call out.

"Don't teach your baby that," I tried to instruct kindly. She was surprised that I understood and could respond in Thai. "Thai people, foreign people, we are all the same. We are all people." She continued to stare at me – study me. And so, I felt compelled to repeat myself. "We are all people, we are all the same."

She had probably never met a *farang* who could speak Thai, and thereby never spoken to one, but this was ridiculous. It couldn't be true.

"What about your nose?" she asked me.

At the bus terminal:

I stood near the door to the bus, waiting for the return of my wife who had gone to the local convenience store to garner snacks for our trip. Across from me stood a young man, probably about twenty, whose job was to take the customers luggage and place it in the compartment under the bus, as he had done for me moments earlier.

An elfin young lady bus attendant bounded between us and through the door onto the bus. The young lad who was attending the customer's luggage had an idea. He looked up at me, and spoke in Thai.

"Do you want a girlfriend?" He asked in reference to the attractive young hostess who was already on the bus.

I thanked him, and explained that not only did I already have a wife, but that she was returning momentarily. He looked disappointed. He looked up at the bus. I pointed to my wedding band and repeated quite simply, "Have wife."

"Don't worry. It's no problem," he smiled agreeably. "She'll understand." He looked up toward the hostess. "She's very easy going."

It's not all funny or pleasant or peaceful. There are moments. There are incidents.

In the next village, not more than a couple of short kilometers away, a group of youths beat a young man, and then kicked him until he died. Motorists are reckless. Motorcycles offer the driver and passengers little protection. Whiskey does not help the equation. More than three people an hour die on the highways.

Village life, Thai life, has restrictions that I do not always abide, accept or understand. My wife warns me against walking alone in the forest. She gets very concerned when I tell her that I walked five kilometers to the Buddhist hermitage in the woods. I tell her I am free, I must be allowed to walk. She worries that a poor person, or someone on drugs, will hit me over the head for what they might hope to find in my wallet. In Bangkok, she has no such concerns.

In our village, during the stone drunk heat of New Year's celebration, there are always fights. This year, one boy held a knife to another boy's throat. He was ready to kill. Someone talked him out of it. After the incident, I asked my wife how it can be that Thai people can be so smiling and friendly one minute, and then, so violent the next. "The blood gets hot," she told me.

And yet, it seems much safer here than in America where inner cities can be frightening, where road side rest areas can be dangerous, where violence is impersonal and random. Here, you must first deeply offend someone; there, you just have to be in the wrong place at some un-appointed moment. I choose not to follow any such restrictions, if I cannot walk freely, then I will die I tell her. This is another reason that my wife thinks that I am crazy.

I Never Vote. It Only Encourages Them

1996 Clinton vs. Dole

My brother wrote a tremendously successful book under the pseudonym "Anonymous". It became a mystery as to who, with such insider knowledge, had written this book. Fingers were pointed. Larry King had a one hour show with a cast of potential culprits, my brother not being one of them.

I knew through my mother. I was sitting in the woods of Pennsylvania, in the middle of nowhere, in a township with more deer than residents, and I was one of about ten people in the world who knew the answer that America was seeking.

I felt special. By this time, I had little contact with and rarely saw or spoke with my brother. He was a celebrity, and his life was viewed in TV appearances and heard about through rumor, spoken casually through phone lines. We could have been a case study of how complete opposites could have originated from the same parents. We looked relatively similar, had the same mannerisms and voice timbre, but our paths were different. I rooted for him from afar.

He sought wealth and fame. I wanted to be free. He was a celebrity. I was the one who was anonymous. He stole my name. I sat alone in the distant woods. He did call me once. I was partially out the door, late for a movie. I rushed back for the phone. When I heard his voice, I asked if all was OK. Yes. I am on my way to a movie, I told him. Can I call you back as soon as I get in?

I don't have time now he told me. I have to go. He hung up the phone having essentially called to inform me that he didn't have time to talk. Younger brother must not be allowed to get off the phone first. I do not fully understand the customs in either country. My brother would eventually get caught, and be branded a liar. I thought that was harsh, but he was playing tackle football with the heavyweights. That's what happens. He was well paid for his efforts. I didn't think he would trade that for an opportunity to take it back.

Clinton did a good job, but was smarmy. Dole seemed to be mean. He came across as a nasty, snarling back room kind of guy, even though I think he spoke truthfully, was smart and might have made a good president. It was easy to revert back to being a non-voter.

In 1997, the final scraps of my marriage dissolved entirely. It wasn't a horrible break-up. It was like waking up one morning and coming to the realization that it wasn't there anymore. We split ten acres, five each and became neighbors. Things weren't coming apart for me; it was an opportunity to resume life in another way and another place. I started spending more time in Thailand, an old favorite country. I would meet my Thai wife a few years later.

Non-Professional Politicians

Not having professional politicians had been my presumed solution to the problems of the nation. I was wrong. In 1996, at age 46, I was ready to do something for my community. I volunteered to serve as secretary on our local, newly-formed Committee to create zoning in our township. We were one of the few townships in the United States that did not have zoning and growth was in the cards.

My job was to write the names of those in attendance, and take minutes of the meeting. Sometimes, I would contribute a joke, which our quite serious Chairman would acknowledge with a wisp of a grin, and then inform me that I was not being helpful. I continued in this non-productive capacity for six months, but my habit of spending long periods of time out of the country was not one of the qualities that they were looking for in a secretary, and I resigned.

An opposition camp emerged due to rumors that the zoning board was goose-stepping into people's lives. Neighbors, knowing of my involvement, were stopping at my house and telling me that they had heard strange things. They were no longer going to be allowed to chop wood, own radios or have wooden lawn ornaments of fat ladies bending over and exposing their underwear. These were big issues.

I, as an unlikely insider, though the meetings were open to the public, would know the goings on of the infidels, and some of the locals came to me. The community was divided amongst the "Newbies" - people like me who had actually purchased our land, and the "Cro-Magnon's" - who were here shortly after man began walking upright, and had inherited staked out claims that were barely distinguishable from DNA.

I felt like a member of my Central Pennsylvania Community as these overall clad farmers would show up at my door. I loved these guys. They were the ones who would pull me out of snowdrifts in the middle of the night as they were just awakening and getting ready for breakfast. They were great neighbors. And I welcomed them with a cup of coffee when they would come to my house with fine manners, and quiet concern, seeking my knowledge of the new zoning regulations. They would tell me what they had heard about no longer being allowed to have relatives stay with them.

I would tell them yes, that was correct. When I would add the word "kidding" - it was too late. Sarcasm has no value on a farm. They didn't recognize it, and responded in much the same way as if a platypus was discovered in their field. A concerned look would creep into their eyes. Kidding, I would repeat, but the look would deepen and become lost in the crevices of their craggy faces. I was a talking platypus.

Doubt ruled. After all, I was a "Newbie" and part of the zoning force. They would rise up and defeat the fascists coming to tell them what to do on their property. Zoning was un-American. Unfortunately, pollution and waste dumps are American, and that was why we needed zoning. It was a difficult issue.

Bud "The Hump" Warner

When you live in a farming community and someone has a nickname like "The Hump" – you don't ask where he got the name. You accept it, especially if you are a "Newbie". But The Hump was one of the more progressive of the Cro-Magnon's. He wasn't totally against zoning. He wanted fair zoning. Who could be against "fair" anything? You could keep your ax, chop wood, have radios, watch wrestling on TV and still have zoning. Almost heaven, Pennsyl-tucky.

The Hump ran the local hardware store, which probably pre-dated tools. His familial history likely included selling sharpened Mastodon bones and grinding Narwhal teeth into powder to be sold as an aphrodisiac, serving the local population for thousands of years. His family once owned all the land between here and way down there, which was interesting because all the Cro-Magnons had the same story, and possibly explicable in that they may have had the same ancestor.

The Hump was funny too. You could always catch a good joke there, as well as any local gossip-mation. He was a solid guy; exactly the kind of upstanding citizen that you would pick from your community to go down to DC and straighten things out. The nickname actually came from his phraseology, which would replace improper curse words with "hump," as in what the hump are you doing? If the system of government were functioning properly, we could send a guy like The Hump to Washington, and we would get our Mastodon bones somewhere else for four years, and then gather at the railway station to welcome back our hero.

I never bought much more than my newspaper at his place. The local hanger-outters were slightly intimidating, but The Hump was always welcoming. I was never sure what the locals thought of me. One day I showed up to buy my morning paper and found the gang sitting on the metal bench which displayed the newspapers outside of the store. They were telling "you just might be a redneck jokes."

I joined in. "If you prefer to sit on the newspapers rather than read them…" well, I didn't buy a paper that day, nobody got up to allow access, and I had already used up my allotment of words. Cro Magnon's have a word quota which kicks in when they are talking to "Newbies."

The Hump informed me of his plans to run for local office and turn this zoning thing around. It was a great idea, and I lent him my vote of confidence. Though I was in Asia at election time, he won in a landslide victory. He would also prove to me the fallacy of my conviction that government should be run by well meaning amateurs.

He started bravely, determined to fix the potholes that had small strips of road between them. He called in several contractors to get bids on the job. One guy told him; "the more I pave the cheaper it gets." The Hump thought that was terrific and hired him on the spot with instructions to keep paving until it was free.

Moose

Moose Forest was inappropriately named. Ape Jungle would have been far more appropriate. He wasn't a Cro-Magnon, and though new to the area, he certainly was not one of the intellectual "Newbies" either. He looked as though he was some sort of missing link, but it would have been a challenge to connect him to anything. He was broad and powerful and very, very hairy. The top of his head flowed mane-like into his thick beard and body hair. I liked him because amidst the hair, his eyes peered out bright and burning with a devilish flare. From whatever species he had descended, he was undeniably alive.

Moose was a community minded citizen who attended all the zoning meetings. He would sit quietly and listen for ninety minutes while I sat bored, doodling figure eights along the edge of the official documents. I had confidence that nobody would ever read these documents again, and so I wrote Victorian type comments in the hopes that maybe someone would stumble on them in a hundred years and use it as a snapshot of the era. "No coffee and cake was served, but a good time was had by all." – A bold-faced lie. I can't imagine that anyone was enjoying sorting out the tangled knots of codes and sections.

About once a month, Moose would ask for permission to speak at the end of one of the meetings. He would rise and talk in a respectful tone with a powerful resounding bass voice:

"The proletariat is not founded under the protection of the neo-conservative, fascist Nazi liberals who were founded on subjugated principles not inherent to the nature of man in an incubatory state that informed prognosticators hadn't inhabited in a perfunctory manner that would inhibit the falsification of prodigious concepts of justice..."

Moose would go on like this for five minutes, and then sit down. There would be a silent pause. The Chief Newbie would thank him for coming and contributing whatever the hell he just said, as it was more of a contribution than any of the other locals who were home watching wrestling on TV while they still had the opportunity.

My returns to America were less frequent, but The Hump had been elected Chief of The Village and urged me to come to an upcoming open meeting. I attended.

The Hump's first act was to trash the existing zoning committee. Two years later, the roads look about the same, so I am not sure there ever was a second act. There was an issue at this meeting about land use. One of the locals was considering opening a kennel in his backyard. The neighbors were concerned about dogs barking in the middle of the night and disturbing their sleep. There still was no zoning in place, fair or otherwise.

The Hump was in the process of appointing his fellow committee members, and I was stunned to hear that Moose, though definitely a community minded fellow, was one of the appointees. This was way over the line. I enjoyed Moose as an electrifying cosmic guffaw, but a public official? He was past any lines that might be drawn and way too far over any ledges. There was immediate opposition. I had been ready to send The Hump to Washington. What if he brought Moose with him? And I guess what I am saying here is that after an incident like this, I have to question my own abilities to appropriately pick candidates.

Linda's Plan

It was the strangest series of phone calls that I had ever received. My publisher called first. A lady in America had read my book, Thailand Stories, and wanted to contact me. It could have been anyone. I was curious.

She had read my book, as had her husband, and wanted to confirm the veracity of a couple of lines from the text in reference to Thai bargirls.

There wasn't a guy in town who could resist the charms when turned on high.

Yes, I had written that. It was opinion. Dramatic license. Surely there were exceptions.

What man could resist the charms of the beautiful, playful, body rattling with giggles Tuk pressed tight against him consumed in frolic?

Well, yes, that too sounded familiar. A theme was starting to develop.

An idea had been brewing and prompted her to propose a Thailand vacation to her husband. She wanted my help. I am too much a gentleman to refuse a lady near anything – and this was quite something.

I met the Rowlands' for the first time in the lobby of The Landmark Hotel. Linda Rowland was fine. Tall, thin, legs that stretched from Bangkok to Koh Samui; she was a looker. My guess was late thirties, though her husband, John, looked older, possibly fifty, a little scarred from business, but an immediate twinkle in his eye as he could not help but notice my attractive young female friend.

I was wearing a blue shirt with white collar as an identifying marker. As the Rowlands' approached, Linda slid a stealthy, knowing smile in my direction. John's eyes went right to Toom, a capricious whimsy in a mini-skirt and glowing Thai smile; a slam bam knock-out; a head turner in any culture, and she was sitting next to me. I nodded back, to let Linda know for sure that I was her connection. There was no introduction.

"I need to go back to the room, why don't you wait here. I'll be right back," Linda deposited her husband in the armchair next to the couch that Toom and I were occupying. He didn't mind, his eyes embarrassingly fixed on my sprite-like booming with energy lady friend. Mrs. Rowland had told me her husband was an ogler - and what a place to exercise the eyeball. Bangkok has to have the most beautiful women in the world, and The Landmark is in the midst of the "district" where you might find ten thousand evening entertainment hostesses in a two block range; a goggling paradise multiplied hundreds of times out, an oasis so vast that the surrounding desert fades to distant memory.

"Was that American English I just heard?" My question was neatly drawn to inform him that not only was I an American, but that I have been here so long that it was a treat for me to hear the sound of my native language. By the looks of my superb young friend, I knew my way around.

We indulged conversation in Mrs. Rowlands absence. In foreign lands friendships amongst compatriots are forged quickly. John was aglow, and I could see his mind whipping through lusty thoughts. I was about his age with a twenty-two year old – and I am fifty-five – though the girls here tell me I look like I am forty. I know they tell that to all the guys, but with me, they are sincere. I really do look forty to them, I know, because they tell me. Who needs more affirmation than that! Though to John Rowlands, I undoubtedly looked my age, and I could see the rascal's thoughts. If a codger like me could do so well, - then a cool guy like him could do better. Maybe even take this girl away from me.

John was chatting gaily, and flirting more than a tad, as Toom's eyes shot sexy hell fire back. There was no doubt that he was entranced. Linda Rowland watched amused from a distant outpost in the lobby. My conversation with John was comfortable and Toom's command of English was paying off, full of meaningless banter, just as you might find in a bar. How old? Where you from? She spoke a few words to me in Thai.

"What did she say?" John knew it was about him.

I hesitated, then with a 'what the hell look' I informed him. "She said you are a handsome man. She can see you are a young man in your heart. Good heart."

John Rowland bought it. He was leaning forward in his chair. His eyes sparkled with youth and Toom's eyes shot back exotic haunts of unexplored realms. Dreams can come true in a world of magic.

Linda strolled back into the lobby. "Honey," she said. "I asked at the desk, and they have a cooking class – it starts in half an hour."

Linda Rowland looked at me. "I see you have made a friend," she noted.

I quickly introduced myself informing her that back in the States – we were nearly neighbors, a thousand miles not much further than ten.

"Don't let me keep you. I am waiting for my wife. We are meeting here for dinner," I informed.

Linda asked me about Northern Thai cooking bringing me in to the conversation. I told her that in Thai language, *Khao soi,* was what you would say to a taxi driver if you wanted to enter a street, and if the tone were changed ever so slightly, *khao soi,* was a famous Northern Thai noodle soup dish. I could never be sure if I were telling the taxi to enter the side street, or stop for food – though the latter never happened. I rambled on nervously until Linda gave me a hard stare which stopped me.

Apologizing, she asked her husband if he would mind terribly if she went to this course. There was a hotel mini-bus that would take her, but he would be left unaccompanied for the evening.

"Well, nothing special, but you are welcome to join us for dinner," I offered to provide the entertainment for a husband left alone on his second night in Bangkok.

My wife arrived on cue. I could see the thoughts racing through his brain. Toom, the luscious, flirtatious young lady was neither my wife nor girlfriend. She thought he was handsome. She would be coming for dinner.

I introduced my wife.

"That's so nice of you," Linda said seeming to barely notice Toom.

"No kidding. Come on along," I urged. "It is just great for me to be able to speak English again. I love the company." He bought that too.

"You don't mind?" John asked his wife.

"No. You have to eat. I'll be sampling the goodies at the course."

"Well, why not," he agreed.

"The course runs until 9:30. They told me the mini-bus usually returns to the hotel about 10:30."

"Enjoy. Take your time."

It was easier than I imagined. John Rowland had the charm turned up high. His feathers were puffed-out in a courtship ritual that would make a peacock proud. He flaired and flaunted and Toom partly retreated, being coy and daring at the same time, her eyes flashing possibility, her hand slipping on to his inner thigh under the table. It had been his wife's suggestion to take this remote vacation, but John was in love with Thailand already. He paid the check with a flourish. The male instinctively knows that his attractiveness is oddly connected to his ability to provide. The dating ritual is not complete without a fine restaurant; a taste of the good life. Ah, the elegant tastes of courtship.

We all have a darkest moment, a worst thing that we have ever done. Profit is a powerful motive. Linda Rowland had assured me of her husband's abusive nature, as well as his large fortune. An unfortunate moment could yield a large dividend in front of a judge.

I did not have to provide much urging as John Rowland invited us up to his suite on the 33rd floor. Linda had insisted on going first class. She wanted the suite, and it was only $20 more. The rest is a swirl in my memory as Linda returned home early from her cooking class. My wife and I were in the living room. A naked Toom was racing from bedroom to living room and back, as a bewildered John had a sheet wrapped around him. It was a fine moment of partly choreographed pandemonium. Toom did a great job, only slightly over-acting. She had a lovely figure I remember thinking. Linda stood with her mouth agog, and the presence of mind to snap a photo.

I paid Toom $100 – twice her usual nightly fee. I paid $50 to the lady who portrayed my wife with quiet reserve and dignity. Linda Rowland, soon to be divorced, paid me. After the handsome retainer, one half percent of the large out of court settlement netted me a cool $20,000 for my evening's work.

A year later, I would bump into John Rowland on Sukhumvit Road, a block away from The Landmark Hotel. I might have run. I might have thrown up an arm in defense, but before the full recollection of his face and the incident set-in, he was smiling and holding his hand out in friendship. He was thanking me profusely, apologizing for the ugly scene and assuring me that being divorced was the best thing that ever happened to him. He was back in Thailand and having the time of his life. Go figure.

He said he had been hoping to bump into me. He had never been able to get Toom out of his head. My thought process was working faster now. I told him that she had never been with a foreigner before, and she had liked him and missed him and talked of him constantly. I told him I would give her a call, and she will be thrilled to see him. She too has been dreaming of him.

If there is a worst thing that you do in life, then by definition, there must be a second worst thing. I called Toom, told her of the incident, and informed her that I wanted 10% of whatever he gives her. She laughed. There was no way that she would give me ten percent. I fixed her up anyway. It was a good deed.

A year later, they were still together. I received a postcard from Kauai six months after that. It just said "Thanks." It was signed Linda.

Writers of fiction are oft served well to be dreamers, and dreamers should be writers. It offers a chance to play out fantasy. Some tales are true, but mostly it is a matter of percent. This one was totally conjured, but it could have been true. And in fantasy, as in life, we have regrets. I should have insisted on a larger percent, a hundred thousand in profit would not have been out of line from a multi-million dollar settlement.

Writing is not a profession that you pursue for profit. You do it for pleasure, yours and hopefully that of the reader. Though my expenses in the village are shockingly minimal in comparison to the USA, the extra money would have been nice.

20

In Bangkok, I stay in a Thai neighborhood. I am undoubtedly twice the age of my waitress, which does not concern her. I am having a plate of fried rice with pork. We exchange greetings, and she sits with me while I eat. Her questions come quickly, her eyes flash unabashed flirtation.

Where are you from? Where do you live? How come you speak Thai? Do you want a girlfriend? – I have a wife. I tell her the truth, which she could have guessed if she had thought about it. Any foreigner who can speak Thai has been here long enough that he would already be taken. I wear my wedding ring every day. She had nothing to lose.

How about a second wife? She asked quickly. I flared my eyes in jest. I have heard this proposal too. Only kidding, she informs me in an effort to save face. I smile which provokes a second opportunity. Unless you want it to be true, she adds.

My waitress is twenty-seven years old and any fifty-five year old would be proud to have her as a wife, first or second. She considers herself old. Finding work outside the family business would be difficult, even in a factory.

Unusual invitations to mate are near daily fare. One creative masseuse penned her phone number on my leg, near my knee, during a foot massage. I must have dozed off. I didn't notice it until the next morning.

While I am in Bangkok, there is rapid progress on the interior of my house. The parquet floors are laid, and a staircase replaces the scaffolding. My request to put the electric wires inside the wall is forgotten or ignored. My requests to put the electric outlets near the floor, as opposed to head high on the wall, meet the same fate. It is too late to change. Everyone shrugs.

The outlets are placed high to be out of the reach of children. The plumbers and electricians in the village are not competent. Problems are inevitable, and when they occur would require the difficult process of breaking-out and opening-up of cement walls.

A month after the water is installed, the upstairs bathroom is leaking into the downstairs. The plumber breaks out the bathroom floor to re-do the work. He sings beautifully, but always the same song, the same line from that one song. Repetition does not bother him. He has returned to do the same job many times.

Jefferson Davis Lee calls from America. He asks about my house construction. He wants to come and visit. We talk about relationships, his favorite topic. He tells me that men are confused. It started with the Women's Movement back in the 1960s. If you opened the door for a woman, you might get a biting reply that she can open her own door. If you didn't, you were discourteous. I think those were the good old days. Things have gone down from there. Logic and reason have no place in a world of cyclonic emotion. He says it is not easy for a southern boy like him. He has been taught that having good manners is important.

I agree with him. If good manners were compulsory, the world would be a much better place. In my wife's version of English language, she has learned to say, 'thank you so much.' She says this cheerfully. Thank you so much. The extra couple of words make a noticeable difference. When she says it, I can see how pleased it makes people.

Relationships are a growing problem in the Western World these days – and it appears a nearly unsolvable problem. Expectations are not met, bickering has replaced conversation. Being wrong all day wears on anyone's nerves. It hardly seems worth it, and most people come to that conclusion eventually and get divorced. I think everyone is overly sensitive. Faults are easy to find. You have to look away.

Here is my solution for Jeff, it is unconventional, but these are tough times. Things are definitely not working, and maybe it is time for something revolutionary. The great beauty in life is that we can be free to transcend convention; the tragedy is that few of us ever do.

A contract should be written defining function and responsibility. A partner will be chosen on the basis of who will be a compatible childrearing associate. Arranged marriages are fine. Since sex and money are the two biggest factors in divorce – sex will be forbidden. Money will be kept separate. Artificial insemination will cut a smooth road through previously choppy seas.

There are two reasons why there is a need for relationships. First, is that two of us together, combining our strong points can bring up children who are better able to cope with the world, and less likely to rob the neighborhood branch of 7-11. The second reason for marriage is companionship. The so called soul-mate who Jeff is seeking does not necessarily need to be involved with sex or money.

All sex will take place outside the bounds of marriage. Whatever goes on outside the house is not an issue for discussion. And since money is the second biggest problem in marriage, then this too will no longer be an issue, because after the cost of unlimited extramarital sex, there won't be any left over.

And, of course, I am only kidding – unless you want it to be true.

21

I was 95% satisfied with the final product when my house was completed six months after breaking ground. There are things that would drive most Westerners nuts. Opening a window is a ten stage process of clips and dead bolts. Sliders would have been better.

Several of the windows do not fit flush into their wooden frames. When it is rainy and windy, water comes in. When we noted this to the builder, he placed cement slabs above the windows so that water would not run down the wall and enter the house through the windows. This did not help. It would have been easier to put wood putty on the few small uneven places, a direct solution.

The house is lovely. It is spacious. Nearly every day my wife wakes early and makes food for the monks and brings it to the local temple. In our house is a half bedroom. It is a Buddha room, and we have amulets and Buddha images placed on a small shrine. A painting of a famous monk hangs on the wall. There are candles and incense for making offerings. It is a place to sit where worldly troubles fade.

Before we spend a night in the house, there is another ceremony with the monks. The family makes food, and we have a party for the village. The men drink beer and whiskey. The neighbor's wife invites me to dance with her. She says it will bring luck and happiness to the house.

I take walks. I ride my sister's motorcycle. I go to a Buddhist hermitage in the woods and sit quietly. I bring paper and pen and write stories. When I write about my past, it can be doleful, though I have had a full and wonderful life. There is something about the writing process that brings melancholy and hurt to the fore. It is easier to write about the present.

A Couple of Days in Mer Nam Noy

Someone always stops along the road to offer me a ride. In certain ways, it's like living in small town America, circa 1950. There is a helpful, friendly atmosphere. Often, it is someone from my village where nearly twenty percent of the population is family, direct or extended. I may not know them, but they all know me.

Our village sits five kilometers off Highway 1, the main north-south highway that cuts through Central Thailand connecting Bangkok with Chiang Mai. After I make my way out to the highway, it is 35 kilometers down the road to Tak, our nearest city and the provincial capital, and like I said, someone always stops and offers me a ride.

It could be our local bus that ferries people to the market and back, or someone who has seen me out walking. The tour buses that ply south from Chiang Mai will sometimes stop for me too; a chance to pick up an extra 30 baht on their way. It might be a car driven by a total stranger wanting to practice their English, or a passing acquaintance. Today, it is Hans, the watermelon-shaped German with the broad smile, who lives up near Bhumibol Dam.

Motorcycles and highways are not a combination of circumstances that I seek out, but here was an opportunity. Hans, in our brief encounters in Tak, always seemed a pleasant fellow, more Schultz than Colonel Klink. I liked him, even though we barely had a word of language in common. And the idea of riding into town with him seemed a nice chance to further a relationship that had so far been nothing more than passing smiles that said, "You live here, I live here too. Wow."

Errors of judgment are part of our daily routine. They rarely matter; just an occasional forgetfulness that sometimes our actions have consequences. The makeshift trailer on the back of Han's motorcycle appeared to add size and stability to the contraption, like a side car, or a stabilizer package that would prevent tipping. And besides, Germans, machines, stability – what could go wrong? And he was the first to stop. That had always been the determining factor in the past. The idea of a mistake in judgment didn't enter the brief equation, until later. It looked like fun.

I swung my leg over the trailer hitch as I mounted the back of the motorcycle, but did not fully clear the connecting rod, scratching my leg inside the knee; a small mistake in judgment right there. I wasn't even on the bike, and blood was trickling down my leg.

Hans smiled, and we were off. It's not easy to understand Hans when he speaks. He has a few words of Thai, and maybe an equal salting of English that he peppers his native language with; all spoken in an accent so heavy that it is difficult to discern which words might not be German. The unsorted mixture spoken from the front of the motorcycle is far beyond comprehension. The words blow past, enjoying the liberation of their moment in the wind. I made out what sounded to be that the motorcycle was old, but a great running machine.

The trailer behind me held a cage with three Rottweiler puppies that he was going to sell in the market. With little momentum, we labored up the first hill, and I noted what looked to be the entrance to a Buddhist temple tucked off the highway. I had never seen it before. I decided to spend my time noticing things, something that motorcycle riders everywhere praise about the experience. It might have been poor judgment to embark in the first place, but once you are aboard, you might as well get the most from the experience.

As we passed the crest of the first hill and began heading downward, I felt a wind. The trailer behind me shifted slightly left, then right, then left, then right, the arcs growing increasingly larger. "Acchh, whoo-aa," exhaled Hans as he slowed and steadied our suddenly unstable means of transport. A large truck whizzed past. The word "jackknife" appeared in my thoughts. Neither one of us had helmets. The concept of waiting for the bus now seemed a far more rational choice. The realization that the trailer was a destabilizing appendage brought apprehension. I could envision my head cracking like an egg on the pavement, all due to a momentary mistake in judgment.

As coincidence would have it, my wife would call me later that afternoon. I was in Tak when she and her sisters found a Buddhist hermitage in the jungle, on a mountain. It was the same entryway that

I had noticed in passing. She said it was peaceful. I told her I wanted to see it too, and the following afternoon, she would guide me there.

Boarding our own small 100cc Honda motorcycle, we crossed the highway and proceeded not more than a kilometer south. We turned down the same small road that I had noted a day earlier with Hans. We followed a choppy, partly paved road, and made a left turn onto a sandy dirt road. We continued on briefly before making another left turn amongst randomly scattered boulders. We parked the bike at a shed and continued on foot through a passageway of large, scattered, near circular shaped rocks that looked like giant dinosaur eggs. The entire area had the look of the American Southwest, combined with a Thai jungle/woodland. It had a secluded, impenetrable aura reminiscent of what I imagined from movie images that "Hole in The Wall" might have looked like during the days of Butch and Sundance.

A pavilion was lodged amongst the randomly scattered boulders in a small clearing. It had four posts and a considerable cement area covered with a tin roof about thirty feet high. Across the front was a platform that ran the entire twenty foot width of the makeshift temple. On the first level were cushions reserved for the monks. On the second level were carved animals and incense, gifts and donations. On the third platform were three larger than life-sized golden Buddha statues. The largest was in the center, and its top neared the peak of the thirty foot roof.

There were brightly colored banners and flags hung about. The decor was bright, but tasteful and well balanced. It was obvious that thought and planning had gone into the positioning of everything. Inside the lengthy pavilion, off to the side, a monk was reclined in repose. My wife presented him with gifts of food and drink when he noted our presence.

The monk was from our village, and welcomed our company. He encouraged us to sit and talk with him, and enjoy the peaceful surroundings. I asked permission to wander the grounds, fascinated by the pathways that led through the boulders that were not evident as Hans and I had passed on the highway the previous day.

Hans was a capable driver. He stayed on the shoulder of the road as much as possible. He did a good job of avoiding the bumps in the pavement that would swing the trailer left then right, left then right, and he slowed the motorcycle so that the arcs grew smaller as opposed to larger. A tour bus would pass, and once more the trailer would swivel from the enormous gust of wind. "Acchhh whooo-a," Hans would exclaim, but then always seemed to steady our ride.

The distant mountains were lovely. Beyond them lies the Burmese border. The fields that carpeted the view were green and lush. A giant Buddha sat on a platform. Stairs led up to the Buddha. The railing was a magnificent Dragon wrapped around the Buddha. All was gold and glimmering in the brilliant sun that was burning my legs. The people who passed on the bus, most likely, would only catch a glimpse of the Buddha. They would not smell the fresh air; they would not hear Hans call out in anxiety, "Acchhhh, whooo-a," as I could feel the arcs grow larger and envision myself in slow motion being catapulted through the air, a projectile in an arc.

The road was far hillier than it ever appeared in passing before. Buses and cars conquered these waves with such ease that the rolling nature of the landscape had previously seemed barely noticeable. I wondered how much of our lives had we built vehicles for to make the hills barely noticeable. From washing machines to nine to five jobs, we have programmed ourselves for regularity, a vain attempt to even out the bumpy road that life certainly holds. And why not? There is nothing wrong with boarding a huge bus if the alternative might be enduring the trepidation of a cracked skull. Some experiences just aren't worth it.

I noted the sign, 20 kilometers to Tak. We were not quite halfway there. My leg burned from the cut, and my rump had been bounced around enough that I was getting saddle sore. The seven a.m. bus from Chiang Mai passes through Mer Nam Noy at about ten o'clock. They have stopped for me a couple of times. The driver and bus hostess know me. Surely they would have seen me and stopped if I remained at the small *sala* on the side of the road. They were more than likely one of the busses that whizzed past us on the highway. "Accchhhh, whoo-a," Hans exhaled. "Heh heh heh," I heard him laugh.

After wandering the grounds of "Hole in the Wall Temple" as I would come to call it, I sat and spoke with the orange robed monk. The stubble of gray hair gave him a look of ancient wisdom, though his age appeared to be mid-forties. His arms had a Popeye bulge at the muscle. His calves were powerful. Sitting on his legs, he could bend backwards at the waist until his head touched the ground behind him.

"This is not my body," he told me in heavily accented English. "This body just come to me," he continued. "I have this body because father and mother are fucking." He didn't smile. He was explaining essence to me. "I am inside, I am my breath."

We admired the beauty of the surroundings together, and then he brought us to the altar. He reached over and found a small baby food-sized jar with a screw-on lid. There were tiny white fragments inside that looked like pearl-colored stones. He told us that they were bone fragments of Buddha; that they are as old as the Thai calendar, over 2,500 years. They looked more like a faux-pearl plastic. He told us that sometimes, at night, the grounds glow as if they had swallowed a star.

There are only a handful of known Buddha relics. These fragments are in museums. The Buddha was cremated and only a couple of teeth exist. One claim from Sri Lanka holds a tooth in a museum in Kandy. Beijing claims a bone fragment. Shwe Dagon Temple in Rangoon re-discovered a hair follicle in 1956. A soapstone casket remains in the Indian State of Bihar. Could there also be bone fragments in a baby food jar in the woods near my village in Central Thailand?

My woods behind my house in America would sometimes glow as if it were daytime in the middle of the night when the moon was reflecting light. However, I wanted to witness his claims. If it were true, then maybe it would provide me with tangible proof to the questions in life that disturb me. I know there is more than meets the eye, but maybe this would be a burning bush of sorts. I want visible proof before I smash my head like an egg due to a mistake of judgment, like getting on the back of Hans motorcycle.

As we approached town there seemed to be more buses and trucks that whined and whizzed past. "Acchhh, whoo-a, heh, heh, heh," Hans would call out now, laughing more frequently, and euphorically, at the near successful completion of our journey. Was it just transportation for him, or was there a special life affirming joy in risking his neck on the highway? We turned onto a side road that would take us into the market. As pedestrian and in-town traffic increased, he seemed to speed up when I thought he might slow down. We were whipping our way through town like maniacs let loose from an asylum. He really was crazy. "Heh, heh, heh," he laughed.

And, as I sat meditating at the "Hole in the Wall" Hermitage, a probably never before used mantra entered my head and helped me to corral my roving mind, and bring my concentration back to my breathing.

"Acchhh, whoo – aa – heh heh heh," I repeated over and again. And it seemed this odd internal chant was working. What is the use of a mantra other than to focus on nothingness? Do the words matter at all if the result is that it gives our overactive brains a chance to rest?

"Acchhh who aa heh heh heh," I chanted to myself.

"Acchhh who aa heh heh heh."

There was a nice rhythm to it. I was becoming very relaxed.

Breathe in – out – slow - deep.

Acchhh who aa heh heh heh.

The monk walked past. I thought he enjoyed the fact that I came and meditated. No. Forget the ego. Concentrate on my breath. Not that the monk was in the vicinity; not that he talked about his parents fucking.

Breathe In. Out. Slow. Deep.

Acchhh who aa heh heh heh.

Achhhhhh whooo aaa heh heh heh.

Oh no. ***My*** parents were fucking too!

Heh heh heh.

I Never Vote. It Only Encourages Them

2000 Bush in Florida

In my opinion, in a free and fair election with voting places open in all communities including Haitian, and with proper ballots that represent the wishes of the voters in West Palm Beach and throughout Florida, one person, one vote – Al Gore wins Florida in the year 2000 by a margin of 30-40,000 votes. My opinion is derived from what I heard through the media, so, you can take it or leave it, but I think it is close to accurate.

One elderly friend told me of moving the ballot around, unable to punch it through a hole. It didn't line up. After the controversy was made public, she wasn't sure who she had voted for.

There has been enough written on this election, and I won't proceed further on the subject, other than to say it seems realistic to me that George W., with the help of friends, stole the election in Florida. Bush was given the election by 513 votes, and later given the Presidency by the Supreme Court.

But it goes further. Gore was a loser. He tried to distance himself from the success of the Clinton administration as opposed to using his predecessor to his advantage. As the winner in the popular vote, he managed to lose the election. As the winner of Florida, he managed to lose Florida. If I were a shrink, I would have concluded that he wanted to lose.

I love the internet, and anybody who lays claim to inventing it is a great man in my book. OK, so he didn't really invent the internet, but I at least like the product that he is claiming to invent, and that might be as close as I ever get to learning about a candidate. I think he liked the internet too. The unfortunate situation with politics is that we can never be sure of the veracity of what these guys are saying. It would surprise nobody to learn that politicians lie. They get away with it far too often.

Bush Sr. was not so lucky when he made a big - "READ MY LIPS" promise not to raise taxes. If it was merely a promise, it would not have mattered too much. When you make "READ MY LIPS" style promises that they can play over and again on the TV news, it is akin to Gary Hartpence prodding the press to follow him around.

I did not think that Gore had the stuff of greatness. I think he proved this by losing the election to a guy who was quite proficient at losing as well. George W. Bush had a record of failure that was colossal. He had failed in business and had done poorly in school. He had a history of being a screw-off and a screw-up. I did not think he would perform well in an IQ test. The choices presented were more embarrassing than any election I have seen. Once more, I did not vote in 2000.

When do we get to choose between winners? When do we get to choose from the best that our society has to offer?

If I had lived in Florida, and if I had registered and voted, what difference would it have made? Suppose I had brought 514 Al Gore supporters with me, would he now be President, or would the Republicans who controlled the state have somewhere found other Bush supporters? I would like to believe that by voting we could have made a difference, but I truly don't.

George W. Bush, after subverting true democracy in Florida, launched a righteous campaign to bring democracy to Iraq. The irony is tragic.

Herman Witkowski

The Millionaire

"I want to be a millionaire," commanded Manny Witkowski, Herman's brother. He spoke as though the decision was final, and voicing it would make it so. Herman looked up from his overloaded desk, bewildered. He was unusually speechless. Did Manny think that he was going to give him a million dollars? Did he not realize that it was tied up in property, inventory, machinery and investments? Did he not realize that it had taken years of hard work and a goodly dose of luck?

"You're a millionaire," Manny added. "I want to be a millionaire too."

"My advice is to make the second million first, because as everyone says, the first million is the hardest." Herman's humor is not always appreciated.

There was a long quiet minute as Herman reflected on life. Not much had changed since the numbers flipped over on his personal balance sheet. Business was business, but he made it fun. He worked too many hours, he had to have fun.

"If you were a millionaire, what would be different?"

The thought was slapped back into Manny's court. He frowned.

"Tell me," said Herman seizing the initiative. "What would be different in your life? What would you do differently?" He posed the question wondering as much for himself as his shiftless brother, who had never allowed work to interfere with his life. "Ok, if you were a millionaire, right now, today, what would you do?"

There was no answer as the two brothers sat in the embarrassment of their imbalance – until finally, Manny had a response.

"I'd go fishing!"

"Fishing!" Herman shouted back. "You'd go fishing?" Manny had a rod and reel. The pier was a short ten miles down the road. There was no admission fee. "Ok, you go fishing. Take the day off and go fishing. Today, you are a millionaire on me, my treat."

Manny left happily. One day of being a millionaire was better than none. And besides, it was Friday. He got over. He would have three days.

Red Lips and Laughing Taxis

Make-up should accent, not draw attention to itself; a subtle blush or dash of color that is not predominant, unless you are a carnival clown. I have that thought everyday as I walk past the lady with the very red lips.

She stands on the hot, sunny side of a Bangkok street, a facial three ring circus in process, squinting from the smoke, and sweating profusely over a hibachi, barbecuing pork *satay*, which she sells three sticks for twenty-five cents. However, with something between a wry expression and a smile, an aura of contentment radiates from her while the burning pork wafts into her face. It looks to me like an awful place to be standing all day, but for her, it seems apparent that life is good – everyday; which leads me to the question: as compared to what?

In a third world country, the stories can be unimaginable. For many, the ice is thin, and the emotional ground they stand on can be as shaky as poverty, and as vengeful as the green chili pepper that you can swallow without noticing its presence in your food.

I tried the pork once. It was stringy and tough. And yet, she is definitely selling it. She never misses a day, early morning until late evening; she is there. And even if she only makes $2-3 a day, though I suspect much more; she has her own business, she is liberated from wherever she came from, whatever it was – and now, she appears to be happy. She is free to get dressed and go to work every day, earn a decent living, and put on as much red lipstick as she likes. Life is good.

Laughing Taxis

I have had any number of unusual taxi rides in Bangkok. One driver had the entire cab decorated in Buddha images and paintings, a veritable shrine on wheels. I have seen television hook-ups during world cup soccer matches and small LCD screens playing music videos. One creative cabbie handed me a microphone so that I could karaoke along with a music video. But, of all the unusual cabs I have encountered, my favorites are the laughing taxis.

They are usually older men, at least fifty years of age, and may be part of an increasingly rare breed. They are the wonderful laughing cab drivers of Bangkok. One might think that the snarl of traffic might make being a taxi driver in this polluted, congested city unpleasant, and for many this is true. When I am lucky enough to flag down a laughing taxi, life turns to pleasure. It is uplifting to be in the presence of such warmth and unfettered joy.

There appears to be a philosophic root to the overtly good mood. At some point, they chose happiness to all the alternative moods and modes of thought. They delight in absolutely everything, and it explodes in brilliant warmth from their wide smiling faces.

"You speak Thai – VERY GOOD! VERY GOOD!" – They might tell me and shine an enthusiastic thumbs-up.

"You have Thai wife!! – Number one!!" and they laugh with a glee that emanates from deep inside and shoots out of every pore. If you have a pulse, your mood elevates.

"She is beautiful?" They ask most assuredly with a smile that stretches from Sukhumvit to Silom Road– or however far you are going.

"Yes, but she is of good temperament too." I relay a fine answer, and it lights-up my laughing taxi driver as if he had swallowed rays of sunshine. "When she was in America, my mother and father fell in love with her," I tell him.

"Poom jai! Poom jai!!" Proud, he calls out, proud, as if it were his own daughter, a daughter of Thailand, and thereby, one of his family as well. This is wonderful news. He is unable to control his mirth.

His assumptions are simple. Everybody has a good heart, is a good person, everybody will make his day, and this enables him to have the joy of living in a world with wonderful people, a world that he has created and maintains with his positive perspective and attitude. He is one of the wonderful laughing cab drivers of Bangkok.

I strive for his outlook on life.

22

The house was finished, and the workers were busily building a cinder block wall to enclose our grounds. There would be a wrought iron gate in front. The builder presented us with a book from which to choose the design for the gate.

We selected a gate that was intricate, but not overly ornate. The builder asked what color we would like the gate painted. I told him that I had seen a gate in Baan Tak, and it was painted black and gold. It was quite attractive, and just right. I had driven my wife past the house, and she too had agreed.

He asked me what color was the gate.

Black and gold, I answered once more.

Black and gold, he repeated double-checking my answer.

Yes, black and gold. *See deum, see thorng.*

He then asked my wife. Black and gold?

Black and gold, she agreed.

Then he decided to take a ride with us to look at this gate in Baan Tak, twenty minutes away. It seemed pointless to me, but I went anyway. I led the way, and we arrived at the house with the black and gold gate.

Ah, black and gold, he said.

Sometimes, I think that this national trait of being agreeable and non-confrontational, creates a permanent state of insecurity. It is impolite not to answer a direct question. Saying 'I don't know' is not commonly acceptable. Wrong answers are endemic. Uncertainty would be a logical result.

Summer 2004

Mike, my staunchly Democratic friend came to visit me in my cottage in the Pennsylvania woods. I lived in a natural paradise, claiming ownership [for tax purposes] of five spectacular wooded acres, sheltered by a mountain and enlightened by a marvelous cascading stream that trips over ice age deposits of boulders, creating waterfalls and total peace. Mike and his family were my last guests there.

When it comes to politics, you can run, but your friends like to talk. As to be expected, in the year 2004, my vote was far more important to Mike than it was to me. I was as annoyed with Bush as he was. We were both anti-war.

I could not understand any of the rationalizations for the war. Nothing made sense. Did this man who subverted democracy in 2000 expect me to believe that he now felt Democracy so precious that he was going to bring free and fair elections to Iraq after stealing the election in Florida? And, if there were free and fair elections – wouldn't the Iraqi's, as most of the Middle East, more likely prefer a fundamentalist Islamic cleric? Though there was no outcry for rebellion, no war waged for freedom, we called ourselves the liberators, and we called them the insurgents.

Abraham Lincoln told a joke about a dog. He asked - if you consider the tail to be a leg, then how many legs does a dog have? People would answer five. He would correct them. It is still four. Just because you call a tail a leg, it does not make it so. It seemed too expensive a proposition to be solely about oil, but the extent of political and financial deviousness often goes beyond my ability to comprehend. I have no idea, and make no allegations. Was de-stabilizing Iraq a means of driving up oil prices, and thereby affording enormous windfall profits to friends in the oil business? Was he trying to finish the war that his father did not in complete in '92? Was it a personal vendetta? Or were they just boys with 'toys of war' that they wanted to use in the same manner in which someone might take a Corvette out onto the highway to open it up and see what it can do. What good is power if you don't use it?

It was an aggressive, un-provoked attack with the horrifyingly juvenile and barbaric name of "Shock and Awe." We proceeded to bomb the Iraqi people into a state of outrage. The rest of the world did not get it. My wife was listening to a radio station reporting opinion from Thailand. The commentator could not understand why America, a rich country that presumably had everything, would start a war. Why couldn't they be content with what they already had?

I don't think there is any country that wants to see the boots of a foreign army walking their streets with machine guns. If it happened in the USA, people would not tolerate it.

I saw a ballooning deficit that seemingly was created before there was time for debate or consideration. Young soldiers were coming home maimed. They were killing and dying, and I could see the country going bankrupt. Was I a Bush fan? No.

And yet - what was my alternative? I would be in Thailand during the election. Absentee ballots played a part in the last election. Mike urged me to vote – if not for his sake, for his son, who would soon be of draft age.

Fish Lunch

The fish was positioned on the table in such a manner that we were eyeball to eyeball. A few years ago, I would have abstained, opting to eat things that didn't have an obvious identity, or at least did not look back at me. However, along with the others, I picked and chomped and looked the fish in the eye, as his body was disintegrating beneath fork and knife. All at the table indulged.

The small gathering of Thai teachers was amused by the conversation. They moaned in disbelief as I told them that the school and property tax on my brother's house in America was $45,000 a year, at least five times more than the average annual salary of a Thai teacher. I went on to explain that a small bag of groceries could be thirty dollars as we rambled through a balance sheet of expenses. Cars, gas, auto insurance, maintenance, usually multiplied by two for most families, is a staple of the American diet; health insurance and home owners insurance that don't always provide the expected coverage, heating oil, electric, cable TV, the price of a meal in a restaurant, clothing, the cost of one nights stay in a hospital - a daunting curtain of expenses rained down on any distant dreams that my lunch partners had of working in America. The costs are too high.

"Having time to breathe is a luxury item," I told the District Director of Schools, a high class, soft spoken man. He laughed. We were under a pavilion at a quaint roadside restaurant. There were six of us. We sat overlooking a large pond on the premises. The tables were picnic style, and the strong wood beams held a grass roof over the swept-clean dirt floor. For me, these types of premises have become routine. I did not know if other Westerners would find it exotic, funky or too dirty to entertain a thought of eating there. Can there be such a thing as a swept-clean dirt floor? The food was delicious, the atmosphere and company, better.

I am spending two days teaching at an English Camp for twelve year olds. They spend more time playing games than they do learning. The children smile and laugh a lot. The games are clever and fun to watch.

The children have opportunities to be funny, and are not punished for having a personality, though mostly they are shy. The teachers laugh too. I don't remember my teachers laughing in school.

I got dragged out of assemblies by the back of the neck for laughing, but, then again, a Thai person would never laugh during the National Anthem. Thailand is the only country in the region that has never been colonized. They are proud. The National Anthem is played twice a day. There are a couple of lines that say:

"Thai people love peace,
But we will not be cowards in war."

I roughly translate this as 'though we are peace loving people, we don't take guff.' They hear this twice a day. Part of being Thai is that you don't take shit.

The tune is a catchy John Philip Sousa type of marching song. It's fun too. Not at all like our difficult to sing Anthem. And it doesn't begin with a stuttering "Oh ho say," which in my mind is halfway to laughing anyway and still provokes an internal grin.

There is not only a Mother's Day and Father's Day in Thailand, but there is a Children's Day. This was not Children's Day, but it could have been. It seemed as though we were there partly to entertain. I taught them to play Simple Simon in English. The two days at camp were a kick, as I pretty much expected they would be, though when invited to volunteer, I had no idea what the program would be. My chatting with the other teachers was mostly in Thai, despite the fact that it was English Camp. We talked about the war in Iraq, George W. Bush, discrimination and food, but mostly we made jokes and smiled. Yes, I could have predicted this and the warm feelings swirling around.

And if I were to be invited to a similar event in America, I would have no idea what to expect. I cannot imagine what a primary school might be like. I would think it would have to be far more serious. American children need to be better prepared to pay bills when they are adults. Thai children will be better prepared to enjoy life, though they undoubtedly will earn and learn less.

And, just as I cannot picture a primary school in America, I cannot imagine what it might be like to sit with the teachers during lunch. I don't have any idea what they might eat or talk about, except I bet there will more than likely be tuna from a can; anything that does not resemble the original animal in any way.

One of my preoccupations in observing Thai people and their attitudes is wonderment at where their easy going nature emanates from. Buddhism has always been my first thought, but now, I think the schools are also a strong factor. If school is a game, then life can be a game too.

I Never Vote. It Only Encourages Them

2004 Kerry vs. Bush

The first thing that caught my attention about John Kerry was that he was so committed to the project of becoming the next president of the United States, that he was taking out a mortgage on his house to use toward his campaign. He made that newsworthy, and I liked that – until I found out that he was married to the billionaire heiress of the Heinz ketchup fortune, and his taking out a mortgage was the equivalent of my borrowing a couple of bucks from a friend to get a Starbucks coffee. It pissed me off. But the Bush War in Iraq pissed me off more.

I listened to the nomination speech: "I'm John Kerry and I'm reporting for duty." Well, where have you been for the last twenty-five years, I wondered? That pissed me off too. But not only was Bush killing loads of innocent Iraqi's and reducing the country to rubble, it was costing us a fortune to do it. We would undoubtedly build it back again too. And besides, he convinced Congress to authorize the use of force, and much to their "Shock and Awe" – he used it. He duped guys like Kerry into supporting the war, and now they were trapped. It pissed me off.

Kerry had said he was for the war, and that left me, and others, to hope that really he wasn't for the war. But that wasn't what he was saying. Pissed again. Bush had squandered the enormous surplus that had been built up and took it three steps further by running up the largest deficit in the nation's history. And what did we have to show for it? We conquered a country that didn't want us there. Most of the world hated us.

In his nomination speech, Kerry promised to add 40,000 active duty troops, double our special forces and provide our troops with the newest weapons and technology. He said we need a strong military, homeland security, care for our children, and protection for our neighborhoods. He would not cut social security. From buying body armor to Veterans healthcare, Kerry was there. Jobs going overseas, health insurance, air pollution, poverty, homelessness, good paying jobs, he was there.

It was a grand vision of America – but not realistic. Who was going to pay for it? He promised everything but to come over to every house in America, and personally cook the chicken that he was putting in every pot.

If you give the American worker a fair playing field, there is nobody in the world he can't compete against, John Kerry told us. What the hell does that mean? Where do we find this fair playing field? Do we buy every worker in China a $150,000 house so that they too will be strapped with mortgage payments? Do we buy them SUV's and present them with bills for gas and liability insurance? Or, do we put Americans in hovels, and pay them two bucks a day and subsidize the price of rice and vegetables? How could Americans not question this stuff?

How could the Democrats have nothing better to throw at Bush than a left- wing Massachusetts liberal in a country that leaned slightly right of center? This did not appear to be a logical path to the White House. My choices on the political spectrum were getting worse.

George W. Bush was such a poor choice of candidate, that even though the Democrats reached into the far left hand side of the party, it was still a close contest decided by the state of Ohio. Though I was in the battleground state of Pennsylvania, it went for Kerry without my help. The fact that Kerry had not come out against the war let me off the hook for the possibility of Michael's son getting drafted. He will be off to college soon.

I didn't vote and I don't feel bad about it. The real question is with guys that piss me off so much, why should I spend my time listening to them and getting pissed off – especially when there are natural wonders to explore and magic to be searched out.

I cannot imagine that I will ever vote again. And here is the reason that goes beyond the Jack Paar story. All politicians lie. Am I supposed to vote for the guy whose lies I like the best? This doesn't make sense to me. It would feel hypocritical. Where is the privilege? Where is the pride?

Herman Witkowski

Through years of being a businessman, Herman Witkowski had always been my "touch stone"- a splash of humor and perspective. When there were problems, he always had the answers. At about the same time, we both liquidated our businesses and faded away from our professional lives. Herman retired to Florida. I moved to Thailand.

In Thailand, people rarely ask what you do for a living. I think they are more interested in who you are, not what you do. All three of my close friends who did not quite fit in, Jan, Bruce and Jane, found this 'what do you do' question a highly intrusive conversation opener. They spent a lot of their time depressed, that was most of what they did, and they did not want to offer this painful fact as an introductory remark.

Herman did not like this question either. His new life as a retiree in Florida was not oriented toward the past. He did not want to discuss his previous occupation, and so, Herman Witkowski went back into business, but not really. Herman had business cards printed with his new company name and logo: **Snow-Go-Way – Snow Removal Services.**

And now, when people ask, he gives them his business card. "We have all the big accounts in Florida," he tells them. "Disney, Sea World." People listen and nod. "Oh yeah, we are the biggest in Florida," he tells them. It sounds very impressive.

One day, at a local restaurant, he dropped his business card into a fishbowl, from which there would eventually be a drawing. A free meal he figured, but there were 1000's of business cards in there. He never thought he would win. A letter came in the mail two months later. Herman was not just the winner of a free dinner. He won the Grand Prize, and his business would be honored and featured at a gala dinner. He thought he might use the opportunity to offer franchises.

And I thought the idea was fun. I thought I would ask him for exclusive rights to the snow removal business in Thailand. I could see my wife shaking her head in embarrassed disillusionment when I gave out my business card – except, like I said, over here, nobody ever asks what you do.

THE S.E.A GAMES 2006

The 2006 South East Asian Games were on TV. I watched as two Vietnamese runners, clad in stylish sunglasses, raced out to the lead in the first lap of a four lapper. A bit more than three quarters of the way around the first lap, one of the Vietnamese runners dropped off to the side.

Was he a pacesetter for the first guy?

Did he succumb to an injury?

As the runners rounded the turn into the final lap, the Vietnamese runner was still in the lead. A Burmese fellow stayed close as the remainder of the runners fell behind, no longer near enough to compete with the leaders.

Then an amazing thing happened. The original Vietnamese runner who had dropped out long ago, joined back into the contest, three laps behind the other runners. My first thought was that it was a courageous effort to finish the race that he had started. Winning was certainly not possible, but he had trained long and hard, and his determination would not let him be denied a chance to finish the race. Good for him, I thought. Even with no chance of being the winner, he was a champion in his own right to continue the race.

This was an errant thought.

It soon became apparent that his purpose was not to finish the race, but to run alongside his teammate in first place down the crucial stretch run. The two, side by side, would create a barrier. His sole purpose in the race was to be a blocker and hinder the possibly fastest man, the Burmese, from winning the race.

He succeeded. A few seconds later, the surprised Burmese runner who did not have the time to swing out and around from behind two men, finished second in the race. He threw himself on the ground in despair. Bruce was never meant to live or compete in a world where this type of behavior exists.

What must it have felt like for the Vietnamese runner to win like this in front of his fans, his family, the world of watchers on TV and the other athletes? I can't imagine that it felt good or heroic. He was a strong runner, just to have been able to be there. If he had finished second, it still would have been a great feat. He might even have won the race legitimately. It certainly would have been close.

The announcer noted the tactic, and thought there should be a penalty, but did not seem appalled. I don't know the final result. I turned off the TV wondering what is wrong with this world, and this gifted athlete, that he would prefer to win by blatantly cheating. I think people are becoming numb. I don't think that George W. Bush, or any of the Republicans, feel soiled for whatever happened in Florida. I am naive to think they might.

It is not an Eastern or Western World thing. There is no external escape from the chicanery that goes down on a daily basis and permeates the society. My escape is internal, a detachment, a mute button of sorts that turns down the volume of the outside world so that you can hear yourself think. Maybe it was that my childhood occurred during a rare period of predominant peace, and there was hope for a new and better world, a tranquil and idealistic time which allowed for Willie Mays to be the most important issue of my youthful days.

I have become comfortable with my own recipe. I live an attached-detachment. I care deeply for friends and family. Suffering hurts. I have trouble watching violent movies. And yet, I am resolved, especially in regards to my own life – that whatever happens is OK. If death is the worst of it, I am ready. Maybe, as I mentioned earlier, it will afford a chance to reunite with friends. Maybe the beyond will be better.

I visit my monk friend at the hermitage in the woods. He came from my village. There are financial entanglements in the USA which remain unfinished. When I get these cleaned up, I will feel more secure that I have done right by my wife and her family, who have proved devoted to me. I tell the monk that I am sometimes lacking peace. I tell him I am concerned that my family will not be OK if I pass on.

He smiles. He says they were fine before you came here, they will be fine after you leave. He places his index fingers together and then moves them apart.

Detach.

23

Writing stories is a pastime. I listen, ask questions, learn and analyze. I shuffle the cards and deal. I write depression from what I imagine it would be for that character, combined with my experiences and perceptions. People can be vivid in their descriptions. The process of putting pen to paper contains a cranial filtration system. There is no non-fiction that is totally true, and there is little fiction that does not have its foot stuck in the fly paper of reality.

There is a painful side to existence, both physical and emotional suffering take their toll. Maybe daily life is a little like a war, all the more ironic for its lack of combat. I feel that was true for Bruce, Jane and Jan. As my parents and their friends suffer through aging, enduring amazing hardships, I renew my hope for a better world beyond. There are so many suffering elderly. Maybe there is a queue.

In this book, I have numbered sections and story sections. The stories have titles. I can be the narrator, but sometimes, I am not. The stories may reveal more about me than the memoir sections telling of my life. Memory refracts like a funhouse mirror. Perceptions distort. Stories well-up from oft hidden crevices within.

The village is a large part of my life. For now, it works well. I have no doubt that the future will bring other places and realities. That is the pattern of my life. I will wander, have adventures and return. Sometimes, being home will be an adventure too. Here's the story of what happened in a period of one week in a small subsistence farming village in Central Thailand.

King Cobra - Rare Medium – Well Done

My wife swears he is part wolf, though I have not heard of wolves being native to the area. Most of the dogs around the village are an odd mix of dingo and breed dogs. They are domesticated, with a Thai-style independent streak. Our dog is furry, not smooth as is predominant amongst the local canines. My wife loves his soft fur. She has a strong childlike side, a Lenny stroking the rabbit facet to her personality. Pookie is smart, but independent. He is playful and a trouble-maker, most often manifest in giving the rooster a startling chase through the yard. He will lie at my feet when I write, and nuzzle my hand when the desire for love and affection overwhelms him. He will, with no remorse, bite the leg off an intruder.

Pookie is all dog. Being protective of territory and family is the job of village dogs, and there is no doubt in my mind that Pookie takes his job seriously. He suffered a broken leg in a tussle with another dog. Three months later, he returned home one morning having lost vision in one eye. For a while, after that, he spent his nights sleeping in the house, maybe it was to test whether we would permit it, or maybe he needed a break from work. He comes and goes according to momentary whim. He is obstinate, and only responds when it pleases him. He once again prefers to sleep outside, within our now gated complex.

I think that certain animals are imbued with majesty of spirit that is easily recognized. Dogs have an abundance of heart and loyalty. Elephants embody a sense of dignity, compassion and a gentle powerfulness inherent in their size. Eagles may soar with regal elegance and grace, but Cobras are King; quite a lofty distinction for a belly slithering snake.

King Cobra images are often used by Buddhists and Hindus to guard temples. The King Cobra is worshipped as a sun deity with power over rain, thunder and fertility. There is a legend that a massive King Cobra came up from behind the Buddha while he was meditating, and spread his hood to shield him from the sun.

However, none of that was happening when I walked out into my front yard and saw Pookie jumping around, barking. He was squared off in confrontation with a King Cobra, hood raised in striking position, darting in and out.

King Cobras are the world's largest venomous snakes. They can release enough venom in one lightning strike to kill an elephant, or as many as twenty people. A bite can paralyze and kill in minutes as the victim's heart and lungs stop, causing suffocation.

King Cobras live in tropical rain forests and tropical deciduous forests and scrub land and apparently, to my surprise, on my front lawn in Central Thailand. When threatened, or on the attack, they rear up and flatten their neck ribs into a hood. This is what was going on when I walked outside:

A King Cobra can see a person 330 feet away. I felt safe at my distance of about ten feet. I had no idea. I am not educated in the ways of tropical poisonous creatures. King Cobras can grow to 18 feet long, though this was obviously a lean, trim juvenile, about 6 feet in length. Cobras are born fully loaded, and some say the young are more lethal for their concentration in size.

It was time to act and calling, "Pookie, Pookie, Pooookkiieee, – Come here boy, atta baby, who is my big boy?" was not doing the trick. He was not about to heed my calls when he had such an animated plaything darting about in front of him. It is not his nature to stand down.

I picked up a piece of petrified wood, [common to our area - I find them along the roadside and bring them home from my afternoon walks] and moved to within a couple of feet of the coiled snake, and in one sudden thrust slammed the rock down upon him.

He wriggled and swerved, though his head looked nearly severed. I picked up the million year old petrified wood which I feel has a powerful dignity to it as well, [most wood just rots away in an all too brief moment in earth's history] and I smashed the King Cobra one more time.

I felt an unexpected exhilaration. Orion stood over his prey with Canis Major at his side. Was that the thrill of the big game hunter? Does the spirit of the vanquished enter into our being? Man, I was high and in control at the same time. I stood tall. I had killed a King Cobra in the wild. It was a calm 'don't fuck with me' power that coursed through my veins and would lodge in my soul and romp with me for the next few days before fading into my past.

* * *

It is a twenty minute ride past the dam and through a pasty scrub of nothingness. We roll down straight roads that cut through fields alongside a dried-out river bed. Second and Third sister had asked my wife and me to come along and visit a clairvoyant. Third sister had an interesting and accurate reading there a few months ago.

Our ride through the countryside concluded in a left turn into a driveway, veering down a small hill to a homestead. There were workers doing construction under the typical Thai-style abode built-up on stilts. A man slept soundly, imperturbable in a hammock. A small thirty-ish year old lady led my wife and third sister upstairs. Second sister watched the baby. I followed along and took a seat off to the side.

There was an altar and a donation box. There were plaster figures of animals all around. The clairvoyant sat behind the altar and held forth a platter that had money and flowers. Third sister placed a donation of 40 baht, $1 on the platter. All of the money goes to the local temple. The medium had her open her hands, palms up, and slapped them gently with a rose. *Satu Satu*, amen, she said to begin the reading.

The clairvoyant is actually a medium. She channels and becomes a young child for the reading. The child dispenses advice through her. She speaks in a high-pitched voice, both charming and odd at the same time.

I cannot follow the conversation too well, but they are talking about the lack of boyfriend situation. Third sister is twenty-nine and beautiful. In America, she would have a line out the door, and a choice of whomever she wanted. In Thailand, her circumstance is not easy.

The young child, being channeled through the medium, suggests that she try the internet. I quirk an eyebrow, as it is a suggestion which

I too have made, though the geographical difficulties of finding a match in the USA are immense. Even Bangkok is a five hour drive.

My wife, sitting next to her sister, interrupts the medium several times, disputing this or that, and asking questions. My wife does not believe in the abilities of the medium. She noted, as did I, that the woman spoke with the child's voice before they went upstairs as well, not just during the reading.

My wife decides to have a reading too. But now, the youth inside the medium comes out stronger and playfully. What do you have in your refrigerator? Do you have lots of snacks? The cherubic imp asks my wife as a curiosity, not a prognostication. Yes. Do you have a lady nearby who sells *Som Tom*? Yes. Why didn't you bring me *Som Tom* or snacks? I like coconut milk! The child inside the medium kept giggling gleefully, and my wife was unsure what to make of this odd turn of events. Finally, the child told her not to play the lottery, and to buy her mother two skirts. She should go to Chiang Mai. I don't like Chiang Mai. I like Bangkok, my wife rebutted. Why didn't you bring me coconut milk? The child pouted.

Second sister came upstairs, and my wife went downstairs to watch the baby. The child medium described my land, and talked about her building a house there. Correct again. This is in the planning stage. Her house will sit alongside that of youngest sister. Then, the child inside the medium confesses to teasing my wife about the snacks. If she comes back another time, a better reading will be provided. Mornings are good. Afternoon is too hot. Even though my wife did not believe in the medium, the next time we would go to town, she would buy two dresses for her mother.

After all leave, I decide to have a reading too. I have difficulty understanding, but the child wants me to ask questions. I have no questions. The child's voice tells me that I have a lingering business problem in America, but it will get better next month, then asks if my legs hurt. Yes. They have been achy for a long time. The child tells me that I am bored. Another lady is waiting for a reading, and I thank the medium and leave.

On the way home, I ponder what she said. Yes. It is true. I am sometimes bored. It is an oft occurring swing in my life cycle.

My house in the village is finished. I enjoy the lack of strife inherent in village life, but there are wants. I like to meet with foreigners. I like to meet with travelers. I like foreign food. So far, it has been a fine mix of a few days in Bangkok, and then a couple of weeks in the village. The lack of distraction makes writing easier. I crave distraction.

I know that soon I will need a "next" project. We are planning gardens, but getting started is a slow boat. We fall into a routine where days pass leisurely, early morning is work time, while hot, dreamy sun-baked afternoon strolls offer time for mind wandering reminiscence. I remember meeting Beer Bobby at the beach a couple of years ago.

"Ken, I'm bored," he told me, barely able to lift his head from a mug of beer. He is young, handsome and floundering, beached along the Gulf of Siam. The original dream was beer and women, a paper-tiger style challenge, each one easily quenched. "Bored," he said over and again through the next half hour. "Ken, I'm bored," he repeated drawing his index and middle finger knife-like slowly across his neck.

"You need to do something different," I told him. He looked at me curiously. This might actually present an answer. He said, "But I have done everything."

'Really' I asked with my eyes. Then I asked, "Have you been to Mongolia?"

Now, this was something. It wasn't just Mongolia. It was a concept. Flee this paradise beach town. Strike out on a journey, a voyage of discovery. Excitement lit a twinkle in his eye. Mongolia. Yes, Mongolia. Mongolia? "What the hell is in Mongolia?" he asked.

"I don't know. When you come back, tell me all about it."

I don't know if Beer Bobby ever went to Mongolia, or anywhere else for that matter. He could still be sitting on the same barstool drunk every night. But, it did get him thinking and me too. Once again, as with my idea for Jane to pursue a life of massage, Mongolia was my passion to pursue – or better yet – let Beer Bobby chase that dream. I'll take Bhutan.

There looms a deeply enchanted world – as untouched as one can expect to find in this jet age of homogenization; the isolated sanctuary, remote and rugged, a haven for solitude and inspiration. Yes, Bhutan, the Kingdom where Gross National Happiness is official policy and placed above Gross National Product, and where psychological concerns are valued above monetary wealth. Dreams are the propellers of my life. Choice is my rudder. Bhutan is a dream.

* * *

The Thai's celebrate three New Years. January 1st, Chinese Lunar New Year and their own, *Songkran* Festival, which is a phantasmagorical festival of fun, the entire country becoming a three-day water fight employing buckets more than pistols.

As the New Year approaches, an otherwise typically hot-season sunny day finds the village in a not unusual state of lethargy, and me, with a heavy heart. A lingering inherited business deal in America has me on edge. It has haunted me off and on for years, far too long. The nightmares and sleeplessness it caused in the past have returned. I mull my options, which are not many or good. This situation leaves me deeply troubled and feeling helpless. I am financially trapped.

My wife visits the monk and returns with a remedy for the nightmares. She teaches me a short chant to repeat before I go to sleep. It works. The next few nights I sleep well, but while awake, my troubles can sap the best hours of the day. The fears of losing everything to this deal turn my thoughts black.

Most religions have a burn in hell punishment for people who commit suicide. My monk friend at the hermitage tells me that suicide victims must re-climb the ladder of incarnation, starting at the bottom. I think there must be a more compassionate fate awaiting them on the other side. Another friend says that their work here is finished, and they are proceeding along their individual spiritual path. This holds a ring of truth for me. My wife says they come back as a crazy dog. A deck of cards holds only one Suicide King, and he is framed in hearts.

* * *

I am cheered by the fact that Jefferson Davis Lee is in Thailand and coming to visit me in the village. He has become an old friend. Though his marriage in America failed, he has a continued interest in the study of relationships. He has dated Thai ladies, and congratulates me on getting along well with my wife, and my understanding of the culture. I tell him the more I learn, the less it makes sense.

Western logic does not always work here. Some things will never make sense in my framework of thinking. I have to accept that, as they have to accept certain things about my behavior that might seem strange. Foreigners who live here must be able to smile and shrug. Not everything can be explained, though some can.

I tell Jeff that I knew a Thai lady in America who explained Thai thinking. Amongst other things, she told me that a Thai lady cannot be happy eating off fine china if her mother is drinking from a coconut shell. Consideration. Respect. Sharing. Children take care of their parents. This is the system. Good children feel good for completing their obligations. A happy wife makes a happy home.

Recognition of this has made my life easier. It has been inexpensive to accomplish, a small monthly contribution to the family circle. Now that I have a car, offering a ride to town or a few days vacation makes me part of the clan. Though not the norm for foreigners with Thai wives, I get along with the family. I try and speak their language. They respect my privacy. They share with me. If they borrow money, it is paid back. There are times to give money, and times to lend. If I need help, they are there for me. We live in harmony, and I have the pleasure of a happy wife.

Jeff has learned a few words of Thai, but feels that reaching a level of proficiency is a job and a half. He wants a life partner, a soul mate to share his innermost feelings. Like I said in the first story, Jeff is a good talker. He needs communication as much as I think he needs the dream of idyllic union. He wants to share without being taken advantage of, a difficult proposition in any culture. Expectations cannot be limited or hindered by warnings or words. They are dreams and appear in the same un-requested manner.

I tell him that with my American wife, we could agree on 98% of an issue, and then the conversation could narrow down to that 2%

where we differed and blossom back out into a fight. There was no fault, just issues. That was how it was. I think it is that way for many couples. I don't like confrontation. Home should be a sanctuary from strife, a refuge from the injustices of life.

Most marital conversations are everyday things. Where is my blue shirt? Why did you tell me you were ready to go, and then leave me standing and waiting for you at the car for ten minutes? I can say that fluidly in Thai. I have no need to explain existential angst to my wife. She knows when I am not sleeping well.

When she sees I am depressed, she chirps "happy, happy, happy," in her high pitched voice. Her intentions are so good, that it actually does cheer me. If we bicker, it is usually about the passage of time or lack of planning. Preparing a schedule is a meaningless activity for her.

My wife will gladly wait for an hour while I get a massage at the temple, and then have me wait for an hour while she gets her hair washed and cut. For me, that is wasting time. For her, it is doing things together. Thai people do things together; they accompany each other on errands or outings. I am accustomed to doing things alone. I think the part of me that is a New Yorker is muted, but will never fall away entirely.

I tell Jeff that my need for intellectual conversation is best satisfied with others, and it need not be part of my marriage. People unrealistically expect everything from a spouse. I tell him I am tired of the anger between the sexes. The geopolitical situation exhausts me. The world seems to be ripping apart at every imaginable seam. There is a weighty weariness, but I don't quit because I still have times of childlike curiosity and awe. And besides, I've never been to Bhutan.

Jefferson Davis Lee commends me for the accomplishment of building a house in Thailand; he congratulates me on making my relationship work. He tells me it is a job well done.

I bring Jefferson Davis Lee to the Buddhist hermitage in the woods. Together we visit the Buddhist Wat on the mountain in the river. It is a pleasantly uneventful couple of days. We talk a lot. The food is good. We take a ride on second sister's 100cc Honda motorcycle through the plush spectrum of rice fields spotlighted by the sun. I love the greens, I tell Jeff. There must be a billion shades.

24

Last night, after midnight, the dog was barking. He woke us up. Pookie was stationed near the door on the front porch, not at his usual outpost near the front gate. There was no question that his focus was on something.

My wife rarely stirs when the dog barks, but there was something different in his tone. She went to the front hallway and stood off to the side, peering out one of the windows. She called me to come and look too.

It is a fair distance to the front gate, near one hundred yards, but there was a clear view as the moon was full and bright. There were large flowing shadows being cast both on the ground, and on the house of youngest sister, as if being thrown off by the wavering movement of large trees in a heavy gust. There are no large trees. The air was still. There was definitely movement, but of what, I could not determine; seemingly wind-blown cloud shadows were dancing with each other in free-form swirls.

I knew that my wife saw the same dark, illuminated visions, and I offered to walk out front and check it out. She said no. She said she saw something. I asked what. She told me she had something to tell me. I asked what. I'll tell you in the morning. Tell me now. We were both awake. No, - in the morning.

We returned to bed. I was drowsy. When I rested my head on the pillow, I met with an unusual, billowy feeling of comfort as I wondered if they had come for me, if they would take me quietly in my sleep. My affairs were not entirely in order, but not too bad. I was at peace. I slept soundly.

In the morning I did remember to ask my wife what she wanted to tell me. She said I told you last night. I said no, you told me last night to ask you in the morning. That's right she said. I told you last night.

I knew what she meant.

Portions of this book were written at the Buddhist Hermittage in the woods.

Readers Comments About

"Thailand Stories – If There Are Places Called Paradise"

I couldn't put it down. I was up in Bangkok and missed happy hour.

Simon from Cha'am

I loved reading Thailand Stories – artful yet not pretentious. The balance of hope and despair, happiness and unhappiness, wealth and poverty, seemed not just real but was also engaging. It kept me guessing as a reader and the payoffs were always welcome. There were profound insights yet the author didn't try to provide all the answers. He let the frayed edges of life flap freely. What a trick to pull off a portrayal of paradise where death is ever present yet not depressing. I liked that.

The author gets at the inner light of the characters – he lights the spark of individuality in them. Thailand Stories is one of the few pleasure reading novels that I will want to read again.

Jon Olson –Penn State University, assistant writing professor

I enjoyed this immensely. Really good stuff. It's funny, sad, crazy… different. It paints a subtle and mature picture of Thailand, and the spicy m lange that results when cultures come together and create diverse relationships. – **Andy Burns**

The book was great! To me, it's a love affair with Thailand and it's contagious as hell. I found myself, many times, making plans to R & R at the beach bungalow. The characters were real and the dialogue often hit a "high hard one."

Kevin Carroll

When I saw that I was past the halfway point, I started reading very slowly. I didn't want it to end. - **Dr. Richard Shainwald**

"Thailand Stories tells it like it is."

Bernard Trink – Bangkok Post